Sarah Mallory grew up in the West Country, England, telling stories. She moved to Yorkshire with her young family, but after nearly thirty years of living in a farmhouse on the Pennines she has now moved to live by the sea in Scotland. Sarah is an award-winning novelist, with more than twenty books published by Mills & Boon Historical. She loves to hear from readers and you can reach her via her website at: sarahmallory.com

THE LAIRD'S RUNAWAY WIFE

Sarah Mallory

MILLS & BOON

First Published in Great Britain 2022
by Mills & Boon, an imprint of HarperCollins*Publishers* Ltd,
1 London Bridge Street, London, SE1 9GF

www.harpercollins.co.uk

HarperCollins*Publishers*
1st Floor, Watermarque Building,
Ringsend Road, Dublin 4, Ireland

The Laird's Runaway Wife © 2022 Sarah Mallory

ISBN: 978-0-263-30171-7

05/22

MIX
Paper from
responsible sources
FSC™ C007454

This book is produced from independently certified FSC™ paper
to ensure responsible forest management.
For more information visit www.harpercollins.co.uk/green.

Printed and Bound in Spain using 100% Renewable Electricity
at CPI Black Print, Barcelona

For Doris Sweet. 1925–2021.
Avid reader and a spirited lady: true heroine material.

Prologue

July 1750

Ardvarrick. He was home, at last. Grant brought his horse to a stop at the edge of the slight rise and gazed across at the house in the distance. The creamy harled walls stood out against the vibrant greens of the trees covering the hill behind and his heart rose at the sight of it. In fact, he realised with a little spurt of surprise that he felt much more cheerful than he had for months.

He had been away on the Black Isle for more than two weeks, concluding a deal that would strengthen the bloodline of his cattle. The success of the excursion had heartened him and, seeing the house with its windows a fiery gold in the low evening sunlight, he was suddenly eager to get home. Back to his wife. Madeleine had been a little quiet when he left, but he had not questioned her about it, being too busy with preparations for his journey. Now he discovered he was impatient to see her again and he urged his horse forward.

'Come along,' he said to Robert, his man. 'We should be in good time for dinner.'

The horses settled into a canter, covering the ground with strong, easy strides, and Grant relaxed in the saddle. He allowed his mind to return to Madeleine and felt a smile growing inside him. He could not wait to tell her about his trip, the bloodstock he had seen and new farming methods he was eager to put into practice. She was always interested to hear his news, however trivial, although there had been so little time for talking in recent months. He felt a small pang of guilt and quickly squashed it, reminding himself how much there was to be done at Ardvarrick. It was his duty, as Laird, to look after the house, the land and his tenants.

But those things could wait until tomorrow. Tonight he wanted to sit down with Madeleine after dinner and enjoy a glass of wine with her, as they had been wont to do before...

'Are you not going that way first, Sir Grant?'

Riding alongside him, Robert jerked his head in the direction of the small stone chapel and burial ground, situated on the edge of the sea loch.

'Not this time. I want to get home'

He saw his man's look of surprise and understood it immediately. In the past year it had become customary for Grant to visit the chapel on his return from every journey. He had made a point of it ever since he had interred the remains of his father, the old Laird, in the family vault. The vault where, only months before his father's demise, he had buried his stillborn son.

He would pay his respects there in the morning, Grant decided, urging his horse on. Today, he needed to give his attention to the living.

When they reached the house the two men left their horses with the waiting groom and ran up the steps into the hall. Robert took their saddle packs on to the bedchambers and Grant turned to greet his mother, who was hurrying across the hall towards him. She was dressed in her widow's weeds, even though it was more than twelve months since the old Laird had died suddenly of a fever.

'Oh, my dear boy.' She stretched out her hands to him. 'You are come back safely!'

'Did you ever doubt I should?'

He caught her fingers and, seeing the anxious

look in her violet eyes, he gave her a reassuring smile. She pulled him close to kiss his cheek.

He went on, 'It has been a most fruitful trip. I have the agreements, signed and sealed, and we have purchased a young bull. I left Andrew in the Black Isle to follow on with the creature in easy stages—but let us go into the drawing room and I will tell you and Maddie all about it.' He looked past her. 'Where *is* Maddie?'

Ailsa's hands trembled beneath his and Grant felt a sudden constriction in his chest. He had a strong premonition that something was wrong. Very wrong. Stepping around his mother, he strode across to the drawing room. It was empty.

'Grant, my son!'

He barely heard Ailsa's anguished call as he dashed up the stairs, two at a time. Robert met him on the landing, a sealed letter in his hands.

'I found this on the table in your room, sir, and was just bringing it to you.'

Grant snatched the paper from him and tore it open, scanning the page rapidly. The words danced before his eyes, but there was no mistaking the message.

Madeleine had gone.

Chapter One

The ball at Tunbridge House was a sad crush. By the time Madeleine arrived, the house was so full she knew it would be considered a huge success. Every room gleamed with the glow of candles, while the Yellow Salon positively blazed with light from the glittering chandeliers suspended above the guests. Madeleine's hand rested lightly on her father's arm as they stood in the doorway to the Salon, waiting for the lackey to announce them.

'The Comte de Vaucluse and Mademoiselle d'Evremont!'

She tensed a little. Would she ever grow accustomed to being addressed by that name again?

'Yves, my dear Comte!' Their hostess swept up to them in a swirl of rose damask skirts, sharp eyes glittering in her heavily painted face. 'And your charming daughter. You are very welcome.'

The Comte bowed low over Lady Tunbridge's hand and Madeleine swept a curtsy, listening to her father murmuring compliments in his smooth voice. She found herself marvelling once again that he had lost none of his charm over the years. Their hostess simpered, laughed and plied her fan like a giddy schoolgirl before waving them on and turning her attention to the next arrivals.

The rooms were hot and crowded. Even in her red-heeled shoes Madeleine could see very little beyond those figures immediately around her. She exchanged greetings, flirted mildly with several gentlemen, but remained at her father's side as he made his way to the magnificent ball-room. A minuet was in progress and they moved around the edges of the room. After a month in London, she was sufficiently acquainted with many of her fellow guests to offer a word here and a smile there to most of those gathered to watch the dancers.

Despite her smiles, Madeleine was not here for her own amusement. This was an evening of business for Papa—secret business that she knew would cost him his life if things went awry. A shudder ran through her at the thought. It was nearly ten years since she first attended such a ball with him. Then she had been fresh from the schoolroom and eager for excitement. In those days she had had complete faith in her father, and relished the added frisson of such an adventure. Now she found no pleasure in it. She was older and her life had changed.

She had had her fill of excitement, adventure and loss.

Lord Tunbridge appeared, all smiles. He greeted them graciously and when her father drew out his snuffbox, His Lordship exclaimed at the exquisite workmanship of the object.

'Quite beautiful, Comte. You are aware, no doubt, that I have a fine collection of my own. It is on display in my closet here and I should be delighted to show you. Lord Froome has already expressed a desire to inspect the snuffboxes this evening and Sir John Belsay, too. Perhaps you would like to join us?'

'My lord, you are all kindness to think of me,' declared her father, bowing low. 'Of a certainty, I shall be there!'

Pocket watches were examined, a time was set and their host strolled off, leaving Madeleine and her father to continue their promenade of the room.

'I take it I am not invited to see this, er, fine collection,' remarked Madeleine, knowing full well the snuffboxes were merely an excuse for the gentlemen to slip away and talk in private.

'*Mais non, ma chère.* You would be slain with *ennui.*'

She looked at him, her eyes wide. 'But how could that be, Papa, if there are such jewelled trinkets to be seen?'

She was teasing him, of course, they both understood that, just as they both understood he would never allow her to know what he was about, as much for her own safety as his. He smiled and shook his head, but before he could respond, a gentleman in a grey peruke and with black patches on his cheek arrived to claim her for the next dance.

Madeleine had moved off to the dance floor and another hour had passed before she saw her father again. She found the Comte in one of the window embrasures and, as she approached, he swept up two glasses of wine from a passing waiter, held one out to her and raised the other in salute.

'You dance like an angel, *ma fille.*'

'*Merci,* Papa.'

'*Écoutes,* Madeleine. It is time. I must leave you for a little while.' He gazed over her head, his eyes travelling across the guests milling around as they waited for the next dance. 'You will mix with these people, if you please. Listen to their chatter and tell me later if there is anything of interest.'

'Must I stay?'

'But of course! What would be said if my lovely daughter was to leave without her papa? Also, you are promised to dance with Sir William.'

'Not *promised*, sir. When we last met, I warned him he would have to take his turn. I will not favour any gentleman above another, Papa, you know that.'

'*Mais*, Sir William Maxton must be accommodated, *ma chère*.'

She hunched a shoulder. 'I am already engaged for every dance until supper.'

'Have a care, Madeleine. Sir William is a very powerful man in London and not one to be crossed. We must remain here tonight until you have danced with him.'

Her father looked cheerful enough, but he sounded unusually sombre and Madeleine glanced about her, suddenly uneasy.

'I did not realise this would be such a grand affair. There are any number of people here with family in the north, connections in Scotland. What if someone should recognise me?'

For a moment his eyes moved to her face and

she glimpsed the cold calculation behind the smile.

'It is unlikely in the extreme that anyone here knows your history, but if you are recognised, we shall deal with it.' He shrugged. 'After all, no one would blame you for leaving that barbaric country and returning to the bosom of your family.'

A sudden pain pierced her, sharp as a blade. Yves d'Evremont might be her father, but it was a long time since she had thought of him as *family*. Those she had loved, those who had been close to her for the past four years, they were her family. Or they had been, but that time was over now. Dead and buried.

The Comte laughed softly. 'You need to look happy, *ma chère*. Remember you are here to enjoy yourself.'

Her lips stretched and curved upwards, but she knew the smile would not be reflected in her eyes.

She said accusingly, 'You told me we should be here two weeks. *Two weeks*, then we would leave for France. I have been in London now for twice that time.'

'Plans change.' His shoulders lifted slightly. '*Mais*, it is only a small delay. And a necessary one, Madeleine'

She held her peace, knowing argument was

futile. After all, it had been her decision to join her father in London. He had taken a house in Surrey Street where he lived in grand style, even insisting that fires should be kindled in the bed-chambers every day, to ward off the damp air coming from their proximity to the river. She had agreed to act as his hostess and it was too late to regret that. Too late to leave him and arouse the kind of curiosity and speculation that could spell disaster.

Besides, where could she go?

As if reading her thoughts, the Comte smiled and flicked her cheek with one careless finger. 'Pray, do not make yourself uneasy, *ma chère*. A few weeks more and this will all be over. Trust me. Now, you will smile and become my eyes and ears while I am with Lord Tunbridge, *non*?'

He drained his glass, gave her a reassuring smile and sauntered off into the crowd.

Two dances later and Madeleine was still waiting for her father's return. When the music ended she thanked her partner prettily and left him, to make her way alone through the crowd. She chattered with the ladies and flirted with the men, but all the time her alarm was growing.

There were blatant signs of Jacobite sup-port everywhere. Portraits of gentlemen in full

Highland dress adorned the walls, on a side table stood a life-size alabaster bust that she suspected was Charles Edward Stuart and the wine glasses were engraved with thistles. Even the white roses embroidered on Lady Tunbridge's gown might be construed as supporting the Young Pretender, Prince Charles Stuart, who had fled the country after the defeat of Culloden. A defeat that had heaped such harsh retribution upon the losers.

However, no one else showed any concern so she tried to put aside her fears and continued to mingle, all the time wondering how much longer she must wait for her father. Not that he would tell her what they had discussed and she knew better than to ask him. It was her role merely to accompany Papa about town, either charming those he wished to influence or distracting anyone who might become suspicious.

Her mind was diverted from its worries by the sight of a familiar figure. A lady of about her own age had entered the ballroom and Madeleine gave a smile of genuine pleasure as she hurried towards her, hands held out in greeting.

'Anne, I had not thought to see you in London!'

Miss McBinnie turned to see who had spoken.

'Nor I you,' she stammered, her face growing pale.

Anne's shock and surprise recalled Madeleine to her situation. She took Anne's fingers and gave them a warning squeeze.

'I am known as Miss d'Evremont here,' she whispered as she leaned forward to press her powdered cheek against Anne's. 'Pray do not betray me!'

'No, no. Of course I will not.'

'Bless you!' Maddie smiled. 'How long have you been in town?'

'We arrived but yesterday. Lady Tunbridge's invitation was waiting for us.' Distracted, Anne McBinnie looked about her. 'My parents are here, too…'

Maddie realised her friend was still looking uncomfortable and she stepped back a little.

'I beg your pardon; you are clearly not happy to be in my company—'

'No, no!' Anne disclaimed hastily. 'A little surprised, perhaps. I was not expecting to find you here, but I am very glad to see you, truly, only… I fear *you* will not be so pleased to see *me* when you know who else is with our party.'

Her eyes flickered towards an approaching figure and, as Madeleine turned to look, her cheeks paled.

The gentleman coming towards them was resplendent in midnight-blue velvet and silver lace.

His long hair was curled and powdered in the fashionable way, but Maddie would have recognised that lean, handsome face and the tall, broad-shouldered frame anywhere. He stopped before her, his dark eyes hard as rock as he made her a low, elegant bow.

'I bid you good evening, madam wife!'

Chapter Two

Madeleine stared up at the man towering over her. Sir Grant Rathmore, Laird of Ardvarrick and her husband. He looked calm enough, but there was no mistaking the cold fury in his gaze. She managed to keep her smile in place, but it was becoming more difficult with every moment that passed. Anne, she noticed, had moved away to intercept her parents who were drawing near and she was now talking earnestly with them.

'You should not be here!' she hissed at Grant, plying her fan to disguise the shaking of her hands.

'Why not?' he drawled. 'My place is by your side. *Wife.*'

He said the last word so quietly only Madeleine heard it. He was smiling down at her, but she felt his rage. It blazed like an aura around him and she took an involuntary step away, as if afraid she might be burned up by standing too close.

She turned to greet Sir Edmund and Lady McBinnie as they came up, but she was all too aware of Grant standing beside them, silent and clearly fuming. She dragged together her chaotic thoughts as the scrape of fiddles announced that the musicians were preparing for another minuet. Who had engaged her for this dance? Ah, yes, young Mr Thrimby. As if conjured by her thoughts, she saw the gentleman making his way towards her.

With a smile, Madeleine excused herself and went off on her partner's arm, but she struggled to maintain her calm demeanour and respond to Mr Thrimby's attempts to engage her in conversation. She was on edge, expecting at any moment to feel Grant's hand on her shoulder. It did not happen, but her spine tingled uncomfortably, all the way to the dance floor.

Grant watched Madeleine walk away, but when he went to follow her, Miss McBinnie stepped in front of him.

'Pray, *think*,' she whispered urgently, 'you must not make a scene!'

'Anne is right, my boy,' Sir Edmund put a hand on his sleeve. 'You must not draw attention to yourself. It is too dangerous, for you and for Madeleine.'

'If she is engaged in any plot of her father's then she is already in danger!'

But Sir Edmund was right. Grant knew it and fought down the furious whirlpool of emotions that threatened to consume him. He had not expected to feel like this—his reaction to seeing Madeleine again had taken him by surprise. He was accustomed to keeping his feelings in check. He had expected to feel anger when he finally tracked down his errant wife, but the sight of her, glorious in a gown of flowered silk and her delicate features alight with laughter, had taken his breath away. She looked beautiful and far happier than he had seen her for a long time.

That is what shook him most. He tried to remember the last time she had been so carefree in his company. It was a long time ago. Before the spring of last year. Memories he had buried deep suddenly surfaced. Memories of Maddie laughing up at him as they danced together at the Ardvarrick gatherings, her radiant face after a particularly hard ride through the glens. How she would laugh happily when he swept her up and carried her to their bed, her blue eyes shining like stars in the firelight…

With a supreme effort of will Grant forced the

memories away, pushing them back deep inside where they could do no harm. That was all in the past. When they had been younger and the future had been full of colour and joy and hope. Before life had become nothing more than a dismal, grey round of duty and hard work. Before the double tragedy of a stillborn baby and his father's sudden death.

Sir Edmund continued to murmur sage advice into his ear. 'You cannot wish to expose her, at least not until you know the reason for her being here.'

'But she is *my wife*, sir.' Granted uttered the words through clenched teeth.

'It is possible we are the only ones in London who know that,' replied Sir Edmund evenly. 'Madeleine did not accompany you when you last came to town. It is highly unlikely anyone would recognise her as Lady Rathmore. Have you considered, my boy? It may be that she is trying to protect your name.'

Grant uttered a savage laugh. 'I doubt it!'

'And if she *is* involved in the latest Jacobite plan,' the older man went on in his calm, measured way, 'she would not wish her fellow conspirators to know that her husband was knighted by King George for his support in the 'Forty-Five. That could put her in grave danger.'

Grant acknowledged the wisdom of his friend's words with a nod, but he made no reply. His eyes were fixed upon Madeleine as she took her place on the dance floor. He watched her shake out her skirts and smile across at her partner and the spike of jealousy in his chest was a physical pain. He had thought he was over her. He had convinced himself he felt nothing for his wife.

For the past year they had been little more than strangers sharing the same house, but Ardvarrick in mourning was a world away from this. Seeing her here in London, laughing and smiling as if she had not a care in the world, had destroyed all his hopes of remaining calm and aloof. She was dressed in that sumptuous new gown, too, one he had never seen before. It was lavishly embroidered with exotic flowers, the colours glowing like jewels in the candlelight.

She had never looked more beautiful. Or more unattainable.

Madeleine performed the steps of the dance without mishap, even though her thoughts were in turmoil. She was sure Grant was watching her and forced herself not to look for him among the crowd. Instead of her partner's smiles she could see only Grant's lean, handsome face with its strong jaw and the familiar dark brows and sculpted lips. A face she had never expected to see again.

When at last she made her final curtsy and allowed Mr Thrimby to escort her from the floor there was no sign of Grant. Perhaps he had left. She desperately wanted to believe that, but it was no real surprise when, a few moments' later, she spotted his tall figure in the crowd. And he was coming towards her.

Madeleine quickly dismissed her partner and slipped away, hiding herself in the crush during the short interval, then seeking out her next partner and hurrying him off to join the set that was forming for the country dance. She was not ready to face Grant yet. His sudden appearance this evening had thrown her thoughts into disarray.

What was he doing in town, why was he not safe in the Highlands? They had shared the same roof, but little else, for the past eighteen months and she had convinced herself that he would be glad to be rid of her. She had certainly not expected to see such savagery in his face. She needed to prepare herself before she spoke to him again.

Glancing up, she caught sight of Grant among the crowd and his murderous glare made her quake. He looked as if he wanted to walk over and physically drag her from the dance floor. She could only pray that he was not so lost to all sense of propriety that he would actually do so.

There followed a fraught game of cat and mouse. Madeleine stood up for every dance and kept her eyes away from Grant, although she knew he was never far away. Whenever the music ended, she kept her eyes fixed upon her current partner and chattered non-stop as she accompanied the bemused but flattered young gentleman back to his friends, where she would remain at the centre of the group until it was time to dance again. She expected Grant to interrupt her, but he seemed content merely to watch, something she found even more unnerving as the evening went on.

By the time supper was announced Madeleine's feet were sore and her head ached with tension. There was still no sign of Papa and she dare not approach the McBinnies, knowing Grant was one of their party. She was not even sure if they would acknowledge her as a friend any longer. Her only chance was to leave Tunbridge House, but she could not do that without first speaking to Papa.

It was then that Grant finally made his move. He stepped in front of her as she was hurrying through the Yellow Salon in search of her father. Madeleine stopped so suddenly that the heavy skirts swayed alarmingly and she almost over-balanced.

'Well, madam, have you danced your fill now?'

Looking up into his stormy face, she saw that his eyes were darker than ever. She knew he was raging inside and the candlelight glinted like angry demons in their black depths. Her lips felt dry and she ran her tongue across them before she even attempted to speak.

She said, 'What…what are you doing here, why are you in London?'

There was a heartbeat's pause before he answered, 'Is that not obvious?'

Madeleine found it difficult to breathe with her heart hammering against her ribs. Despite all that had gone before, she could not prevent a sudden flare of hope that he had come to reclaim her. However, the very thought of it made her even more anxious for him.

'It is not safe for you here,' she told him, her eyes flickering over the crowd. 'Almost everyone in this room is a Jacobite.'

His lip curled. 'Do you think I do not know that?' He glanced about him, shrugging. 'Even though I was honoured by the Hanoverian usurper

I did fight for the Stuart himself in 'Forty-Five. I believe my credit will suffice. And, naturally, I am eager to learn of this latest venture.'

Her eyes flew to his face. 'What do you know of that?'

She opened her fan and began to cool her heated cheeks while she waited for his reply, but before he could speak, Lady Tunbridge came bustling up to them, her good-natured countenance alight with smiles.

'Ah, Sir Grant, so you have met Miss d'Evremont. She is our newest and brightest star.'

'Brightest?' Grant's brows rose. He made the word sound more insult than compliment and Madeleine held her breath, wondering if he was about to denounce her as a fraud. She saw his eyes narrow, but he said merely, 'Yes, we are acquainted.'

Their hostess looked as if she would know more, but a sudden resurgence of chatter nearby caught her attention and, after uttering the hope that they were both enjoying themselves, she sailed off.

The Yellow Salon was emptying and as there was now no one close enough to hear them, Madeleine braced herself and waited for a tirade from Grant.

'I should have guessed I would find you here,'

he said, his tone scathing. 'Masquerading as a single lady, too.'

She flushed. 'My father thought it would be best I use my former name.'

'Ah, yes.' He looked up, his eyes scanning the emptying room. 'Where is the old reprobate? You must introduce us, my dear. I think it is time I met my father-in-law, don't you?'

She put up her chin, 'You can have no interest in the Comte de Vaucluse.'

'Oh, but I have,' he said softly.

There was no humour in his smile and the menace in his eyes caused Madeleine to clasp her hands tightly about her closed fan.

She said, 'Not here. Not tonight, Grant, I beg you!'

'Why not tonight?'

'Someone will be sure to notice. They might guess at the connection...'

'You should have thought of that before you set out on this charade. It would not be difficult for any interested party to discover we are married.' His lip curled. 'No doubt you thought you were safe. After all, no one in London would know or care about an insignificant Highland laird. By heaven, I doubt any of these mincing, painted fops have even heard of Ardvarrick!'

The bitterness in his voice smote her. She suddenly felt like weeping.

'Please Grant, do not become embroiled in my father's machinations. I would not have you put yourself at risk.'

'No? I am touched by your concern, madam. Very well, then you and I must talk.'

He held out his arm to her and she took a step back.

'No. Not tonight.'

'Yes, tonight! Let us have this done with as soon as maybe, that we may both get on with our own business.'

His whole demeanour was so fierce that Madeleine feared he would physically drag her away if she did not comply. She placed her fingers on his sleeve and he escorted her back through the salon and away from the supper room. He murmured softly and when she looked up she saw he was smiling, as if entranced by his companion, but his eyes were still hard. This was purely for the benefit of anyone watching and she responded in the same vein. To an observer this was merely a little flirtation, nothing at all out of the ordinary.

Nothing that Madeleine had not done a dozen times before at the balls, routs and parties she had attended during the past few weeks. Those flirtations had been harmless, conducted in a corner, a window embrasure or even on the terrace, but always in full view of other guests. Now Grant was slipping a silver coin to one of the footmen and asking where he might speak privately with the lady. Madeleine's face flamed at the implication, but she put up her chin and fixed a smile in place. There was no way of avoiding this now without attracting unwanted attention.

Chapter Three

⚬⚬⚬⚬⚬

They were shown into a small sitting room illuminated by only the two branched candlesticks on the mantelshelf. As soon as the door had closed behind them, Madeleine dragged her hand free from Grant's arm and moved away.

'Very well,' she said, turning to face him, 'tell me now why you are here and what it is you want to say to me?'

Grant did not reply immediately. Instead he tried to quell the tumult of rage and bewilderment churning inside him. She was the only reason he had come to London. Not out of love—no, by heaven, she had killed any possibility of that! He had seen it as his duty to find his wife and discover just why she had left Ardvarrick. But their unexpected meeting tonight had thrown him completely off balance. The McBinnies had asked him to come with them to Tunbridge

House and he had accepted out of courtesy. He had thought to find some diversion in the company. What he had *not* expected was to find his wife, sumptuously attired in an expensive silk gown and with her dark, unpowdered curls glistening in the candlelight, being fêted and admired by everyone.

As soon as he had seen her, the anger he had kept under control for the past weeks had boiled over. Now, as she fixed him with a haughty look from those sapphire-blue eyes, he was damned if he would give her the satisfaction of knowing he had travelled hundreds of miles just for her sake.

'I need to know what you and your father are doing in London.' Good, that sounded calm enough. He went on. 'Sir Edmund told me he had received a letter from an old acquaintance, a Lord Elibank. It was carefully worded, but Sir Edmund knows the man to be an avowed Jacobite and it was clear something is afoot.'

'Yes, I met Lord Elibank here this evening.' She looked about her, as if afraid someone might be hiding in the shadows. 'I had not thought the McBinnies would want anything to do with such plots.'

'Sir Edmund never believed the 'Forty-Five could succeed, but he told me His Lordship's arguments were persuasive and he was intrigued.

It seems there is a new plot afoot and, coupled with the growing dissatisfaction with the Prince of Wales, Elibank believes the Stuart might now have a greater chance of succeeding in England.' Grant looked directly at her. 'Is that why your father is here?'

Those smooth white shoulders lifted in a shrug.

'I think so, but Papa deliberately does not share all his plans with me.' She eyed him uncertainly. 'Please, Grant, I do not know the whole, but I have no doubt there is great danger. I would not have you embroiled in any of this.'

If you are involved, then so am I!

But he could not bring himself to say as much and after a moment's silence she spoke again.

'Papa has many contacts both in England and France. I believe he is acting as go-between for the Stuart Prince's followers and those in Government who can help them. Men of power and influence.'

'And what is your role in all this?'

'As always, I watch, I listen. He calls me his eyes and ears.' Her lips twisted a little. 'A lady and gentleman may whisper together at a gathering such as this without arousing much interest at all.'

'You are playing a dangerous game, madam.'

She gave a little sigh. 'With Papa, it was ever thus. He says it will be over soon.'

'And if you are caught?' He saw the stubborn set to her mouth and felt his anger growing again. 'The penalties for treason are dire, madam. You could be burned at the stake for what you are doing!'

She was pale, but still looked defiant. 'That is no concern of yours.'

'You are my *wife*, madam. Whatever you do is my concern! I am taking you back to Ardvarrick, away from all this.' He reached out and caught her wrist. 'I have lodgings in Henrietta Street. You will come there with me now.'

'Oh, no, I will not!'

She struggled against his hold and with a growl he pulled her closer. 'Do not goad me too far, Maddie. I'll pick you up and carry you if needs be!'

'No, let me go! I cannot leave Papa; I have given him my word.'

'Then you will break it.'

She stopped struggling and looked up at him, her large eyes dark, luminous pools in the candlelight. He breathed in sharply as her perfume filled his senses. It was tantalisingly familiar and quite suddenly he recalled how it used to be between them. How much she had entranced him in those early days of their marriage. When desire could flare with just a touch, a glance.

Grant's anger was turning into something much more dangerous. His heart was pounding now. He felt light-headed, giddy with the need to crush his lips against hers and lose himself in her. She was so close, her mouth soft and inviting…

'Please, Grant, *please*. I cannot leave London yet!'

The distress in her voice sobered him. She did not want him, or his kisses. Love, or whatever it was they had once shared, had long since died.

'I cannot leave,' she repeated, her voice low and not quite steady. 'My father has no choice but to do this, his life is forfeit if he does not.'

'A pretty tale!' he muttered, releasing her and swinging away towards the fireplace.

'I believe this time it is true. Oh, you know as well as I that Papa has always been engaged in one intrigue or another, but this time it is different, I am sure of it. He tells me very little, but I think, I *believe*, he had no choice but to carry out this assignment. I have never known my father to be so anxious, although he does his best to hide it from me.' She stopped and he heard her draw in a breath before she said in a quiet, desperate voice, 'He needs my help, Grant.'

'He is using you.' He threw the words at her over his shoulder. 'Yves d'Evremont abandoned you during the last Rising, have you forgotten that? You owe him nothing!'

'He is my *father*! He may be a most unnatural parent, but he is the only one I have. How can I refuse?'

Her appeal caught Grant on the raw. The loss of his own father last summer was still a painful memory. He gripped the cold marble of the mantelshelf and stared down into the empty hearth. There was a whisper of silken skirts as she came closer.

'Please let me stay, Grant. No one here knows we are related, apart from the McBinnies, and I am sure we may trust them not to disclose the truth. There is no reason why anyone else should discover it. And if they do, I shall tell them I have left you.' A moment's silence, then she said quietly, 'I give you my word I shall not do anything to bring shame upon your family. When this is over, I will go to France with my father and you need never hear from me again. You will be free of me.'

'You begged me in your letter not to follow you,' he said bitterly. 'I should have taken heed of that and left you to your fate.'

'Oh, how I wish you had, sir!'

There was such sincerity in her voice that Grant knew it could not be clearer. The ties between them were irrevocably severed. He straightened, keeping his back to her as he lifted his eyes to the mirror above the fireplace. In the dim light his reflection stared back at him, a stranger with grey-powdered hair and fancy lace at his throat. When he spoke, his voice, too, did not sound like his own.

'Very well,' he said. 'Stay if you must. Assist your father. I shall importune you no further.'

He walked to the door and was about to open it when she said, 'Promise me you will quit London now, Grant. Go with all speed. You must not risk Ardvarrick by becoming involved in this conspiracy.'

He turned to look at her. 'Ardvarrick is already at risk, but whatever I choose to do, madam, it is no longer your concern!'

And with that, he went out, closing the door upon his wife.

Madeleine sank down on a chair, shaking too much for her limbs to sustain her. Why had Grant come here? Their marriage was dead and her carefully worded letter should have ensured he would not want to follow her. After Culloden he had vowed never again to be caught up in the machinations of government or the Jacobites. He had worked so hard, improving Ardvarrick, for himself and his people. It made no sense that he should risk it all now.

She must try to think clearly. Grant had said Sir Edmund had come to town to discover what this latest plot could mean for them—was it so very extraordinary that Grant should be interested, too? Madeleine dropped her head in her hands. Having talked to him, heard the cold disdain in his voice, it was far easier to believe he had come to London intrigued by a Jacobite plot than to find her.

The door opened and she looked up to see her father had come in.

'*Tiens*, Madeleine, you did not appear at supper. Thus, I come in search of you! What do you do in here, alone?' The Comte walked across to her, the boned skirts of his gold damask coat swaying. He reached down for her hands and gently pulled her to her feet. 'But what is this, *ma fille*, do I see tears?'

'No, no, Papa, I had something in my eye and came in here to deal with it.' She disengaged herself. 'Is your business finished, can we leave now?'

'Not quite yet, that is why I came in search of you.' He held out his arm. 'Supper is over and the dancing is about to recommence. We must return to the ballroom before you are missed.'

'First, Papa, there is something I must tell you. Grant Rathmore is here tonight.' His brows went up and she added hastily, 'Not to find me. He came with our...with *his* friends, Sir Edmund and Lady McBinnie.'

'*Vraiment?* I did not see him, but then, we have never met.' He laughed softly, 'We might have brushed shoulders this evening and I would not even know of it. Very well, let us go and find him. I am most eager to meet this Scottish laird!'

She hung back. 'Papa, take heed, I will not have Grant drawn into your plans.'

'No, no, *ma fille*, but he is your husband, and it is most natural that I should have a great desire to meet him. And his friends.' He smiled at her, all innocence, and put out his arm. 'Shall we go?'

Squaring her shoulders, Madeleine placed her fingers on his sleeve and accompanied him out of the room.

Chapter Four

The McBinnies were standing near the open doors to the ballroom, so close that ignoring them was out of the question, but Madeleine was nervous as Papa carried her inexorably forward. They were such old friends of Grant and his family. How would they react to meeting her father?

Sir Edmund saw them and bowed to her. 'Ah, Mademoiselle d'Evremont! I am so glad to see you again tonight. It was most remiss of me not to tell you earlier what a charming surprise it is to find you here.'

He was smiling at her with such understanding that she could breathe again and perform the necessary introductions. Papa was all charming complaisance and while the two gentlemen conversed, Madeleine looked uncertainly at Lady McBinnie, who gave her a reassuring smile.

'We are *truly* pleased to see you, my dear,'

she said, taking Maddie's arm and drawing her away a little. 'It was such a shock when we heard that you had left Ardvarrick, but I know that this past year or so has been very trying for you and your husband.' She lowered her voice a little. 'Ardvarrick has left, now, if you were worrying about seeing him again.'

'He is angry with me, but that is not surprising.'

'No, but he will come round, I am sure—'

Maddie put up her hand. 'Pray, ma'am, say no more. I hope very much that you and Sir Edmund can persuade Grant to return to Scotland, and as soon as maybe.'

'Without you?' Lady McBinnie's brows went up. 'I am sure he will not do that.'

Madeleine hesitated, torn between loyalty to her father and concern for her friends.

At last, she said quietly, 'It is not safe for him to be here.' She added, with an urgent, warning look, 'Or for you, ma'am.'

My lady gave her another smile. 'I understand your concern, but rest assured, we are in London purely on a visit of pleasure. It is a treat for Anne, who has never been to London. Is that not so, my dear?' Lady McBinnie turned to her daughter, who was standing silently beside them.

'No, it is my first time and I am enjoying it

very much.' Anne chuckled. 'Although I am beginning to wish we had not brought Eilidh with
us! You will remember my maid, Maddie, she is
quite outraged that we should come here rather
than Edinburgh!'

'Poor Eilidh,' said Lady McBinnie, smiling.
'She still sees the English as our enemies and
cannot look at the King's head upon the coins
without a frown.'

It is quite true!' Anne stifled a giggle and
leaned closer to whisper to Madeleine, 'She even
has a white cockade sewn to her garters.'

Even Madeleine could not forbear a smile at
that. 'Oh, dear,' she said, 'that could be very
awkward for you.'

Anne shook her head. 'No, not really. She is
a clever girl and knows that she must not display her Stuart sympathies while we are in town.
And she is certainly the best dresser of hair that I
have ever had. I really could not do without her.'

'I still urge you all to be careful,' Madeleine
replied earnestly. 'Please do not allow my father
to persuade Sir Edmund into…to do anything he
does not like!'

'No, of course not,'

Lady McBinnie was quick to reassure her and
Anne stepped up to take her arm in a gesture
Madeleine found immensely comforting.

'You must not worry about us, my dear friend,' said Anne quietly. 'Papa knows what he is about. He will not do anything to put us into danger.'

'Charming people,' remarked the Comte du Vaucluse, when he and Maddie finally moved on. 'Sir Edmund is very well connected, you know, even though he prefers to live so quietly. He could be a most valuable acquaintance.'

She knew that thoughtful tone and said quickly, 'Pray do not ask my friends to be a party to your schemes, Papa.'

He laughed gently. 'These are not *my* schemes, Madeleine, not this time. Ah, and here is your next dance partner.'

Madeleine followed his glance and her mouth turned down in an expression of distaste.

'Sir William Maxton! He is not my next part-ner as I have not agreed to dance with him. I have told you, Papa, I cannot like the man.'

'It is not necessary to like all of one's asso-ciates, but one must be polite to them,' stated her father. 'And you *will* dance with him, for my sake.' He led her inexorably towards a large, stocky gentleman in a powdered bagwig and a coat of sage-green damask. 'Sir William! *Je suis votre serviteur.*'

Even with the crowd jostling them on all sides, her father's bow was a masterpiece of elegance.

'Comte.' Sir William bowed low before turning to Madeleine. 'And Mademoiselle d'Evremont.' He took her hand and brushed her gloved fingers with his lips. 'You look quite charming this evening, ma'am. I hope you will honour me with your hand for the next dance?'

Aware of her father's eyes upon her, Madeleine dropped a curtsy, all graciousness.

'But of course, Sir William. With pleasure.'

Maddie smiled and said all that was proper, but never had a dance seemed so long or so tedious. Her head was still reeling from her meeting with Grant and she parried her partner's attempts to flirt with a distracted air that was in no way assumed. She could only hope it would give Sir William a distaste for her company.

Striding away from Tunbridge House, Grant declined all offers of a chair and walked the short distance back to Henrietta Street. It was still early and he was not accosted, although his mood was such that he would have welcomed the opportunity to lash out at something, or someone. His head was full of Madeleine, the sweet, musical tone of her voice, the subtle perfume she wore that always reminded him of summer.

Those deep blue eyes that had once slain him with a glance, or sparkled with laughter and sent his heart soaring.

It was the shock of seeing her again, he told himself. He was immune to her charm now. For more than a year—eighteen long months!—he had fought against it, throwing himself into his duties at Ardvarrick. He had ignored the siren call of the marriage bed for so long it had become second nature to keep her at a distance, even though, at times, all he had wanted was to drag her into his arms and lose himself in her kisses.

They had become little more than polite strangers, sharing the same house. He had convinced himself he was content with the arrangement, but some small, tormenting devil told him he was wrong. He wanted her now, more than ever. Even though it was clear she did not want him. Grant muttered a savage curse, causing a passing stranger to step quickly into the gutter and hurry on his way.

Having reached his lodging, Grant made his way up to his rooms. His man was dozing in a chair and jumped up hurriedly when the door opened.

'Sir! I was not expecting you for hours yet.'

'There was nothing to stay for. Fetch me some brandy, Robert, will you?'

Grant waited until he was alone, then he shrugged off his coat and waistcoat and loosened the lace at his neck. Those first years of marriage at Ardvarrick had been so full of joy and laughter. How had it come to this? What had happened to destroy their happiness?

Her father called and she left you. Yves d'Evremont had only to snap his fingers and she abandoned her duties as your wife to go to him.

'It was a mistake to come here,' he muttered savagely. 'I will go back to Ardvarrick and leave the woman to her fate!' He looked around impatiently. 'Robert! Where are you, man, where's that brandy?'

He threw himself into a chair, feeling even worse for roaring so angrily at his manservant. Robert had been his valet and personal servant for the past four years, ever since they met in Edinburgh, soon after Grant's marriage. Robert's previous employer had just died, leaving him without employment, and Grant had taken him on. Despite the fact that Robert was an Englishman, they had become close friends and Robert was now a trusted confidant. He had been a quiet but steady support following the unexpected death of the old Laird, Grant's father.

That tragic time was still fresh in Grant's memory. He had needed to stay strong for his mother and for Madeleine, who was still recovering after losing their baby in childbirth. Ailsa and Maddie were his responsibility, his alone, and he could not add his own suffering to theirs. He had buried his grief deep and looked after everyone, his people, his land, his family. And how had he been rewarded? Madeleine had left him. She had returned to the glittering salons and intrigues of her father's world.

Robert came back in with the brandy. He put the tray down on the table beside Grant's chair and silently poured a measure of the amber liquid into a glass. Grant gave a nod of thanks.

'That will be all,' he said. 'You may go to bed. No need to wait up for me.'

'Are you sure? I am happy to—'

'No questions, I pray you. Goodnight!'

'Very well, sir.'

'Oh, and, Robert…we will be leaving London as soon as maybe. Tomorrow, if it can be arranged.'

'So soon? I beg your pardon, sir, I thought… And will my lady be joining us?'

Grant was already refilling his glass and he swore as he spilled some of the precious spirit on to the tray.

'No. We return alone.' He sat back and glared up at his man. 'Be ready to leave at dawn.'

'That may be a little difficult, sir, tomorrow being the Lord's Day.' Robert coughed. 'If I might suggest postponing your departure until Monday, sir? It will give you time to consider your position.'

'Damn you, there is nothing to consider!' His words were met with silence and the look on Robert's face said clearly he did not agree. Grant scowled at him. 'You think I should stay?'

His man picked up the velvet coat and shook it out before tenderly laying it over his arm.

'It is not my place to say, sir,' he replied woodenly. 'However, I should not want you to do anything you will later regret.'

With that he gathered up the discarded waistcoat and went out, leaving Grant to his thoughts and his brandy.

Chapter Five

⁓⁓⁓

The following day was Sunday. The Comte de Vaucluse and his daughter did not attend church, but in the afternoon they did take an open carriage to Hyde Park. It was only to be expected that the park would be crowded on such a fine day, after all, it was the end of August and who knew how many more summer days there would be? Madeleine sat up beside her father, her parasol unfurled to shade her face from the sun, as they made their slow progress around the Ring. She smiled and said all that was necessary to everyone: a nod to Mr Thrimby when he passed them on his prancing bay horse, a smile to Lord Froome and his lady as they strolled by. They paused to exchange greetings with Lady Primrose, who was taking the air in her carriage, and she reminded the Comte he was engaged to join her little soirée at the end of the week.

'And you must bring your charming daughter,' declared my lady. 'Mademoiselle d'Evremont will give an added lustre to the evening.'

'Thank you, ma'am.' Maddie inclined her head. 'After such a compliment, how can I refuse?'

She smiled, but it was an effort and she was relieved when their carriage moved on. After seeing Grant last night, she wanted only to crawl away into a corner and hide from the world. To grieve for all she had lost.

'How much more of this, Papa?' she muttered as they continued on their way.

'Patience, *ma fille*.' He grasped her hand and squeezed it. 'Another week, two perhaps, and this will be finished. We will go to France and you shall meet your new mama. The Comtesse is anxious to see you and you will like her, I think. She has no daughter of her own and means to spoil you, there is no doubt of that. You will be a lady again, Madeleine.'

'I am already a lady,' she reminded him.

'Pshaw, your husband's knighthood, bestowed by a usurper! It means nothing, as little as his estates in the cold and barren north. In France you shall have riches and comfort beyond your dreams. You will want for nothing.'

'Except my husband.'

Even to her own ears the words sounded desperately sad and Maddie was obliged to blink back the hot tears that were threatening to spill over.

'You will forget him, *ma chère*. He was never worthy of you.'

'Some would argue it is the other way around, Papa.'

'Then they are fools of the most ignorant! *Non. En France*, you will have your pick of the gentlemen. I do not doubt you may take any man you choose for your lover.'

'I have told you before, Papa,' she retorted, 'I will be no man's mistress. Ever!'

He looked at her for a moment, then he gave a little shrug.

'Si tu veux.' He smiled, but she knew his attention was already wandering.

Lady Tunbridge was approaching in her landau. The Comte waved in greeting and both carriages stopped. As Madeleine listened to her father's fulsome compliments to the lady, thanking her for the most delightful ball the previous evening, she knew that her problems were already banished from his thoughts.

They moved on and completed another full circuit of the Ring before the Comte suggested they should alight and walk a little way. Madeleine regarded the fashionable throng strolling beneath the trees and suddenly felt overwhelmed by the sight of so many people in one place. She had a strong wish to be back at Ardvarrick, striding out across the hills and moors. The heather would be at its best now, vast swathes of purple, vibrant in the sunshine. She had missed the blaeberry season, but there would be blackberries in the hedgerows and then the elderberries. How busy she would be in the stillroom, if she was at home.

It pierced her, like a knife through the heart, to remember that Ardvarrick was no longer her home.

The Comte ordered the carriage to stop. 'Come, Madeleine, we shall walk. I see a number of our friends, it will be *très amusant.*'

Bowing to the inevitable, she climbed down and took his arm.

The purpose of this promenade was to see and be seen. The Comte strolled along with Madeleine, idly swinging his cane from his free hand. They paused often to exchange niceties with this acquaintance or that, to indulge in a little gossip and even to agree arrangements with Sir Evelyn and Lady Molton to make up a party for Vauxhall. Madeleine said all that was expected of her, but she felt little interest in anything or anyone, until she spotted Sir Edmund coming towards them with his wife and daughter.

The Comte stopped and bowed to the McBinnies, all easy charm. He turned to walk with Sir Edmund and Lady McBinnie, leaving Madeleine and Anne to follow behind.

'Have you heard from Grant?' Maddie asked, angry with herself for caring, but unable to resist. 'Is he leaving town?'

Anne looked anxious. 'I have no idea. He left Tunbridge House early last night and without a word to us.'

'That was my doing,' said Madeleine wretchedly. 'We argued and I begged him to return to Ardvarrick.'

'Ah, I see, and I am sorry I cannot help you. We have heard nothing from him. I am sorry, too, that you and Grant have quarrelled.'

'Thank you.' Maddie hesitated. 'I am very thankful that you and your parents have not cut my acquaintance.'

'Why should we do that?'

'Because you and Grant are such old friends. I thought, having left him…'

'He has never asked us to choose between you, Madeleine.' Anne took her arm and gave it a little squeeze. 'You and I have been friends

ever since we first met, when you brought Grant
to our house after he had been wounded by the
redcoats. I would not abandon you now, just because you have had a little falling out.'

'If only it *was* such a small thing,' said Madeleine, trying hard to sound calm. 'We are…
irreconcilable. He made that very clear to me
yesterday evening.'

'He did? We thought…' she glanced towards
her parents '…we *hoped* a few weeks apart would
have given you both time to think again and resolve your differences.'

'I am afraid not. I return to France with my
father.'

Anne regarded her for a few moments, then
she sighed. 'I shall miss you very much, Maddie. When do you leave?'

'It is not yet decided. In a few weeks, perhaps,' she answered vaguely. Papa had not divulged his plans to her and nor would he, until
departure was imminent. That had always been
his way.

'Then we must make the most of your company while you are here!' declared Anne. 'I shall
call for you tomorrow and we will go shopping
together.'

'Oh. I am not sure…'

'Do say you will come,' Anne urged her. 'You

will know much better than I which are the best shops.'

Maddie laughed and shook her head. 'I do not think so. My only visit to London was many years ago, Anne. Before I was married.'

'Did you not come here with Grant when he received his knighthood—?' Anne broke off, covering her mouth with one hand, then saying remorsefully, 'Ah, no. I had forgot. You were not well…'

'I had just discovered I was with child.' Maddie lost all desire to smile. 'We agreed it would be best if I did not travel, after what had happened. The first time. Not that the outcome was any different.'

The memory of that first miscarriage was still strong. The disappointment she had felt, the conviction that she had failed Grant, although he had been quick to deny it. The pain had been intense, but it was nothing to the agony of the stillbirth that followed. That had happened in March last year and, three months later, Grant's father had died suddenly of a fever, throwing the house deeper into mourning. Looking back, the past year and a half had been full of grief and loneliness.

Maddie gave herself a little shake and summoned up a smile for her friend.

'Let us not think of that now,' she said. 'I should very much like to go shopping with you. Do, please, call for me tomorrow and we shall go exploring. We will discover for ourselves the most fashionable places to spend our money!'

Discussions about their proposed expedition diverted them until the little party had returned to the point where the Comte's carriage was waiting. When the young ladies divulged their plan to the others, it was met with approval.

'You do not object, Papa?' Madeleine asked her father. 'You have no other engagements that require my presence?'

'Nothing, *ma chère*. I am very happy for you to spend the day with Mademoiselle McBinnie.' His beaming smile encompassed them both. '*En effet*, it is most acceptable, because I have at this moment invited Sir Edmund and his lady to join us for dinner tomorrow!'

Having agreed everything, they took their leave of Sir Edmund and his family and the Comte helped Madeleine into the carriage, but as soon as they had resumed their drive she turned to frown at him.

'What are you about, Papa, inviting the McBinnies to Surrey Street?'

He gave her a look of pained innocence. 'I

did it for you, *ma fille*. I thought you would be pleased to spend more time with your old friends.'

'Fustian! You do nothing if it is not in your own interests.'

He shrugged. 'It is true that I wish to discuss certain matters with Sir Edmund. I think he could be very useful.'

'I have told you, I would rather you did not involve them in your machinations!' She grasped his arm, saying earnestly, 'These are my friends, Papa. I would not have them dragged into danger.'

'The very fact Sir Edmund has come to London at the behest of his friend Lord Elibank tells me he has an interest in what is afoot.' He patted her hand. 'You may be easy, Madeleine. I coerce no one into helping me, you know that.'

'No,' she said bitterly, remembering the letters he had written to her. 'You coax and cajole people into going along with your plans!'

He looked at her, one pencilled brow arched in enquiry. 'Are you saying I encouraged you to leave your husband, *ma chérie*? *Non*. You were unhappy and I merely offered you a way out of your predicament.' When she did not reply he laughed softly. 'You are my daughter, Madeleine. Admit it, you crave excitement, adventure, not *la vie ennuyeuse* that you lived with your Scottish laird!'

Madeleine twirled her parasol and stared ahead of her, refusing to answer. Perhaps her father was right—she had been running away, but not because she was bored. Only now, seeing Grant again, did she realise that it was not so easy to escape from heartache.

Chapter Six

⁓⁓⁓⁓⁓⁓

Shopping with Anne McBinnie proved a welcome diversion for Madeleine. By the time she had arrived in Surrey Street, a month ago, her father had already acquired the magnificent gowns and dresses essential for her stay in London and all that had been required was a seamstress to carry out any necessary alterations. She had quite forgotten the pleasures of visiting a fashionable mantua maker, or browsing through the wares of the silk mercers in Spitalfields to choose her own fabrics.

She spent hours with Anne in various establishments, selecting hats and gloves, new boots for driving and pretty heeled shoes for dancing. As she sent yet another footman back to the carriage with his arms full of her purchases, she was disturbed by the idea that her father might be right after all; perhaps she did want more than a quiet life at Ardvarrick.

'Do you have a riding habit, Madeleine?' Anne demanded, breaking into her thoughts.

'Why, yes. I wore it to travel to London.'

'I do not mean your woollen broadcloth,' said her friend, dismissively. 'It is very serviceable, I agree, but you have had it for ever and it is hardly modish. You must order a new one before you go to France,' Anne declared. 'I have heard no one can compete with the London tailors for fit and elegance. Only think how well it would look!'

'Perhaps.' Madeleine was non-committal, but as they continued to stroll past the fashionable shops, she allowed herself to consider Anne's suggestion.

Her riding habit was four years old, having been made as part of her wedding clothes, although she had had little use for it in the past two years. It had been put away before her last confinement and not fetched out again until she had dressed to leave Ardvarrick. She remembered now how she had hoped, once she began to recover her health and her spirits in the weeks following the stillbirth, that she and Grant might start to ride out again together. But then Logan Rathmore had died and all her hopes had faded away like morning mist.

Once Grant became Laird of Ardvarrick Madeleine had seen very little of him, except at dinner. He spent much of his time riding over his lands, but he had never invited her to go with him. In fact, whenever she had suggested going out together he made excuses not to do so and when he did come home he shut himself away with his books and ledgers. She could not accuse him of cruelty, or neglect. He had never refused a request to purchase anything, whether it was for herself or the house, and he was always perfectly polite, but she felt as if he had withdrawn from her.

As for the nights, Grant showed no sign of wanting her back in his bed. Her mother-in-law was distraught after Logan's death, so there was no shortage of work to be done in managing the household and Maddie had found some solace in that, but it did not fill the aching void she felt inside at the loss of Grant's company. It was several months before Ailsa started to take an interest in anything, but by the spring her grief was easing. She had even begun to play her beloved harp again and, encouraged by this, Maddie confided her anxieties about Grant.

'Be patient, my dear,' Ailsa had advised her. 'He has lost a son and a father and is struggling to come to terms with everything. Give him time and he will come around.'

But Ailsa had been wrong. Spring gave way to summer and still Grant remained cold and distant. Madeleine was anxious not to cause Ailsa any further distress, so she did not mention her own unhappiness or the growing restlessness. Maddie knew Grant's love for her had died, there was no child, and no hope of one, to keep them together. Their marriage was over.

'There is no perhaps about it!' Anne declared, interrupting these dismal musings.

'About what?' asked Maddie, dragging herself back to the present.

'You must have a new riding habit,' said her friend decisively. 'My father will know the best tailor to make one for you, we will ask his advice when we get back to Surrey Street.'

'Yes, very well. That is a good idea,' Madeleine agreed and thrust aside her unhappy thoughts. After all, she would have to make the long journey back to her father's home in France. A new and stylish riding habit would be better for travelling. And for meeting Papa's wife, the Comtesse, for the first time.

'Good, then that is settled,' said Anne, taking Madeleine's arm. 'Now, there are some very pretty bonnets in the window over there that I should like to look at.'

'Another milliner, Anne?' Maddie teased her. 'You have already purchased two new bonnets today. When will you find time to wear them all?'

'Oh, Mama intends that we should stay in London for at least another month,' replied her friend. 'Come along, let us cross the street. And afterwards, we will take the carriage to the warehouse she suggested.'

Laughing, Madeleine accompanied her friend across to the milliner's shop, where they browsed through the assortment of caps, hats and bonnets and later they drove on to visit a selection of warehouses. As Anne chattered away about the parties she had attended and the new acquaintances they had made while in London, many of them introduced by the Comte de Vaucluse, Maddie became increasingly uneasy.

She was afraid her friends were being drawn into a dangerous game, partly, if not wholly, of her father's making. The British government would surely consider any overt support for Charles Edward Stuart to be treason. Papa had also hinted at powerful men behind the schemes, men who would not tolerate the failure of their plan. If that was the case, then she feared the threat to those involved was increased considerably.

However, she did not want to worry Anne, so she decided she would mention the matter to Sir Edmund later. For now she pushed aside her doubts and threw herself into the pleasures of shopping. Maddie would very much prefer her friends had nothing to do with any plan involving her father, but one thing she had learned from her years as Yves d'Evremont's hostess was how to put on a brave face. Confidence was essential to the success of his schemes and, very much aware of the risks to the McBinnies and to Grant, she could not afford for this one to fail.

Visiting so many shops and warehouses took up a considerable part of the day and it was not until very close to the dinner hour that Madeleine returned to Surrey Street. After assuring herself that all was in readiness in the dining room and below stairs, she ran up to her room and scrambled into an evening gown of holly-green silk embellished with lavish quantities of gold lace.

Her maid had just finished dressing her hair when she heard the knocker, announcing the arrival of their first guests. She flew from her stool, snatched up her fan and ran quickly out of the room. The chatter from the hall below told her the guests were divesting themselves of their outer garments and she was already on the stairs, words of greeting on her lips, when she heard a smooth deep voice that there was no mistaking. She stopped and quickly moved back on to the shadowy landing.

Madeleine heard a movement behind her and looked around to see her father approaching. She caught his arm and drew him back into the corridor.

'What is the meaning of this?' she demanded in a furious whisper.

'Oh, what, *chérie*?'

'Grant Rathmore is in the hall with the McBinnies!'

'Is he? *Très bon.*' Yves d'Evremont nodded, quite unperturbed.

'You knew he was coming?'

'*Mais oui.* When we did not meet at Tunbridge House I was *désolé*, but Sir Edmund introduced us this afternoon and I invited Sir Grant to join us. I am eager to further my acquaintance with my son-in-law.'

'After all that has happened?' She glared at him. 'After I told you last night my marriage is at an end, you still want me to sit down to dinner with him?'

He eyed her for a moment, then said in a more serious tone than he was wont to use, 'There are matters at stake here of far more importance than your marriage, *ma fille*. Also…perhaps you should prepare yourself for the fact that Sir Grant Rathmore's reason for coming here tonight may not be to see *you*.'

His words were gently spoken, but they sliced into Maddie. Not that she would ever admit that. She concealed the hurt beneath a veneer of indifference.

'Very true,' she said coldly. 'Nothing has ever been more important to you than your latest scheme, has it, Papa?'

Suppressing any sign of anger or mortification, Madeleine fell into step beside her father and they went down the stairs together. She wanted Grant to leave London, not only to save her the pain of seeing him again, but also to remove him from harm's way. If he became entangled in her father's plans, then she was very much afraid of what would happen to him.

'My poor girl, are you quite worn out from traipsing all over town with Anne today?

Lady McBinnie was the first to greet Madeleine as she entered the room.

'No indeed I am not, ma'am. I found it prodigiously enjoyable, I assure you.'

She was relieved how steady her voice sounded. She was also pleased to find she could walk so calmly across to a sofa and sit down with Anne and her mother, although she was painfully aware of the three gentlemen talking together on the far side of the room.

Sir Edmund was dressed with his customary neatness in a dark coat, in marked contrast to her father, who looked magnificent in ruby velvet embroidered with gold thread. But although she would not allow her eyes to dwell upon Grant, it was he who held her attention.

He had been talking to Anne earlier, smiling and seemingly untroubled, until he turned to acknowledge Madeleine's entrance. He had given her the briefest of nods before walking away to engage Sir Edmund in conversation.

Now, she kept her head high and her eyes averted. Not for the world would she admit how much Grant's cold indifference hurt her. Lady McBinnie was eager to hear about their shopping expedition and she threw herself into an animated description of the fabrics they had seen, the gloves and ribbons they had purchased and the changes she had noted in the town since her last visit. She would show Grant Rathmore that he was not the only one who could be carefree!

Across the room, Grant tried hard to concentrate upon what Sir Edmund was saying, but he was all too aware of Madeleine, laughing and chattering with the other ladies. He wished now he had not come, but after spending Sunday mulling over the situation he knew he could not return to Ardvarrick and abandon Madeleine. Her father was a rogue and Grant did not trust him to keep her safe.

Not that Grant had planned the meeting with the Comte de Vaucluse earlier that day. He had been in one of the coffee houses near Devereux Court, where for a small fee one could read all the pamphlets of the day as well as the latest news sheets. Sir Edmund had recommended the place to him, so he was not surprised when that gentleman came in. What he was not expecting was for him to be accompanied by Yves d'Evremont.

The introduction had bordered on the farcical. Sir Edmund presented Grant to the Comte de Vaucluse as if he had been no more than a passing acquaintance and all three men had conducted themselves accordingly. Grant saw before him a lavishly dressed man of middling years in a powdered bagwig and he searched beneath the maquillage of the once-handsome face for any resemblance to Madeleine. He recalled hearing her say that she had something of her mother's looks, but he could detect a likeness with her father, too. It was there, in a fleeting expression or a sudden twinkling of the eyes.

They sat down to drink coffee together, but only the Comte appeared at ease with the situation, expounding easily upon any subject that arose. However, when he referred to his lovely daughter, Grant could not help himself.

'Ah, yes, *Mademoiselle* d'Evremont,' he said, trying not to grind his teeth as he uttered her name. 'I do not quite understand, Monsieur le Comte. You speak often of your Comtesse, so why was it necessary to bring your daughter with you to London as your hostess?'

If Grant was hoping to discompose Yves d'Evremont, then he was disappointed. The Comte merely laughed softly and waved one white hand.

'A question most reasonable, Sir Grant,' the older man replied cheerfully. 'Madame la Comtesse does not enjoy the travel. Even more, she does not like to travel abroad. My daughter has played hostess for me for so many years and she is most accomplished at the task.' The smile deepened in his grey eyes. '*Vraiment*, I do not know how I would go on without her.'

It was a blatant taunt and Grant resisted the urge to make a riposte. He knew his anger was not caused by jealousy. Without love there could not be such a thing. But he was not an ogre and he did not want Madeleine to come to any harm.

Listening to her now, here in the Comte's drawing room, he felt again that sense of unease. There was danger in this house. He knew it and wanted to warn her, to save her, but how could he, short of dragging her forcibly back to Ardvarrick?

The irony of it, he thought bitterly. He was her husband, yet he was almost powerless to help her. If the Comte had been Madeleine's lover, he would have challenged him to a duel and run him through, but he could hardly do that to his father-in-law. From everything he had heard about the Comte he had always thought the fellow a scoundrel, albeit a charming one, but he was still Madeleine's parent. She had travelled hundreds of miles to London to join him and Grant knew he must tread warily.

Chapter Seven

By the time they went into dinner, Madeleine's head was throbbing. As hostess, her place was at the end of the table, opposite her father, but when the Comte directed the others to their seats, her heart sank to find Grant taking the place beside her. The arrangement only added to her anxiety, knowing that an unguarded word or gesture could so easily give them away. No one had made any direct reference to their relationship, they all knew it was safer not to disclose these things before servants, especially staff hired with the house for the Season. One could never be sure of their loyalty.

The dinner took the form of an elaborate charade. Whenever it was necessary for Madeleine and Grant to speak to one another, they were punctiliously polite, but for the most part they behaved like strangers with very little in common. Madeleine smiled and laughed, but inside she was as brittle as fine glass.

When the ladies had returned to the drawing room, the Comte dismissed the servants, declaring his guests were perfectly capable of pouring their own brandy. Grant displayed a spurious interest in some diverting tale his host was recounting, but all the time his mind was racing. Yves d'Evremont was trying to charm his guests, attempting to draw them into revealing their allegiances. He casually dropped Jacobite references into his conversation, hinted gently at future plans, and it had not escaped Grant's notice that the Comte wore a single white rosebud on his coat. It was all very subtle, giving his audience the opportunity to comment, to show themselves as supporters of Charles Stuart.

Sir Edmund was polite but cautious, posing the occasional question, but Grant was having none of it. He remained silent and would not commit himself. Indeed, the more he thought of it the more he disliked the idea of leaving his wife in this house a moment longer. If her father was plotting some new and traitorous scheme, the risks to Madeleine, and to his own family, were great indeed. She must be removed from danger at all speed, whether or not she was willing.

* * *

When the gentlemen returned to the drawing room, Grant sought an opportunity to speak in private with Madeleine, but she steadfastly evaded his every attempt to draw her away from the others. At last frustration got the better of him and he jumped to his feet.

'By heaven, I have had enough of this!'

The room fell silent. All eyes turned towards Grant, but he ignored them and strode across the room to stand in front of Madeleine.

'A word in private, madam, if you please.'

There were no servants present, but even so, Lady McBinnie glanced nervously towards the door. Sir Edmund coughed.

'Grant, my boy, be careful,' he said in a low voice.

'Confound it, I have been *careful* for far too long!' Grant turned back to Madeleine and held out a hand, saying imperiously, 'You will talk with me. Now.'

'My dear sir,' drawled the Comte, stepping forward, 'if my daughter does not wish—'

'Your *daughter*?'

Grant ground out the word and was about to remind Yves d'Evremont that Maddie was first and foremost his wife when she jumped to her feet in front of him.

'Very well,' she said, opening her fan with a quick, angry snap. 'We will go to the morning room.'

A prickling fear ran down Maddie's spine as she led the way across the hall. Grant was following her, his pent-up anger palpable, but she was angry, too, and in no mood to be browbeaten. She stalked into the morning room and waited until she heard the door click shut before turning to face him.

'Well, what do you want of me?'

'I want you to come back to Ardvarrick.'

Her chin lifted. 'Why?'

He hesitated, but if she had expected him to plead and utter soft words to persuade her, she was disappointed. He had never looked colder or more disapproving.

'How much do you know of your father's business?'

'As much as it is prudent to know.'

He came closer and said in a low voice, 'I believe what he is planning is *treason*.'

She knew that. It had caused her many sleepless nights, but she had her answer ready.

'Then disown me. There is no need for your family to be caught up in this. In fact, you will recall that I begged you to return to Ardvarrick.'

'I cannot leave without you. You are *my wife*.' He sucked in an angry breath and took another step towards her. 'Hell and damnation, woman, I could *beat* you into submission if I so wished!'

She might be furious with him, but that brought a wry smile tugging at her mouth.

She said gently, 'You *could*, Grant, but that is not your way.'

His eyes narrowed dangerously. For a brief, searing moment she wondered if he would prove her wrong, but he made no attempt to carry out his threat and she let her breath go in a sigh.

'My father needs me, Grant. Pray do not ask me to leave him.'

'Needs you? Oh, yes, I am sure he does, but it is purely for his own advantage, madam, not for yours.'

She clasped her hands together, desperate to make him understand.

'This is not a plan of his making. It was forced upon him. His life is forfeit if he doesn't comply.'

'Hah! He told you this, I suppose. *Who* is threatening him?'

'He would not say, but I believe it is true. This time, beneath his insouciance, he is worried. I have never known him to be so in the past.'

Grant folded his arms and looked down at her.

'What do you know of this plan?' he demanded.

She frowned. 'He tells me very little, but there have been many meetings. With men from France and also with men I believe are very powerful in this country, some with connections to the government, I think. They are expecting a visitor to arrive soon. From France.'

His lip curled. 'With news of the Pretender, no doubt!'

Madeleine raised a hand in warning.

'The Comte has very few of his own servants here,' she muttered, glancing around. 'It is best not to say too much.'

Cursing under his breath, Grant caught her shoulders.

'Confound it, everything you say tells me that you *know* how dangerous this whole affair is for you!'

'But more so for my father. Please, Grant,' she begged him, 'do not force me to leave him now. Papa needs me here. He is surrounded by enemies and I am the only one he can trust completely. If he should fail, his life is at risk, not only from the British, but his paymasters, too.

'I truly believe that he will only be safe if the plans succeed and if for that he needs my help, how can I refuse?' She shrugged him off and turned away. She said in a low voice, 'You should return to Ardvarrick, sir. Forget me. Once this is over I shall disappear and you need not be troubled by me again.'

'How the devil can I do that?' he demanded furiously. 'We are man and wife in case you have forgotten.'

'I have not forgotten, but there is a way.' She was obliged to swallow the lump in her throat before continuing. 'Under your Scottish law, in four years' time you can divorce me for malicious desertion.'

Silence followed her words. It hung thick and heavy between them and seemed to stretch on for ever, although it could only have been moments.

'Is that you want?' he said at last.

'Yes.' Maddie felt the tears pricking at the back of her eyes and blinked hard. 'Since we no longer love one another, it is best for both of us that we do not continue with this unhappy marriage.'

Grant stared as the dainty figure standing with her back to him. In this dimly lit room she looked like a creature of the night, the green gown as dark as a moonless sky and her lustrous black hair glinting in the candlelight. There was resolution in the proud tilt of her head and her straight shoulders and he knew it would be futile to argue. They had not shared a bed for more than a year. In fact, they had not shared anything: hopes, fears, feelings. Nothing save the roof over their heads.

'You are right.' He rubbed one hand across his eyes. 'It is time we put an end to this farce.'

'Then I may stay?' she asked. 'And you will return to Scotland?'

'No, I will not leave London. You can do as you please, madam, but if this madcap adventure should go awry your actions could bring down my family as well as yours. I will do what I can to avert that. I must remain in town until it is finished.'

'But you will not force me to leave my father?'

'No. If that is what you wish.'

He waited, part of him still hoping she would see sense and agree to leave with him, but he was not surprised when she did not. Her loyalty to her father was as strong as ever, even though the rogue did not deserve it! Accepting defeat, Grant walked to the door and held it open.

'Shall we re-join the others?'

Without a word, or a look in his direction, Madeleine unfurled her fan, lifted her chin a fraction higher and preceded him out of the room.

Chapter Eight

Soon after midnight the McBinnies rose to take their leave. Chairs were summoned for the ladies, together with link boys to light the way. Sir Edmund invited Grant to walk with him.

'We can go via Henrietta Street and your lodgings, my boy,' he said. 'I hope you will bear me company that far, if you are leaving now?'

Realising there was nothing to be gained by remaining any longer, Grant accepted and the little party set off.

'What do you think to our host and his plans?' he asked Sir Edmund, as they followed the chairs through the darkened streets, far enough behind that there was no danger of being overheard.

'An interesting character, but from the little I have gleaned about him, not one to trust too far. I believe too close an acquaintance with the Comte could prove dangerous.'

'You have the right of it,' replied Grant with a crack of humourless laughter. 'I think he is preparing the ground for a visitor to London.'

Sir Edmund glanced around him. 'An emissary for Charles Edward Stuart?'

'I believe so, yes. Tell me plainly, would you support the Prince, if he made another attempt to win the throne here?'

'I was intrigued by Elibank's letter, I confess it, but 'pon reflection, I do not believe there is sufficient support in the country. Oh, I know there are those who flaunt their views and statues of the Young Pretender are sold quite openly here in town, but I cannot like it. I have heard, too, that the King of Prussia has a finger in this particular pie, trying to stir up trouble. No, I think the time has passed and I want no part in it. In fact, much as my wife and daughter are enjoying themselves, I am minded now to cut short our visit and go back to Scotland.' He looked at Grant. 'What are your thoughts on the subject?'

'It has always been my opinion that one should stay well clear of the Comte and everything associated with him!'

'I thought as much.' As they passed a street lamp Sir Edmund cast a shrewd look at his companion. 'I was never convinced it was the Jacobite cause that brought you to London.'

Grant's jaw tightened. 'It was my mother who suggested I should come.'

'Ailsa!'

'Aye. When Madeleine left, my mother was racked with guilt because she had not given sufficient care to her. She blames herself for not seeing how unhappy my wife was.'

'Ah, poor Ailsa, how could she notice anything when she was herself distraught with grief? Logan being taken so suddenly. I never knew such a devoted couple. You, too, must have felt the loss most deeply.'

Instinctively Grant's hand came up, as if to keep at bay the memory of that black time, and he did not answer immediately.

Eventually, he said, 'My mother has convinced herself that Madeleine still cares for me. She thought I could persuade her to return to Ardvarrick.' He scowled and kicked a stray stone into the gutter. 'She was quite wrong about that.'

'Are you sure?'

'Perfectly.'

'Grief affects us all in different ways,' remarked Sir Edmund, weighing his words carefully. 'Your father dying before you and your wife had recovered from the loss of your child, it must have been a very hard time for you both.'

'Thank you, sir, but that has nothing to do

with it,' Grant retorted. 'It is quite evident from talking with, with *my wife* tonight that she no longer wishes to remain with me. She has decided to go back to France with her father.'

He stopped and pressed his lips together, fighting against the thoughts and feelings welling up inside him, but the words could not be contained. They burst out of him.

'Reason tells me I should quit this place and go home, but how can I? The devil of it is, you know as well as I that if the Comte's scheme should unravel, he and his associates might well be arrested for treason. I cannot leave London until I know Madeleine is safe.'

They had reached Henrietta Street and Sir Edmund stopped with Grant at the door to his lodgings.

'Then we shall stay, too,' he decided. 'You may need someone in town whom you can trust.'

'I thank you sir, but I would rather not drag you into this business!'

'Our families have always been friends and through darker times than these. If we can help you or Madeleine in any way, you only have to say,' replied Sir Edmund. He added quietly, 'Remember, we are here to help, if you need us, my boy.'

Grant clasped the proffered hand. 'Then I thank you, sir. And I will not forget.'

They looked at one another for a long moment, then Sir Edmund nodded, turned on his heel and strode away to catch up with his family.

As soon as all their guests had departed, Madeleine declared that she would retire.

'I bid you goodnight, Papa.'

'Not quite yet, my dear. I need to talk with you.'

Surprised, she returned to her seat. 'Very well.'

She folded her hands in her lap and waited while the Comte sipped at his brandy. He looked at her over the rim of the glass.

'What did Rathmore say to you?'

'He asked me to go back with him. To Ardvarrick.'

'From his demeanour when you returned, I assume you refused him?'

'I did.' She looked down at her fingers, clasped so tightly together that the knuckles gleamed white. 'I told him I intend to go with you, to France.'

He nodded, but his searching gaze was still fixed upon her and Madeleine felt a flush mounting her cheeks.

'I told you, Papa, there is nothing for me in Scotland. Seeing my husband here this evening only confirmed it. For us both.'

'Will he be leaving London now?'

Madeleine's shoulders lifted a fraction. 'I am not privy to his future plans.'

'Hmm.' The Comte tapped thoughtfully at his chin. 'But it is unlikely he will be of use to us. That is a pity. Having the Laird of Ardvarrick as an ally would be a strong encouragement for others in the far north to show their hand.'

'I do not think it a pity at all!' she retorted, with spirit. 'I do not *want* him to be your ally. Nor Sir Edmund.'

'Then you may rest easy, *ma fille,* neither of these gentlemen shows any inclination to help our cause.'

'I am relieved they have such good sense!' she retorted. 'I have gone along with everything until now, Papa, but this is not *my cause* and I will tell you to your head, I will not have my friends caught up in your schemes. If you make any further overtures towards Sir Edmund, I shall warn him to have nothing to do with you.'

Her father opened his eyes wide at her. '*Mais, ma chère*, have I not already explained, most clearly? My purpose in inviting them here to-night was only to please you.'

Maddie knew better than to argue, but in any case, there was no opportunity, for almost immediately he continued, 'Pah! Enough of this. We must prepare for our very important dinner next week. You look surprised, *chérie*, did I not tell you of it?'

'You know very well you did not,' she told him crossly. 'What day are you planning for this dinner? You will be well served if I had made other arrangements.'

'But you have not done so,' he murmured, reaching for his snuffbox.

'No.' She glanced towards the mantelshelf, which was littered with gilt-edged cards. 'There are invitations aplenty, but I have no fixed evening engagements, save Lady Molton's rout tomorrow.'

'*Bien.* That pleases me. You are a dutiful daughter. Madeleine, and we shall attend Lady Molton's together. There will be some there I wish to see.'

'More plans, more intrigue!' She waved an impatient hand. 'Tell me about your dinner. What night will it be and who is to be invited?'

'Thursday, I believe, although I cannot yet be certain. I shall know more in a day or so. As for guests, Sir John Belsay and Monsieur Thrimby will be dining with us. There must be ladies, too, to keep you company, so my Lords Froome and Kelty will bring their wives. You might even invite Sir Evelyn and Lady Molton, when we see them tomorrow.' He paused to take a pinch of snuff and delicately wiped his fingers on his handkerchief. 'Maxton, too, must be invited.'

'Sir William!' Madeleine grimaced.

'I know you dislike the gentleman *ma chère*, but you will receive him with courtesy.'

'It is not only dislike, sir. I do not trust him.'

'All the more reason to keep him close.'

'I would rather have nothing to do with him.'

'That, however, is not possible.' He saw her little moue of distaste and added, 'It is a matter most important to me that you do not provoke Sir William, Madeleine.'

His tone and manner were unusually grave, which could only mean that Maxton was even more dangerous than Madeleine had suspected.

'Very well, Papa, I shall be polite to him, you have my word.' She inclined her head and, bidding him goodnight, went off to bed.

She felt very dejected and could not shake off a feeling of melancholy. She told herself it was natural that she should feel low after her meeting with Grant. It was beyond all doubt now that their marriage was over. She might even allow herself a few tears tonight, but in the morning she would put her unhappiness aside. It was important that she should be able to concentrate upon her father's plans. She would need all her wits about her if she was to be of any help to him.

Chapter Nine

Grant decided that for his own peace of mind he should keep away from his wife. Madeleine stirred up too many emotions within him and his thinking became muddled when he was with her. Part of him wanted to snatch her up, despite her protests, and carry her to safety. He would do so, too, if matters became desperate, but that was very much a last resort. Grant prided himself on being an enlightened man, like his father and grandfather before him. They had treated women with kindness and respect and had brought him up to do the same.

Leaving it to Robert to keep a watchful eye on Madeleine and her father, Grant spent his days visiting the coffee houses he knew were frequented by supporters of the deposed Stuart king. Rumours were flying around, but although there was plenty of gossip about the flamboyant

Comte de Vaucluse, Grant could discover no evidence of any current Jacobite plot. In fact, when he compared notes with Robert a few days later, they concluded that the Comte and his daughter were behaving no differently from the dozens of other visitors who flocked to the capital to enjoy its delights. They drove in the park, visited the theatre, attended balls and entertained friends.

Grant found himself wondering if he was wrong. Perhaps he was being far too suspicious about the Comte, but Madeleine had said her father needed her and she had appeared to be genuinely worried. Grant's inner demons whispered that it was all a ploy. That she was merely trying to persuade him to leave her in London, but he could not bring himself to believe that. And neither could he bring himself to abandon her, if she was in danger.

A week later Grant was no clearer about what was going on. There were nebulous rumours among Stuart supporters that something of great importance was about to occur, but that was nothing new and the Comte continued to go about very much as before. According to Robert and the little band of trusted men he had hired to help him keep watch, there were no mysterious visitors to Surrey Street. The Comte paid frequent visits to local coffee houses but he met no one new or suspicious there. Madeleine, meanwhile, drove about town, shopping or visiting her friends and almost every evening she attended parties of pleasure with her father. Worryingly, the parties were hosted almost exclusively by known Jacobites.

It was all most frustrating. Grant wished Yves d'Evremont would quit Surrey Street and take his daughter back to France, but until that happened, he felt himself obliged to remain in London. Not that he wanted to see Madeleine. She had made it very plain it was all over between them, but until he was sure she was safely out of the country he could not be easy. Having decided he would be best avoiding her company, he spent most evenings in the clubs and coffee houses that abounded in the capital, but since he was no gambler, he occasionally craved a more varied society and he thumbed through the various invitations he had received until he found one he thought it safe to accept.

Lady Elizabeth Wallington was an elderly widow who lived on the edge of town and was renowned for her grand entertainments. Grant had been introduced to her when he had come to Court to receive his knighthood. She had taken a liking to him then and, learning that he was in town, she'd invited him to bring a party of friends to her firework display on Saturday. Such a display would prove most diverting, he thought. Moreover, he knew that Anne McBinnie had never seen fireworks and, since Lady Elizabeth was known to be a staunch Hanoverian, he suggested the McBinnies might like to join him.

It was not quite dark when Grant's party arrived at Wallington House, an impressive mansion some ten miles out of London on the Great West Road. They were shepherded into a large gilded reception room where the wine was flowing freely and a selection of fancy cakes and sweetmeats was spread out on long tables for the delectation of the guests, while they waited for the firework display to begin.

Grant and the McBinnies mingled with the crowd, introductions were performed and one or two acquaintances renewed, but in the main there were few people here whom they knew, although Sir Edmund recognised a number of the guests.

'Our hostess is very well connected,' he remarked as they gathered together at one side of the room. 'The cream of society is here tonight.'

'I am aware,' replied Lady McBinnie, her eyes bright with interest. 'At least two government ministers have been pointed out to me and a royal duke! I—' She stopped, staring fixedly at a point over Grant's shoulder and he turned to see what had caught her attention.

The Comte de Vaucluse was standing in the open doorway, resplendent in velvet and gold lace. Madeleine was at his side and almost immediately her eyes locked with Grant's. It felt inevitable, he thought, his heart contracting painfully. They had always had a connection, an awareness that was like an invisible cord between them. It was still there, powerful as ever.

Had she missed him this past week, had she spent the days thinking of him, where he was, what he was doing? He made himself look away from Madeleine and dragged his thoughts away, too. He was merely being fanciful, there was no connection between them and the sooner he realised that the better.

Grant concentrated on the Comte, watching as his gaze swept over the assembled guests and came to rest upon Sir Edmund. He saw that the Comte was about to move towards their little group, but Madeleine put a hand on his arm and stopped him. Her father dipped his head as she murmured something in his ear then, with a shrug, they moved off in another direction. And that was a good thing, too. He had no interest in the lady any longer. Only in the damage she and her father could do to his family and his friends.

When Grant turned back to his companions, he found that Anne and her mother were regarding him anxiously.

'I beg your pardon,' he said. 'I had not expected to see the Comte here tonight, or I should never have suggested…that is, I would not have your evening ruined because the Comte and his daughter are here.'

'I am so sorry, Grant.' Lady McBinnie laid a gentle hand on his sleeve. 'I know you would rather not meet with your wife at present.'

'Or ever!' He realised how bitter he sounded and forced himself to smile. 'I do not wish to involve you in the unpleasantness of my marriage.'

'But we are involved, my boy,' replied Sir Edmund gravely. 'We are very fond of you both. You know that.'

Grant said quickly, 'Thank you, sir, I appreciate that. And I am hopeful the Comte's presence will not spoil the evening. In a large house such as this, there is every possibility that our paths will not cross again.' He spoke with finality, to indicate the matter was closed, then looked over their heads and continued cheerfully, 'I see people are beginning to make their way to the gardens. Shall we go?

He ushered his party outside, where they joined the guests milling about on the lawn, waiting for the display to begin. A few minutes later a fanfare of trumpets blasted through the night air, followed by a whoosh as the first rockets shot upwards and burst into a thousand stars. It was a magnificent spectacle. A covering of cloud obscured the moon and provided the perfect backdrop for the colourful flashes. Grant gazed upwards, but his thoughts were not engaged by the entertainment. What was the Comte doing here? Lady Elizabeth's allegiance to the Crown was well known and he would find few Stuart sympathisers among the guests.

And Madeleine. Grant dearly wanted to know if she was here at her father's behest or if, perhaps, this had been her decision. It was not impossible she had come to meet an admirer. That disagreeable thought stuck in his head and destroyed any pleasure he might have felt at the dazzling display taking place in the sky above him.

Chapter Ten

Madeleine watched the display and tried her best to join in with the applause and gasps of delight as the fireworks soared and burst like stars against the night sky. It should have been an enjoyable evening. Papa had told her they were there purely to be entertained, but she was not sure she believed it.

Her thoughts kept returning to Grant. She had not been expecting him to be here, yet she had seen him as soon as she entered the room. With his tall figure elegantly clad in blue velvet and that rich auburn hair unpowdered, how could she not notice him? Then he had turned and looked at her and just for a moment the world had stopped. She had experienced a wave of yearning so strong it almost knocked her off balance.

She had persuaded her father not to approach

him, but any attempt to divert her own thoughts away from Grant Rathmore had failed dismally. Even though Grant was now lost in the darkness she could *feel* his presence. She had seen him with Sir Edmund and his family and she assumed they had come here together. Was he even now standing beside Anne, had she jumped, as Madeleine had done, when that first, particularly noisy rocket exploded above them? And had Grant placed a reassuring arm about her shoulders?

Madeleine fought down a wave of jealousy. Anne was her friend; she would not think ill of her. Neither should she be angry with Grant. After all, she had chosen to leave him. She closed her eyes for a moment. Their love was dead. They were both agreed on that. It was only grief she felt now and that would pass. It *must* pass.

'*Ma chère*, I must leave you for a little while.'

Madeleine's eyes flew open as she heard her father's voice, close to her ear.

'But you promised me,' she protested. 'This was to be an evening of pleasure!'

Not that she felt much pleasure.

'And so it is,' he responded soothingly. 'You have nothing to do tonight but enjoy yourself. *Mais, hélas*, there is someone I must talk with.'

He patted her hand and smiled down at her. 'I shall return shortly.'

Her eyes narrowed. 'How long will you be gone?'

'I shall return as soon as I am able, *chérie*. Trust me.'

'Trust you? I am finding it increasingly hard to do that, Papa, since you tell me nothing.'

He was not a whit disturbed by her anger and merely chuckled.

'*Doucement*, Madeleine. You know it is for your own safety that I share nothing with you. That way you may be easy and enjoy the entertainment until I return.'

With that he sauntered away, leaving Madeleine to glare after his retreating form. She hunched her shoulders and turned back to look up at the sky. It was useless to argue with Papa, he would go his own way. Unstoppable, like the rocket that had just whooshed and exploded into a golden starburst. She watched as the dazzling shower of lights twinkled and faded away in the darkness.

It had been a mistake to join Papa in London. She should have known better than to put her faith in him, but life at Ardvarrick had become so unbearable that when she received his letter, asking for her help, she had seen it as a way to escape. What a fool she was to have joined him. She had allowed herself to be embroiled in a scheme that she was certain endangered not only their lives, but Grant's too.

Another rocket burst and bloomed overhead, this time filling the sky with blood-red stars. Maddie shivered and looked away, feeling quite sick with regret at her foolishness. Her hostess was standing nearby with a group of friends and Madeleine walked across to her, hovering until she could catch Lady Elizabeth's attention and draw her apart. Then she asked if there was a quiet corner somewhere that she might rest.

'A sudden headache,' she explained, making her tone a little tremulous.

'Oh, my poor *mademoiselle,* but of course you must go inside.' Lady Elizabeth beckoned to a passing footman. 'John will show you to the library. You will not be disturbed there.'

Inside, the whoosh and crackle of the fireworks was muted and the house itself was eerily quiet. Maddie followed the servant into the library and waited by the door while the man put a lighted taper to some of the candles in the room. As soon as there was sufficient light to see her way, she dismissed him with a word of thanks, then she sank into one of the high-backed chairs that flanked the marble fireplace and, with a little moan of despair, dropped her head in her hands.

'I saw you come in here.'

Maddie jumped to her feet. Grant was standing in the doorway, his tall frame blocking the light from the hall.

He said, his voice rough with concern, 'What is the matter, are you ill?'

'A slight headache, that is all.'

Warily she watched him close the door and cross the room towards her.

'You were never one to suffer with headaches.' He took her shoulders and turned her to the light. 'What is it, Maddie, what is wrong?'

His gentle tone almost overset her. She shrugged him off.

'We are agreed I am no longer your concern,' she said coldly.

He continued to stare at her and she felt her energy sagging. She turned away from him and rubbed a hand across her eyes.

'Please, Grant, go away.'

'I have brought the McBinnies here tonight, I cannot leave without them.'

'I am not talking about tonight.' She waved an impatient hand. 'Go back to Ardvarrick. Forget all about me.'

'If only it were that easy!'

'It *is*,' she insisted. 'It has to be.'

'Why?' he countered. '*Why* must it be?'

'Because we are no longer in love!' The words were wrenched from her. She took a breath. 'Where there was warmth and affection between us there is now *nothing*. I thought—hoped—that even if you no longer loved me, we might at least live together as friends, but lately we have been more like strangers.' There was a constriction in her throat and she had to swallow painfully before concluding, 'You do not need me.'

'I am sorry if you think that…'

'It is why I left you,' she went on as if he had not spoken. 'I have no place in your life now.'

'What you really mean is that I have no place in *yours*!' he accused her, his voice dripping with scorn.

'No!'

She swung around, ready to protest, but the sight of his face shocked her into silence. The candlelight cast black shadows across the flat planes of his cheeks and highlighted the strong jaw, clenched now in anger. Beneath the frowning brows his eyes glared at her, reflecting the candles' flames like dancing devils.

He gave a savage laugh. 'This is nothing to do with me! You wanted an excuse to go back to your life of luxury, where you can revel once more in your intrigues and deceits—'

'Stop it, Grant! How dare you taunt me.' She drew herself up and fixed him with a steely glare. 'I want you to go. Leave me, now.'

'Very well.' He came closer, 'To quote the poet, "Since there's no help, come let us kiss and part."'

He was smiling, but the angry glitter had not left his eyes. Maddie refused to be intimidated and she raised her chin, staring up at him defiantly, willing him to go away. Before she realised what he was about, he swooped. She stood frozen, unable to move or speak as he brushed her lips with his own. It was the merest graze, but her whole world shifted.

Grant had meant the kiss as an insult, a gesture of how little he cared, but as his mouth touched hers heat surged through him. It shocked him. He felt as if he had been burned. Dazed, he lifted his head to find Madeleine was staring at him, her sapphire eyes dark and wide with shock. He should not have done that. He must apologise.

The thought had barely crystallised before she reached for him. She caught his face between her hands and dragged him back, capturing his mouth with her own in a kiss that set his already shaken senses reeling. The passion smouldering inside burst into flame. He pulled her to him, his lips parting, and their tongues danced together, setting his blood on fire. His heart was pounding, carrying hot and urgent desire into every part of his body. It consumed him. All he could think of was the woman in his arms. She was kissing him passionately and pressing her body against his while her fingers drove through his hair and held him a willing prisoner.

When the kiss ended he did not pull away. His lips began to trail over her face, her eyes, her cheeks, then he began to place a line of kisses along her jaw. She threw back her head, inviting his roving mouth to explore the slender column of her throat. He kissed the erratic beat of the pulse beneath her ear before his lips moved down to the soft swell of her breasts. They pushed against him, ripe and ready for his touch.

And then, with bewildering speed, everything changed. She was struggling against his hold, pushing him away. Grant released her immediately and she stumbled back a couple of paces, gasping.

'How *dare* you!'

His body and his head on fire, a ragged laugh

escaped him. 'I think, lady, you will find you kissed *me* that time!'

'I was overwrought,' she said, furiously, wrapping her arms about her. 'You took advantage of me!' She tossed her head. 'You should go now.'

She was glaring at him, cheeks and eyes aflame, dark curls in disarray. She looked…glorious. His body was still hard and aroused. He could not have walked away if he had tried and he really did not want to.

'After what has just happened between us?' he said, playing for time.

'That was nothing more than lust.' Her eyes slid away from him. 'You are not to think that only men have such…moments.'

'You know I don't think that,' he said, recalling her eager responses during the passion-filled nights—and days—they had shared together at Ardvarrick. Remembering her cries of pleasure, and his own, when she had learned to rouse his body to the brink of ecstasy.

But that time was past now. Bitter memories quashed his desire as surely as a dousing of icy water and the heat inside him turned quickly to rage. At Madeleine for tempting him, at himself for succumbing so easily. He had seen her dancing with other men. Flirting with them. How could he be sure she did not feel the same desire for them?

He would not share her with anyone, but now he had to clench his fists tightly at his sides to stop himself reaching out for her again.

'Very well, madam,' he said, his voice clipped, controlled. 'I accept what you say, that what occurred was the result of lust, and I can only regret that I allowed myself to be so easily, so foolishly, tempted.'

He strode to the door, but stopped there as another line from the poem came to him.

'"Nay, I have done, you get no more of me."' He looked back at her, his lip curling. 'A fitting quote with which to leave you, is it not?'

And with that he went out, taking inordinate care not to slam the door behind him.

Chapter Eleven

Grant made his way back to the garden, cursing his weakness for the jade. And undoubtedly, a jade is what she was. The sooner her father took her off to France the better it would be for them both!

The firework display had ended and the guests were now drifting back into the house, where their hostess had laid on an elegant supper to carry them through to the early hours of the morning. Grant had no appetite for food. His senses were still full of Madeleine, the taste of her, the feel of her body pressing against him. Even her scent. It was all so familiar and his body ached with longing.

He raked a hand through his already disordered hair. He had to fight this. Madeleine was lost to him. It was madness to yearn for her like a lovesick schoolboy. He sucked in a lungful of the cool night air and squared his shoulders. He was damned if he would dance to her tune a moment longer.

Grant said very little on the journey back from Wallington House with Sir Edmund and his family. Madeleine had proved herself intractable. She did not want him and if that was so, there was little reason to torture himself by remaining in town. She had told him to disown her and he would do just that. He would place an advertisement in the newspapers, absolving himself of all responsibility for her debts and her conduct. Then he could return to Scotland and forget he ever had a wife!

A night's restless sleep brought little cheer for Grant. Throwing open the shutters, he gave a grunt of satisfaction at the rain beating against the window. It showed no signs of abating and that would preclude Lady McBinnie inviting him to join her and Anne in Hyde Park for their usual Sunday perambulation. He was in no mood for social chit chat and preferred to spend his day planning how to disentangle himself from Madeleine and her father. However, his attempts to draft a suitable declaration failed miserably and he eventually gave up, deciding he would appoint a lawyer to do it the following day.

* * *

In the event, he was thwarted in that endeavour, too. Early on Monday morning, Sir Edmund had furnished him with the name of a reliable and discreet attorney, but when Grant had arrived at his office, he discovered that the fellow was out of town until Thursday. It was disappointing, but there was no help for it; he knew of no one else who could be trusted to carry out such a delicate matter.

Grant returned to his lodgings, where the invitation to the ball at Clifton House that evening caught his eye. The gilt-edged card was on the mantelshelf, propped up behind a Meissen pug dog with a particularly mawkish expression. Even a crowded ballroom would be better than spending another interminable evening alone with only the brandy bottle and his imaginings for company.

He had been planning to send his regrets, but now he changed his mind. Robert had discovered that the Comte was engaged to dine with Lady Thanet that evening so Grant thought it would be safe to put in an appearance at the Clifton ball. Sir Edmund and his family were going so he would join their party.

He walked into the ballroom just as a dance was ending and saw Madeleine immediately. She was being escorted off the floor by a young buck who was clearly smitten by his partner. Grant choked back an oath. How presumptuous of him, how crassly foolish to think she would go everywhere with her father. It was too late to withdraw and, giving a little shrug, he moved on with a show of nonchalance.

Taking a glass of wine from a passing waiter, Grant watched as Madeleine's partner led her to the side of the room, where they were joined by several other gentlemen, all of whom appeared to be vying for her favours. Just the sight of her made the blood pound through his veins. He could not help reliving that kiss at Wallington House. The touch of her lips, the feel of her soft, pliant body against his own.

Despite his better judgement he moved closer. Madeleine was using her fan to good effect, flirting lightly with all her admirers, a smile for one, a roguish look for another. His jaw clenched. If she was acting, it was a damned good performance! He had not seen her look so happy for...

Memories surged up and overwhelmed him. He recalled how joyous those early years had been. Even that first miscarriage had not totally dimmed their happiness. They had grieved together and although the loss had never been forgotten they had accepted it and life had carried on. The experience had brought them closer, they had laughed and loved and worked together as they had done before.

Until the much-anticipated arrival of their son. The stillbirth had left them both distraught and, as if that cruel blow was not enough, the tragedy had been followed by the sudden death of Grant's father only months later. After that nothing had been the same. The joy had never returned.

Resentment flared as he watched Madeleine now, enjoying the adulation of her admirers. Was this his reward for the sacrifices he had made then? He had assuaged his feelings of loss by throwing himself wholeheartedly into his duties, but all the while he had kept his grief hidden, not wanting her to suffer more than she was already. Afraid to allow her too near him lest the mask should slip. It had been his duty as Laird not to show weakness when everyone was depending upon him to be strong, but it had been a painful, lonely time.

'Ah, Sir Grant. You are admiring London's latest beauty.'

A hand on his shoulder and the cheerful voice of his host jerked him back to the present. He managed to reply with reasonable calm, 'As you say, Lord Edgecott, a veritable beauty.'

'Come along, my boy, I will introduce you.'

'What?' Grant's thoughts were still caught up in the past and he struggled to gather his wits as Lord Edgecott's hand moved to his arm. 'But I already—'

It was too late. The words faded away and he found himself being propelled forward.

Madeleine had not seen him. She was laughing at something amusing the overpainted fop beside her was saying, damn his eyes!

'Mademoiselle d'Evremont,' Lord Edgecott addressed her, 'I have a gentleman here who wishes to meet you.'

She looked around then, but apart from a slight widening of her eyes she gave no sign of discomposure at seeing him. Her smile remained in place as she responded.

'*Mais*, you mistake, *milord*. Sir Grant and I are already acquainted.' He noticed that her enchanting French accent was more in evidence tonight.

Their host gave a merry laugh. 'Then he was too smitten to inform me of the fact!'

That caused some amusement among the group, much to Grant's chagrin, but he reined in his temper and managed to reply lightly, 'I doubt I am alone in my admiration for Mademoiselle d'Evremont.'

'Indeed, you are not, sir!' tittered one of her

coterie, a macaroni in a tall powdered wig and with a plethora of fobs and seals about his person.

Grant wondered how soon he could extricate himself from this damnable situation. Having declared himself enamoured, he could hardly walk away from the lady now.

At that moment the musicians began tuning up for the next dance and he gave thanks for his deliverance, thinking he might now walk away. Several of the gentlemen were stepping forward, begging for the honour of leading *mademoiselle* to the dance floor, but Madeleine seemed disinclined to accept any of them as her partner. She fluttered her fan and held it high, so only her teasing eyes were visible.

'*Non, non, messieurs*, how can I stand up with any of you?' she teased, 'It is a fact well known that Englishmen cannot perform this dance!'

'But you are too cruel, *mademoiselle*!' cried Lord Edgecott gaily. 'How can you deny us the pleasure of watching you perform the gavotte?'

The gavotte! 'Fore Gad, thought Grant, would the memories never stop? The images were playing in his head so vividly it was as if he had been transported back to Ardvarrick.

It was a chilly spring evening and he and Maddie were in the drawing room with Logan and Ailsa. Everyone was happy and relaxed, but Maddie was trying to persuade him to learn a new dance and he was being encouraged to do so by his parents.

'I know enough dances,' he had argued, reluctant to move from his comfortable chair beside the fire. 'It was part of the gentleman's education you insisted I should have, Mama, do you not recall? I might be more accustomed to dancing the reels and jigs of the local ceilidhs, but I am also adept at the minuet and courante, as well as the fashionable contradances performed in the very highest society.'

'You are not, however, familiar with the gavotte,' remarked his father, grinning. 'And Madeleine is determined to change that.'

'*Mais oui*, Papa Logan, I am,' she declared, her eyes sparkling, 'Because it is a *danse galante*.' Grant remembered how she had turned to him then, those delectable lips pouting prettily. 'It is a very elegant dance, *chéri*, and we shall dance it properly, in the French manner.'

'Aye, you should learn it, my son,' declared Logan with a smile. 'You will be going to the English Court in October, to be knighted by the King. I should like above all things to hear that you and Madeleine dazzled them with your brilliance on the dance floor!'

Grant's objections were overridden. He helped his father to push back the furniture and roll up the carpet while Madeleine sang the melody to his mother. As an experienced harpist, Ailsa only needed to hear a tune once and she could repeat it faithfully on the *clàrsach*. But even when Ailsa started playing the stately melody Grant held back. Maddie came up to him.

'Come now, *mari,*' she said, taking his hands. 'The gavotte began as a peasants' kissing dance and we shall conclude with a kiss, as they were wont to do. Surely that will tempt you?'

And it did. Grant allowed himself to be coaxed into the centre of the floor and they walked through the first section of the dance, Madeleine instructing him as they went. It was complicated, but they persevered. By the end of the evening his head was ringing with her calls of *jeté, chassé-croisé* and *jeté vite*, but they completed the whole dance sequence and he was rewarded with his kiss.

He remembered, too, how Madeleine had rewarded him again, later. When they were lying between the cool sheets of their bed.

'You did very well, *mon cher,*' she murmured, pressing her shapely naked form against him. 'But we must continue to practise. I want you to be *l'homme le plus élégant* when we dance the gavotte together.'

'If you wish.' His body was already hardening as her hand moved over his chest and began to roam down across his stomach. 'As long as I can have my kiss at the end of every dance.'

'Oh, I think I would like more than that,' she whispered, her voice low and seductive. Then she began to kiss him, starting with his mouth, but moving down with light, butterfly caresses to follow the trail her hand had taken. Kisses that left his skin on fire and his blood boiling with desire.

The dancing lessons had continued throughout the summer, but by October Maddie was pregnant and Grant had gone to London alone. They had never danced the gavotte together in public.

Pain seared Grant. It brought him crashing back to the present, to the crowded ballroom full of laughing, chattering strangers. And Madeleine. The gentlemen clustered around her were still protesting, begging her to favour them, and suddenly Grant found himself speaking up.

'I will dance it with you.'

Madeleine's eyes flew to his face. She looked astonished, as was he.

The macaroni tittered again. 'Beware, sirrah,

the lady has declared the dance impossible for our barbaric nation!'

'But I am not a barbaric Englishman.' For some reason Grant could not control his mouth. Or his actions. He held out his hand. 'Will *mademoiselle* do me the honour?'

He noted her reluctance, but with everyone watching them a refusal would have caused a stir. The sort of attention she would be anxious to avoid. After a tiny hesitation, she placed her fingers in his and allowed him to lead her on to the dance floor.

Grant only hoped now that he might remember the steps.

Chapter Twelve

Why was he doing this? Madeleine had looked up into Grant's face when he had said he would dance the gavotte with her. His eyes were near black, but this time they were not hard and cold. They were full of emotion, as if he, too, remembered how they had practised this dance together, perfecting the steps, turning every touch, every glance into a message of love. The chaste kiss at the end was merely a promise of the night to come, when he would pull her into his arms and caress her until she was swooning from the sheer pleasure of his touch.

Her body was shaking even now at the memory of it. She breathed deeply, trying to maintain her calm as they took their places on the floor. There were very few couples standing up, the gavotte being less popular in England than in

France, and Madeleine felt far more exposed to the eyes of the watching crowd.

She hoped her limbs would not give way as she stood, one dainty foot arched and pointed, counting the beats before the commencement of the dance. This was not what she had expected this evening. She had noticed Grant as soon as he entered the ballroom, looking far more elegant in his plain velvet coat and unpowdered hair than the painted and bewigged gentlemen who clamoured around her. She had been determined to avoid him at all costs, but here they were, standing up together for a dance that held such precious memories for her.

Why on earth had he suggested they should dance it here, now? It was more than two years since she had taught him the gavotte and they had never danced it in public. It might all go disastrously wrong and she knew she must ensure that did not happen. Madeleine uttered up a silent prayer of thanks for the French dancing master Papa had hired upon her arrival in London. She was well practised now and it was up to her to make sure they made it through the dance without embarrassment.

As the first beat sounded, she cleared her mind of everything except the execution of the dance. She gave her full attention to her performance, the correct arching of the foot, the elegant placing of an arm, the turns and timely jumps. She suspected that Grant was concentrating as hard as she upon the steps, because he gave her no flirtatious glances or meaningful looks. She was immensely relieved, knowing that such behaviour would have broken through her resolve and sent her running from the ballroom.

Miraculously, they completed the dance without mishap and excitement fizzed through Maddie's blood as she sank into the final curtsy. She felt as if she had been balancing precariously on a high wire, her nerves were stretched to the full and, although there had been no physical danger, she felt an immense glow of satisfaction at successfully negotiating a most complicated set of dance steps with her partner.

The joyous mood vanished as soon as she put out her hand for Grant to raise her up, for at that moment she recalled only too clearly how they had always concluded this particular dance. She put up her chin and turned resolutely away. The final kiss would not happen this time. It was sheer foolishness to feel any pang of regret.

As they walked off the dance floor some of the guests were applauding. Madeleine managed a smile as she tried to steady her breathing and her emotions.

'An excellent display,' cried Lady Edgecott, beaming at them both. 'I have never seen it performed better. You danced it just as you would in France, *mademoiselle*!'

'Not quite,' Grant replied. 'I believe if one is performing it *correctly* in the French manner, the dancers should exchange some token of affection.' She saw the glinting challenge in his eyes. 'A flower or…something.'

How dare he mock me?

Her shredded nerves found relief in anger. From somewhere she dredged up a little laugh.

'Perhaps, among the peasants,' she said, injecting a touch of scorn into her voice, 'but never in the *best* society.'

She withdrew her hand from his arm, swept a curtsy that conveyed nothing but contempt for him and sailed off with her head high.

Grant watched her retreating figure and felt a grudging admiration stirring. He had not meant to remind her about the kiss, but the success of their performance on the dance floor had sent his spirits soaring. It had made him reckless and the urge to tease her was irresistible.

He should not have asked her to dance with him. He had no idea what had possessed him, what particular devil it was that had made him do it. If she had ripped up at him, as he fully deserved, the consequences could have been disastrous. But she had kept her calm and it came as a shock to realise that he had always known she would. They had travelled the Highlands together after Culloden, facing many dangers, and she had never let him down. That soft, womanly body hid a core of steel.

Something very like regret rose up in Grant, but he swiftly pushed it down. Too late for that. No point in dwelling on what was dead and gone.

Madeleine had a headache. The ballroom was hot and stuffy, the company tedious and she wanted nothing more than to go back to Surrey Street and take to her bed. However, that was not possible, at least until after supper. She felt out of reason cross and berated herself for ever agreeing to come tonight.

If only Papa had not arranged for her to join Lord Kelty's party for the Clifton House ball before taking himself off about his own business that morning. Even then, she had been minded to cry off, but when the carriage called for her, Lady Kelty was so kind that Madeleine had not the heart to say no. And having come, it would be ill mannered and ungrateful of her to ask them to leave early.

There was also another reason she must stay: it would give rise to just the sort of speculation she wished to avoid if she left directly after that very public gavotte with Grant Rathmore. Thus, she pinned on her smile, danced a minuet with Lord Froome and after supper she stood up for two country dances before declaring herself completely fatigued. She spent the rest of the evening sitting with Lady Kelty and her friends at the edge of the dance floor, where she had the dubious pleasure of watching Grant tread a measure with Anne McBinnie.

Madeleine tried to convince herself that she did not care in the least, but she did. Not that she was jealous. Oh, no. She liked Anne; they were friends. And Grant had known Anne since they were children, so why should they not dance together? But she could not rid herself of the tiny voice in her head that suggested Anne McBinnie would make a far more suitable partner for the Laird of Ardvarrick than his present wife and she could not deny that punctured her self-esteem.

Maddie tried to interest herself in the conversation going on around her, but could not deny it was a relief when at last Lady Kelty declared she was ready to drop and sent her husband off to order their carriage.

Grant opened his eyes. Bright sunlight was filtering in through the cracks in the shutters, but he had no inclination to leave his bed, even after Robert had brought in his morning coffee. They had arranged to visit Surrey Street, to talk to the watchers Robert had employed, but that could wait an hour or so. He thumped his pillow to make it more comfortable, then lay back down with his hands behind his head, thinking again about his encounter with Madeleine at Clifton House last night.

He was surprised at how much he had enjoyed standing up with her for the gavotte. It had been a gamble—if they had made a mull of it then it would have meant humiliation for both of them, possibly even exposure, but the danger had only added to the enjoyment. He had been exhilarated by the success of their performance, although it was clear Madeleine had not felt the same, for she had swept away and avoided him for the remainder of the evening.

He should be grateful to her for walking away, he thought as he threw back the covers and swung himself out of bed. The pleasure he had gleaned in standing up with her could only be compared to that of a moth dancing around a candle, moments before it is consumed by the flame.

After breaking his fast, Grant put on an old coat and muffler and set out with Robert for Surrey Street. They found the watcher in position, dressed in shabby clothes and carrying a broom. The man swept a crossing for them as he divulged that no one had left the house so far that day.

'But I am expecting the Comte to go out soon, sir,' he added, pocketing the sixpence that Robert handed him. 'He and the young lady regularly take the air in the park on a sunny day.'

'Then we shall wait,' said Grant.

'An' another thing,' said the man, as they went to move on. 'There's been a few other coves hanging around here in the past few days.' He sniffed and scratched his head, looking at the ground as if pondering a question. 'They wears plain coats, but to my mind they's soldiers. One can allus tell. Too stiff by half, they are.'

'Oh?' Grant resisted the urge to turn his head and look for them. 'Are any of them around here now?'

'One's up there, on the corner with the Strand.'

Throwing the man another coin, Grant linked

arms with Robert and they sauntered on towards the Comte's house at the end of the street.

'What do you think, sir?' said Robert. 'Government men?'

'Aye, but which government?' mused Grant, recalling what Sir Edmund and Madeleine had told him. 'It could be that the French are watching d'Evremont, or mayhap some other foreign power. It is quite possible there is more than one country behind this current escapade. See what you can discover about these fellows, Robert, but carefully.'

'Aye, I will, sir. And you?'

'I am going to the river. There is something I have been wanting to look at for some little time now.'

He gave his companion a nod of farewell and headed for the narrow opening in the building across the end of the street. Passing through the arch, Grant found himself on a set of ancient steps leading down to the river, where a dilapidated wooden jetty projected out over the water. Robert and the men he had left watching the street had not seen anyone from the Comte's house using the stairs, even in the dead of night, yet this was the ideal place to land if one was crossing the river from the south side. Or coming ashore from a ship.

The river itself was busy with traffic, but the old posts of the jetty were worn and rotten, as if it was rarely used these days. Grant looked upstream and saw a skiff pushing off from the next jetty along, the one at the end of Strand Lane, and he waved, beckoning the oarsman to come over.

'Do you have time to row me a little way along the river?' he called. He saw the waterman staring dubiously at his rather threadbare greatcoat and patted his pocket. 'I have money.'

The man plied his single oar and brought his little boat alongside the jetty.

'What can I do for 'ee, sir?'

'I'd be glad for you to take me along the embankment as far as the Arundel Stairs.'

The waterman gazed along the riverbank, as if wondering why anyone would wish to pay for such a short journey, when they could as easily walk to it through the nearby streets, but he shrugged and gestured to Grant to get in.

They set off and Grant kept his attention on the narrow river bank. The end wall of the terrace of houses in Surrey Street towered over them as they moved away from the jetty. The waterman plied his oar and the little boat floated on until they were passing the garden wall. On the river side of the wall there was a narrow strip of embankment and Grant noticed that the weeds and rushes were flattened, as if they had been trampled.

'Looks as if one of your people ran ashore there recently,' he remarked casually.

His observation was met with derision by the oarsman.

'We don't spend seven years learnin' our trade just to do sich a thing,' he retorted. 'Only a looby'd do that. A cod's head!'

Grant begged pardon and said no more, but although he looked relaxed, his attention was firmly fixed on the river bank. He had seen something in the rushes. Something that looked very like a ladder. That would be useful for anyone wishing to scale the garden wall, he thought, and the perfect way to smuggle someone in or out of the end house under the cover of darkness. But who would need to arrive in such secrecy, and was it merely a coincidence that the end house was taken by the Comte de Vaucluse?

When they reached the Arundel Stairs, Grant handed a silver sixpence to the waterman before hopping on to the jetty and setting off to walk back to Surrey Street. If his suspicions were correct, then this was a far more serious plan than he had first thought. A plot of such daring that, if they were caught, both the Comte and his daughter would be guilty of treason. He would not be able to save her then and he was convinced that any number of disclaimers or repudiations from him would not save Ardvarrick.

He cut through Howard Street and had just reached Surrey Street when an empty open carriage swept past him and pulled up at the painted black door of the Comte's hired house. Grant stopped on the corner and patted his coat as if in search of something, all the while keeping his head low and the brim of his hat shadowing his face. He saw Yves d'Evremont come out of the house, closely followed by Madeleine. She was wearing another unfamiliar outfit and he supposed that the Comte had purchased her clothes for her, since she had taken very little money with her when she left Ardvarrick.

He gazed now at Madeleine, studying the jacket of palest dove-grey wool. It had a soft, flat collar and wide revers, like a man's frock coat, but there was nothing mannish about the lace collar and frivolous blue bow at her neck. Her hat, in the same rich shade of blue as the bow, was a shallow-crowned creation with a wide brim and trimmed with a white ostrich feather.

Grant's mouth thinned as he watched the carriage pull away and disappear around the corner on to the Strand. They were going to Hyde Park at the fashionable hour and there was only one reason for such a frivolous ensemble. It was designed to attract the eye of every man who saw her. And much as he was reluctant to admit it, she looked utterly enchanting.

He did not want to watch the fools falling under her spell, but he knew he must follow. He hurried out to the Strand where he was fortunate to flag down a passing hackney coach. The promise of an extra coin persuaded his driver to make haste and follow the elegant open carriage that was just ahead of them. Grant knew the hackney was not permitted to drive through the park, so he divested himself of the muffler and greatcoat and stuffed them under the seat. By this time they had reached the gates, where he quickly jumped out and paid off the driver before setting off to follow the carriage on foot.

Chapter Thirteen

Such was the number of carriages parading through the park that progress was necessarily slow. Grant had no difficulty in keeping his quarry in sight, although he was obliged to avoid the traffic moving in and out of the park. However, his luck held and it was not long before the Comte's carriage stopped and its occupants alighted. They began to stroll along towards the Serpentine River. The track in that direction was less crowded, away from the main drives and, once they reached the river, far more secluded. Perfect for illicit meetings.

He could not believe it was mere chance when two gentlemen strolling in the opposite direction stopped to converse. Keeping his hat low, Grant carried on walking, confident that in his riding coat, buckskins and shining top boots he looked no different from dozens of other young gentlemen enjoying a stroll in the park. He did not slow his pace until he was some distance ahead, then he stepped off the path and rested his back against a tree trunk, his gaze fixed on a family of ducks near the riverbank.

At the very edge of his vision he could see Madeleine's pale skirts and knew the moment the little group began to move again. A quick glance showed him that the Comte was engaged in an animated conversation with the men, while Madeleine had dropped behind and was walking alone.

As the little group approached, Grant shifted around, until the broad trunk of the tree was between him and the path. He heard the low murmur of the men's voices, but no one looked his way as they strolled past him, and he seized his chance.

Maddie was lost in thought. She was not acquainted with the two strangers talking to her father, but they were conversing in French and she had heard mention of the imminent arrival of a ship. She wondered if it would bring a messenger from the exiled Stuarts. Her father was certainly waiting for *something* to happen and, much as she wished for it, she doubted that the ship in question was coming to take them back to France. She would have liked to hear more, but Papa had drawn the gentlemen close and indicated that she should drop back and leave them to their machinations. He had no use for her, for the moment.

They reached a point where the path divided and the Comte guided his companions along the left fork, a riverbank walk that ran between the water and a narrow line of trees and bushes. Madeleine followed, but just before the paths diverged, she suddenly felt the hairs rise on the back of her neck. She had no idea why, until she looked around and saw that Grant was on the other track. The next moment he was beside her and gripping her arm, forcing her to stop.

'I need to talk to you.'

He spoke quickly, but thankfully his voice was too low to reach the gentlemen ahead of them.

'Not here, not now!' she whispered, trying to shake him off. 'My father—'

'You will not be going very far out of your way. The paths meet up again after a while.' His grip tightened. 'Or do you want me to say what I have to here, where your *friends* might hear?'

She glanced again towards her father, but he was walking on, still deep in conversation with the strangers. Another few steps and they would be lost to sight. With a little nod of acquiescence, she accompanied Grant on to the other path.

'Well, what do you want of me?' She had already lost sight of her father, but still she kept her voice hushed. 'I am sure there is nothing more for us to say to one another.'

'I am asking you again to quit town. If you will not come back to the north with me, then so be it, but I beg you to go away and quickly. London is not safe and it is not only you at risk if you stay here.'

'I am aware of that, but I explained it to you. I cannot leave Papa.'

They fell silent as they passed a couple strolling in the other direction. Madeleine thought that if she had not been so anxious, she would have found the path delightful, with its view through the trees to the brightly coloured crowd gathered at the Ring, where the rich and fashionable were parading with their showy horses and open carriages. She had hoped to drive there today and meet up with Anne McBinnie. How much more pleasant that would have been than this!

'Your father!' Grant said scornfully. 'The man is not worth your concern.'

Madeleine noticed a little group sitting on a rug. Two nursemaids, she surmised, out of doors with their young charges and enjoying a good gossip.

'You should leave him, Madeleine.'

'He is my father!'

'If you wish to risk your life for his madcap ventures that is your affair,' he ground out, 'but what he is doing is *treason*, madam. Do you realise what will happen if you are caught?'

She swallowed. 'Yes.'

She heard his indrawn breath, as if he was controlling himself with an effort.

'It is not only your own life at risk. I cannot, will not, allow you to put Ardvarrick in danger. My family, our tenants and staff. They will all suffer. Surely you do not want that?'

No, Madeleine did not want that. She was very fond of Ailsa, her mother-in-law. She loved Ardvarrick and its people. She knew if her father's plans went awry, if she was found guilty, then by association her husband and his family would lose everything.

At that moment one of the children, having escaped his nurse, hurtled towards the path and into Grant.

His attention fixed on Madeleine, Grant did not notice the little boy until something cannoned into his leg. He looked down just as the small child rebounded and fell back on to the grass. When he started to cry, Grant quickly scooped him up into his arms.

'There, there, my little man, are you hurt? No, just winded, eh?' he concluded, as the wailing was reduced to an occasional hiccup.

'Master Rupert! Oh, you naughty boy, to be troubling the gennleman so!' The nursemaid came running up, breathless and red with mortification. 'Beggin' yer pardon, sir, I never noticed he'd gone—'

'Master Rupert, is it?' Grant had settled the little lad on his arm and was engaged in wiping away the tears with his own handkerchief. 'No harm done,' he said cheerfully, handing the child back to his nurse. 'But if I were you, I'd watch him more carefully in future; he is a lively little fellow.'

'Yessir, thank 'ee, sir,' stammered the nursemaid, clutching at her charge.

She hurried away, clearly relieved at escaping so lightly from the encounter, and Grant turned back to Madeleine.

'Shall we continue our walk?'

He was obliged to repeat the question because she was lost in thought and when she did respond, he could see it cost her an effort. He wanted to ask what was troubling her, but they were approaching the point where the riverbank walk emerged from the sheltering bushes and joined the main path again and Grant knew he did not have much time to make his point.

'To return to our discussion,' he said. 'You must see that I cannot leave you in London.'

'But you *must* leave me here.' There was a note of quiet desperation in her voice. 'I will swear an oath that you had no knowledge of my actions.'

'Hah! Do you think anyone will believe that?'

'They are more likely to do so if you disown me and go back to Scotland.'

'I cannot go while you are in London.'

'And *I* cannot leave my father!'

'How can you say that, when he abandoned you in Inverness on the eve of a bloody battle?' he demanded angrily. 'He left you alone, with the country in turmoil. He has not shown the slightest interest in you for the past four years, until he needed your help to save his own skin! Hell and damnation, Maddie, you owe him nothing!'

'You do not understand.'

'You are very right, madam, I don't.'

The Comte de Vaucluse and his companions had come into view. Grant saw that they were looking about them. Searching for Madeleine, he suspected. Their time alone was running out. He stopped and turned to her.

'Tell me then. Tell me why you cannot leave him.'

She stared at him, her eyes swimming with tears.

'Don't you *see*?' she said, her voice choked with emotion. 'I have lost my babies. I have lost *you*. Papa is all I have left!'

With that she hurried away to join her father and his friends, leaving Grant to stare after her.

Madeleine walked as quickly as she could towards the blurred figures ahead of her. She knew one of them was her father, she had seen him before tears had obscured her vision. Tears that she dared not allow to fall. Instead she must call upon every ounce of willpower and school her face into a look of unconcern. She must look happy and explain to them that she had been enjoying a little dalliance while the Comte went about his own business. Papa, of course, would have recognised her companion but she could only pray that his associates had no idea Grant Rathmore was her husband.

As she drew close her father put out his hand and greeted her in his native tongue.

'Ah, Madeleine, my dear, have you been flirting with your admirer?'

She replied in the same language, and with a roguish look, 'With *one* of my admirers, sir!'

'Without doubt,' said one gentleman gallantly, 'Mademoiselle d'Evremont will have any number of gentlemen at her feet.'

That required a flutter of the fan and a small curtsy.

'La, you are too kind, *monsieur.*'

Both gentlemen smiled and bowed, and after a few more pleasantries they took their leave. The Comte watched them for a few moments, then turned and held out his arm to Madeleine.

'You told me all was at an end between you and Sir Grant,' he remarked as he escorted her back to their carriage.

'It is, but when I saw him walking towards us I thought it best to divert him on to a separate path. You would not have wanted your conversation interrupted, I am sure.'

'You are very right, *ma chère*. Fortunately, the gentlemen are new to London and know nothing of the Laird of Ardvarrick, or his connection to you.'

'Thank goodness for that, I dread to think how dangerous that might have been for him!'

Her response was so heartfelt that the Comte stopped.

'Can it be you still have a *tendre* for your husband?' he asked, his eyes searching her face. 'You have changed your mind about coming to France with me?'

'Not at all, Papa. In fact, this latest encounter has made me even more determined to leave England.'

It was true. When she had seen Grant gather up that little boy, heard him speak so gently, she had suffered again a fierce stab of grief at losing her babies. The aching sadness of it had never completely left her. She felt it whenever she saw a young child or heard the cry of a baby.

She thought sadly that Grant would not understand that. He had been a soldier and, to him, death and loss were like physical wounds to be bound up, healed and forgotten. Not that he had ever reproached her for her own mourning. He had always been very kind and given her all the time she needed to recover while he continued with his duties. Indeed, they had not spoken of it again. He had never burdened her with his concerns, or his grief. Even when the old Laird died Grant had not allowed her to comfort him. Instead the distance between them had increased.

Seeing Grant with that little boy, she thought

now that he would be such a good father. Was it any wonder he had been so cold to her this past year, so detached, when she had failed to provide him with a child of his own? His love had withered and the best thing she could do for him was to disappear, to go to France and allow him to divorce her. Before she could do that, she must help her father. He had told her his life was forfeit if his plan failed and she would do everything she could to prevent that.

After all, as she had told Grant, he was all she had left now.

Chapter Fourteen

'Well, what did you discover?'

Grant asked the question as soon as his man walked into their rooms at Henrietta Street.

'The Comte *is* being watched,' said Robert, unwinding his muffler. 'I spoke to one of them. Definitely a British military man.'

'You are sure he could not be in the pay of the French?'

Robert shook his head and smiled a little. 'I've seen enough redcoats in my time to know one, even if they are trying to hide the fact. And this fellow was not experienced at subterfuge. A loyal subject of King George, I'd stake my life on it.'

Grant cursed under his breath. 'It is serious, then.'

'Aye, sir. And it puts my lady in even more danger.'

'Thank you, Robert, I do not need reminding of that!'

He walked slowly across to the window and stared into the street. He wanted to save Maddie, had considered carrying her off by force, if necessary, but would she ever forgive him if he stopped her from helping her father? Since returning from the park earlier that day, he had been haunted by her final words to him.

I have lost you.

There had been something in her tone, in her eyes... He raked a hand through his hair. Could it be that she still cared for him? If there was any possibility of even a spark of love left, then he would do anything to preserve it. Forcing Madeleine to abandon her father to his fate would most certainly kill it.

'If the British are watching the Comte, then there is little hope of his plans succeeding,' he muttered, giving voice to his thoughts.

'It must needs be abduction then, sir.'

'No. Not yet. Let me see Lady Rathmore again first. Talk to her.'

Even as he spoke, he felt the grim reality pressing in on him. He could see little possibility of keeping Maddie *and* Ardvarrick.

His quarry proved elusive. The following morning he had called at the Comte's house, only to be told that *mademoiselle* was not at home. And, no, the footman could not tell him when the lady would be receiving callers. Grant had gone to Broadwick Street, but neither of the McBinnie ladies could tell him of Madeleine's movements. He was perturbed to learn that she had written a hasty note to Anne, cancelling their proposed outing that day, but giving no reason.

In desperation, he had returned to Surrey Street later in the day and learned from the crossing sweeper in his employ that the Comte had taken a ferry across to Southwark and not yet returned.

'Also,' the man went on, somewhat apologetically, 'I saw *mam'selle* leaving the house with her maid, soon after you'd gone this morning, sir. I sent a boy after them, but he lost 'em somewhere in the City.'

Frustrated, Grant went back to his lodgings and, after a solitary dinner, he put on his finest coat and charmed his way into the house of every hostess he knew who had any connection with the Comte. He was welcomed everywhere, but gained no news of Madeleine or her father, nor did he hear a whisper of intrigue. He returned to Henrietta Street in the early hours of the morning and fell into bed, exhausted, but none the wiser.

* * *

He was woken by the sound of Robert coming into his room, carrying his breakfast tray.

'So there you are,' Grant muttered, sitting up. 'Where the devil had you got to, when I came back last night?'

Robert put the tray down on the bed, in no wise disturbed by his master's wrathful greeting.

'After you had gone out, I decided to go back to Surrey Street, to see if I could discover anything.'

'And did you?' Grant yawned and reached over to pull the tray on to his lap. He drank the coffee while he listened to his man.

'Not much activity in the street, sir. My lady returned at about six and did not go out again, but there had been no sign of the Comte all day. However, once it was dark I decided to go and keep watch on the stairs. At about nine o'clock, I was fortunate enough to see a small craft approaching. It was not one of the watermen. This was quite different, bigger. And there were four men rowing.'

'Go on,' Grant ordered, his breakfast forgotten.

'I drew back a little, thinking they were making for the jetty, but instead they ran the boat up against the embankment and two passengers alighted. They climbed over the wall into the garden.'

'Using the ladder that had been hidden among the reeds.'

'Yes, sir.'

'Then I was right,' muttered Grant, nodding with grim satisfaction. 'They could enter the Comte's house through a back door.

'Aye, sir. The bank is worn away completely from that point on up to the Surrey Street stairs. No one could step off that jetty and walk along under the wall without ending up in the river, so the chances of anyone spotting the ladder are very small.'

'Very good. Anything else, Robert?'

'Well, it was too dark to see clearly, but one of the gentlemen looked to be the height and build of the Comte and very agile for a gentleman of his age, if I may say so.'

'And the other?'

'A younger man, I believe. As tall, but of slighter build than his companion.'

'No one else?'

'No, only the oarsmen, who remained on board and went away soon after. The two men who alighted had a large bundle with them. A bag perhaps, the sort that a sailor might use to carry his possessions.'

'Hmm. Could this be the emissary from France that the Comte was waiting for?'

'Aye, sir. I think that is very possible.'

Grant jumped out of bed.

'Then the game's afoot,' he said, thinking quickly. 'We need to know what is going on. Robert, you go now to the Comte's house, I can dress myself. And see if anything has occurred overnight. I will visit the coffee houses, see if I can discover anything more—'

'There is something else,' Robert interrupted him. 'A letter was delivered here this morning. I put it on the tray for you.'

Grant turned. He had not touched his food, but how had he missed the folded cream paper tucked beneath the edge of the plate? He snatched it up and broke the seal to find enclosed a second sheet, which he quickly unfolded.

I, the undersigned...

His eyes scanned the rest, then he slowly tore the paper into small pieces. It was Madeleine's sworn statement, exonerating him from any knowledge of or involvement in her actions. He said slowly, 'Now I know what my wife was doing in the City yesterday.'

'Bad news, sir?'

Grant shrugged, unable to trust himself to say anything more. He tucked the pieces back into the wrapper and refolded it, then held it out.

'Put a fresh seal on this and return it when you go to Surrey Street this morning, will you?'

He almost thrust it into Robert's hands before turning away. He did not trust himself to take it in person.

'Very well.' His man coughed. 'It is Thursday, sir. You said you were going to Lincoln's Inn this morning; do you want me to call you a cab before I leave?'

'No. I have changed my mind about seeing that attorney.'

The irony of the situation was not lost on Grant. He had been planning to disown his wife, but she had done it first. Yet, strangely, Madeleine's statement had crystallised his thoughts for him. He knew now there was no way he would abandon her.

Chapter Fifteen

Grant spent a fruitless morning in the coffee houses, where he learned nothing to his advantage, then he joined Sir Edmund and his family for their daily promenade in Hyde Park. He had begged Anne to keep up her friendship with Madeleine, knowing she would be a reliable source of information for him, although his conscience had pricked him at using her in this way, as he admitted to Anne while they strolled together along the crowded path.

'It is understandable that you wish to know how Maddie goes on,' she replied. 'I only wish I could help more, but at all our recent meetings she could not be persuaded to tell me anything other than the veriest trifles. I wish she would be more open with me.'

'She suspects you will pass on your information to *me*,' said Grant.

'It is more that she does not wish to embroil either of us in her affairs.' She squeezed his arm. 'She still cares for you, Grant, I am sure of it.'

'I am not. I handled our last meeting very badly.' He tried to smile. 'Pray do not attempt to be kind to me, Anne. All I want is for Madeleine to be safe. It matters not what she thinks of me now.'

'Surely you cannot mean that, Grant. I—oh!' she cried, stopping suddenly.

'What is it?'

'I have something in my eye.'

'Look up and let me see…ah, yes, I see it. You have dust in your eye. Here, let me.'

He pulled out his handkerchief and proceeded to carefully wipe away the speck. So intent upon his task was he that the carriages rattled by without his noticing. Including the smart equipage hired by the Comte de Vaucluse to carry his daughter through the park.

Madeleine was alone in the open carriage. Papa had advised her not to wait up for him the previous evening, so she had retired early and risen to find her father had already gone out, but he had left orders that she was to drive in Hyde Park. He had been very specific about the time she was to go and the route to be taken. She was also instructed to be sure to use the new blue and white parasol he had purchased for her. It was clearly intended as a signal to someone and she wondered what would have happened if the English weather had lived up to its reputation for being changeable and it had been raining. As it was, the balmy September day was quite perfect for the task.

She had seen Anne walking in the park and, wanting to make amends for having cried off from their meeting yesterday, she had been minded to order the carriage to pull up. Even when she recognised her friend's companion, Maddie thought she could do it, if only to show them both that Grant Rathmore no longer meant anything to her.

Anne and Grant were such old friends and it was only natural that he should be with her, reasoned Madeleine. He had probably told the McBinnies by now that his marriage was over and she should be grateful for that because it would save her the pain of divulging it to them. But before she could order her driver to stop, the couple paused and she saw Grant cup Anne's chin and gently tilt it up towards him. As if he was about to kiss her.

Madeleine quickly averted her eyes. How dare he! Gross impropriety and in such a public place, too. She remained silent and the carriage swept on without slowing. She also tilted her parasol to block the couple from her view, not that she would have seen very much, for she had to blink regularly to clear her eyes of the hot tears that threatened to spill over.

By the time the carriage left the park some ten minutes later, Maddie was beginning to wish that she *had* stopped the carriage and berated them both, until she remembered the declaration she had signed, effectively renouncing Grant. He was no longer her concern and if he had fallen in love with Anne McBinnie then she should be glad.

Only she was not. Not at all.

The day proceeded to go from bad to worse for Madeleine. The tailor recommended by Sir Edmund had promised to have her new riding habit finished today, but when she called at the workshop in New Bond Street, she discovered they had not incorporated the special little pocket she had requested and she was obliged to come away empty-handed.

Then, arriving back at Surrey Street, she discovered her letter to Grant had been sent back. She carried it up to her bedchamber to open it and when she did, the torn pieces of her statement fell to the floor. Quickly she gathered them up and burnt them in the fire.

The Comte had not yet returned, but she found a new gown that he had purchased for her laid out on the bed, together with a note to say she was to wear it for their dinner party that evening. At any other time she would have been delighted with the golden robe *à la Française* with its silk chenille appliqué and scalloped flounces on the sleeves. Now, the lavish attire and her father's postscript that she was to order another place to be set at the table only roused her suspicions.

She was sure that Papa was planning something momentous this evening. It had not escaped her notice that her father's personal servants were on edge. When she cornered his valet, he was persuaded to tell her that the Comte had returned late last night with a visitor, but more than that he would not say. Madeleine's imagination was left to run riot with fevered speculation.

As evening approached, she arrayed herself in the sumptuous gown but when she left her room shortly before the dinner hour, she was greeted with the news that the Comte was delayed. It would not be the first time she had been obliged to welcome dinner guests in his absence, but her brittle nerves tonight made it more of a struggle to smile and present a carefree face to the world.

The Froomes were the first to arrive, followed by Richard Thrimby and Sir John Belsay. Then Lord Kelty and his wife came in with Sir Evelyn and Lady Molton. Maddie hoped the Comte would appear before their last guests arrived, but it was not to be and she schooled her countenance into a smile of welcome as Sir William Maxton came up the stairs. He was accompanied by a slender, dark-haired young man whom he introduced as Alexander Murray.

'I beg your pardon for intruding at short notice,' Mr Murray greeted her, looking hesitant. 'I believe the Comte sent word about my coming...'

She held out her hand to him. 'He did, *monsieur*, and it is no trouble, *je vous assure*. I am a little acquainted with your brother, Lord Elibank...'

Conversation was made easier by relief. Maddie had feared she might find herself entertaining a French emissary for dinner. In her opinion, that would have been a far more dangerous guest to have in the house.

Madeleine sent word to the kitchen to put dinner back another hour and ordered more wine to be served. The company were all in good spirits and there was no lack of conversation, but try as she might she could not avoid Sir William Maxton for long. He drew her away from the others and suggested she might like to step out into the garden with him.

'It is such a warm night,' he remarked, 'I am sure you would benefit from a little air.'

She disclaimed with a little trill of laughter, 'La, sir, I am not at all uncomfortable here.'

'And yet you have been fanning yourself most assiduously since I arrived.'

'But of course. Did you not know? The fan is a lady's most powerful weapon.' She raised her own and peeped at him over the top of it.

He laughed. 'One of them, undoubtedly. Tell me, who was the gentleman you were dancing with at Clifton House the other night? A tall man. Dark red hair. Unpowdered.'

She pouted a little. '*Vraiment*, how am I supposed to remember every man who speaks to me?'

'You will not have forgotten this one. You danced the gavotte with him.'

Madeleine opened her eyes wide at him. 'How can you know these things, Sir William, when you were not even there?'

He looked pleased and leaned in a little to purr into her ear.

'So, *mademoiselle*, you noted my absence?' She did not reply but lowered her eyes demurely and he chuckled. 'No, you would not admit as much, would you? But to answer your question, it was Lady Froome who mentioned it. She said the fellow was very…attentive. From her description, I believe I have seen him with you on other occasions. At Tunbridge House, for example.'

'Let me think.' Madeleine pretended to consider. Sir William clearly knew too much for her to plead ignorance. 'Ah, that would be Sir Grant something…' She fluttered her fan dismissively. 'I really do not remember much about him, save that he was not long come from the north.'

'And yet Her Ladyship tells me you and he were flirting prodigiously.'

'I flirt with many men, Sir William, it does not mean I remember them all.'

She gave him a saucy look and he laughed again. 'Minx!'

She looked away, seemingly very pleased with this term of endearment, then she said, innocently, 'Why do you ask?'

'Because I like to know who my rivals might be.'

'*Alors*, you will be very busy, sir, if you are

going to show an interest in every chance acquaintance.'

Her tone was light, but in truth Madeleine was
seriously alarmed. It would not do for anyone to
look too closely into the link between her and
Grant Rathmore, especially Sir William, whom
she feared was more likely than most to discover the truth. The door opened and she swung
around, relieved at the interruption.

'Ah,' drawled Sir William, 'here is our host
at last.'

Never had Madeleine been so pleased to have
her conversation interrupted. She hurried across
to her father, hands held out and chiding him
gaily.

'Fie upon you, sir, where have you been hiding? I was obliged to put dinner back by an hour
and I have no doubt our guests are quite fam-
ished by now!'

'A thousand apologies, *ma chère*, and to you,
my honoured guests. I hope you will forgive my
being so late, once I have explained myself.'

'You have news of a…er…certain gentleman?'
exclaimed Mr Thrimby, stepping forward eagerly.

The Comte glanced behind him, to make sure
the servant had withdrawn and the door was
closed. Then he bowed.

'There is news, *monsieur*, but this is not the time to discuss it. Madeleine, my dear, you will order dinner to be served *toute de suite, s'il te plaît*. And afterwards, I have a treat in store for everyone.' His beaming smile swept over everyone. 'We are all invited to attend Lady Primrose's soirée!'

Chapter Sixteen

It was only a short stroll to Essex Street, but the Comte insisted upon chairs for the ladies. There had been no opportunity for Madeleine to speak with her father alone, but his smiles and high spirits during dinner made her wonder, as she squeezed herself and the heavy skirts of her gown into the small space of the sedan, just what mischief was afoot this evening.

When they reached Lady Primrose's residence, they were shown upstairs to a crowded salon that was very warm, despite the windows being thrown wide. Maddie knew better than to cling to her father's arm and she soon found an excuse to move away from his party. She walked off to greet a slight acquaintance she had spotted across the room, smiling and talking with an insouciance she was far from feeling.

Madeleine was troubled and not only by anxiety for what the evening might hold. There was also the nagging memory of Grant and Anne in the park. She had convinced herself she was no longer in love, yet the sight of him showing such attention to another lady had let loose a little demon of jealousy that gnawed away at her. She was being unreasonable, she knew that. If Grant could find happiness with a good, kind woman like Anne McBinnie, then she should be glad of it. Instead, she felt the most alarming desire to scratch Anne's eyes out.

When Madeleine looked for her father a short while later there was no sign of him, although the rest of their party were still in a little group. Sir William Maxton was conversing with Mr Murray, but she noted the way his eyes were constantly moving over the assembly. Not wishing him to see that she was currently on her own, she quickly turned and made her way through to another room.

She found herself in a large salon, with little clusters of men and women standing around, laughing, chattering and drinking. The panelled walls were painted a soft green and intricate carvings had been picked out in gold leaf, which glinted in the candlelight. At the far side of the room, in front of the shuttered windows,

Lady Primrose was sitting in regal state, talking with her friends.

Madeleine stopped, her eyes widening in surprise and alarm. It was not the sight of her hostess or the magnificent decor that caught her attention, but the painting hanging above the chimney piece. It was the portrait of a handsome young man in a powdered bagwig, his gentle brown eyes set in an almost boyish face and the faintest hint of a smile on his lips. He wore a blue sash across his coat of rose silk damask and the Order of the Garter was emblazoned on his chest. Fear and excitement caused her heart to contract: she had seen too many paintings not to recognise the subject.

Swallowing hard, she tore her eyes from the portrait and turned away, alarmed that a likeness of Prince Charles Edward Stuart should be displayed so prominently. Surely Lady Primrose risked being accused of treason if this came to the ears of the government. She took a glass of wine from a passing waiter and, as she lifted it higher, the candlelight illuminated the delicate engraving of a rose, another reminder of her hostess's allegiance. Her senses prickled with fearful anticipation and she took a sip of wine to calm her nerves.

It was at that moment that her father came in,

accompanied by a tall stranger. The two men made their way across the room towards their hostess, who had risen from her chair to greet them. Madeleine heard her father present the gentleman as *Mr Smith* and she took another quick glance at the portrait. Any remaining doubts were dispelled when she observed the deep curtsy Lady Primrose was making to the gentleman. This was the Stuart Prince whom almost everyone in that room considered to be the rightful heir to the throne.

The chatter had died down to an excited muttering. Madeleine moved into a corner, trying to be inconspicuous. She guessed that this had been her father's mysterious guest last night, but why was he making his appearance here, with Lady Primrose, rather than in Surrey Street?

The answer came to her almost immediately. Papa would not take responsibility for hiding the Prince while he was in London, although she had no doubt he would be happy to accept the credit for spiriting the Young Pretender into the capital. A slightly hysterical laugh bubbled up. This was madness, but one had to admire her father's aplomb as he escorted his companion around the room. The low bows and deep curtsies were far in excess of what was required when meeting a plain Mr Smith, but no one here was in any doubt that they were in the presence of royalty.

When the Comte caught her eye and beckoned, Madeleine came out of her corner to be presented to the Prince. He was not as slender as the figure in the portrait and his long face was weather-beaten, although still handsome. He looked older, his features more careworn, but his tawny hazel eyes held a merry twinkle and his smile, she had to admit, was charming.

She gave him her hand and sank into a curtsy. 'Welcome, *monsieur.*'

'Your father has spoken often of you, *mademoiselle.*' He raised her up, his words uttered in impeccable English. 'I find the Comte has not exaggerated your charms.'

'You are very kind, *monsieur.*'

Maddie struggled through a little conversation until the Comte softly reminded his companion that there were others waiting to meet him and she could retreat back into the crowd. She understood why his followers found him so charismatic. She herself was torn, because she liked the man, but was fearful of the danger he presented.

'Well, Madeleine, are you now a convert to the cause?'

She turned to find Sir William Maxton at her side.

'The...*gentleman* is very amiable,' she replied cautiously.

'Your father has created quite a stir this evening.'

She considered his words, then said, 'It was not entirely a surprise.'

'True. We all knew the Comte was up to something, but he gives damned little away.' He paused. 'Does *Mr Smith* lodge with you tonight, do you know?'

'I know no more than you. My father has not informed me of the fact, but as you say, sir, he gives very little away.' With a smile and a nod she turned to go, but Sir William put his hand out to detain her.

'I should like to know more of your father's plans, my dear.' She tensed, her brows going up, and she looked coldly at his fingers gripping her arm. He released her and continued, with a little laugh, 'If he should confide in you, that is. I would not want such dangerous knowledge to rest solely upon your beautiful shoulders.'

'Neither does my father want that, Sir William. It is precisely the reason he does not confide in me,' she replied before making good her escape.

* * *

It was late. The first grey streaks of dawn were in the sky before Madeleine and her father left Lady Primrose's soirée. Again, he insisted she take a chair, to protect her gown from the filth of the streets, so it was not until they were in their own house and walking up the stairs together that they had any opportunity to talk privately.

'How did you like our visitor, *ma chère?*'

'Mr Murray?' she replied, deliberately misunderstanding, 'He was pleasant enough, although I did not speak to him a great deal.'

'I mean Mr Smith, Madeleine, as you well know.'

'But he was not *our* visitor, sir—that honour goes to Lady Primrose.' She went on, dropping any pretence, 'I cannot deny I am relieved he is not staying here. In truth, I would rather we had nothing to do with this at all, Papa.'

'*C'est impossible, hélas.* It is only for a few days, however, and your role will not be particularly onerous, *chérie.*'

She stopped. 'My role?'

'*Mais oui.*' He tucked a hand under her arm and urged her to continue up the stairs. 'Mr Smith is here on business, but there will be moments of relaxation, too, when he will require entertaining. For example, he has expressed a desire to see a play.'

She laughed. 'That must surely be out of the question.'

'*Mais non, ma chère,*' her father replied, a note of triumph evident in his voice. 'I have procured a box and we shall attend the theatre tomorrow night.'

Madeleine was speechless. She had thought herself inured to her father's audacious actions, but this was too much! She said nothing as they walked on, but when they reached the door of her chamber they stopped and the Comte chuckled.

'I see you are astounded by my daring, but you know my ways, *chérie*. It is skulking in corners that attracts the eye. Better by far to be hiding in full view, where one is least expected.'

She stared up at him and her hand went to her throat, as if she could feel a noose already tightening around it. The Comte noted the action, but he merely smiled. Then, with a little flick of her cheek, he bade her goodnight and sauntered off to his own bedchamber.

The morning brought Madeleine a note from Miss McBinnie. It was an invitation to go shopping and it seemed Anne was determined she would not be gainsaid, for she even stated the time she would be calling at Surrey Street to collect her friend.

The memory of seeing Anne and Grant together in the park was still fresh and Madeleine was reluctant to agree, but she was even more anxious to avoid spending the day at home. The proposed visit to the theatre weighed heavily on her spirits and she badly needed a distraction, so she went upstairs to change into her walking dress.

Chapter Seventeen

'I am so pleased you could spare the time to come out with me,' said Anne, when Madeleine climbed into the carriage. 'Mama has the headache and although Eilidh would come with me, she would not enjoy it. She is still very disapproving of the English. Besides, shopping with one's maid is not nearly as enjoyable as with a friend.'

'I am surprised you did not ask Grant,' Maddie replied, trying not to sound waspish. 'You are such great friends, after all.'

'Grant!' Anne gave a little trill of laughter. 'You are a great joke-smith, Maddie—you know as well as I that Grant has no taste for shopping! Although,' she continued with a warm smile, 'if he had known *you* were coming…'

Studying her happy, guileless countenance, Madeleine wondered if she had been mistaken in what she had seen yesterday. Some of the anger and pain inside her melted away, but her reply was still rather sharp.

'He would have made sure he had another engagement. He has no more desire to see me than I him.'

'That is not true.' Anne reached across and put her hand on Maddie's arm. 'He is very anxious about you, you know.'

'Anxious lest I put his family in danger,' she retorted as the carriage came to a stop outside a fashionable milliner's shop. She looked out of the window. 'Oh, we are here already!'

Madeleine was relieved that Anne did not pursue the subject of Grant and she tried her best to forget about him. It was not easy when almost everything brought him to mind. A stray dog running through the streets with a leg of lamb clamped in its jaws made both ladies laugh and she wanted to store the memory to share with him later. Then, when she called in upon the tailor to collect her new riding habit and save him the trouble of delivering it to her, his apprentices were working on a riding coat in Grant's favourite colour.

As if that was not bad enough, she forgot herself to such an extent that when they passed a snuff shop advertising bound books among its wares, she wondered if there were any she could buy to add to their growing library at Ardvarrick…until she remembered she would not be going back.

After that it was a struggle to remain cheerful. When Anne expressed a desire to look closer at a pretty shawl in the haberdasher's window, Madeleine urged her to go in alone, saying she wanted to look at the prints in the neighbouring shop window. She was thus engaged when she heard someone addressing her.

'Mademoiselle d'Evremont?'

She swung around to find herself looking at a tall, upright gentleman soberly dressed in top boots and a dark riding jacket. A man she had not seen for four years, not since she and Grant had been fleeing across the Highlands after Culloden.

'M-Major Rutter! Forgive me, I had not expected to see you here!'

He gave a stiff little bow. 'No, of course not. Although, it is Colonel Rutter now.'

'Really?' She fought down her nerves and summoned up a friendly smile. 'Then I must congratulate you upon your promotion.'

'Thank you, *mademoiselle.*'

His smile was perfunctory, but she read little

into that. The man had always had a rather sober mien. She glanced again at his plain riding coat.

'You are, perhaps, on leave, sir?'

'No, unfortunately I am not.'

'Oh.' She waved a hand. 'But you are not in uniform…'

'I have been assigned to Whitehall for the present time.'

'You have?' Oh, heavens, worse and worse! Madeleine forced a laugh. 'I hope your duties are not too onerous!'

'I am merely making enquiries upon certain matters,' he said vaguely. 'May one enquire what brings you to town?'

'I am here with my father, the Comte de Vaucluse.'

She thought she detected a spark of recognition in his eyes at the name, but it was gone in an instant. Her thoughts raced. The last time she had seen Major Rutter, she and Grant had saved his life and secured a hoard of Jacobite gold for the Crown. It was Grant's heroic actions that had earned him his knighthood, but would that be enough to protect him if Colonel Rutter should suspect he was caught up in a Jacobite plot?

'I thought you would be in Scotland with your brave Highlander,' the Colonel went on. 'In fact, I thought you would marry Grant Rathmore.'

She swallowed. It would be useless to deny it.

'I did,' she said quietly. 'But we are estranged.'

'Ah, I see. I am very sorry to hear it.'

'Thank you. That is why I am in London and why I have chosen to be called Miss d'Evremont while I am here,' she explained. 'My father is taking me back to France.'

He inclined his head. 'The Comte de Vaucluse, you said?'

A tinkling bell signalled her rescue and Maddie turned to smile at her friend, who had stepped out of the shop carrying several brown paper packages.

'Ah, there you are, Anne! You will remember Major Rutter?' She shot her a look full of warning. 'Only he has been promoted to colonel now, you know.'

'Of *course,* I remember!' Anne came forward, holding out her hand. 'How could I forget, when you were billeted with us for some weeks in 'forty-six?' She smiled to show she meant no offence. 'What a pleasant surprise. You are on leave, Colonel Rutter?'

'No, alas, I am here on duty, Miss McBinnie.'

'I said exactly the same, Anne,' exclaimed Madeleine playfully. 'One cannot but wonder what business it is that brings the good Colonel to London.'

She looked at him encouragingly, but Colonel Rutter was not to be drawn. He afforded her question no more than a slight smile.

'It is best not to wonder about government business, ma'am,' he replied solemnly. 'However, my days are not uniformly onerous.' He gestured towards the parcels Anne was holding. 'Do you not have a manservant to carry those for you?'

'We had to send him back to the carriage,' said Anne, twinkling up at him. 'What with the hats I have bought, and Maddie's new riding habit, he was already laden with so many parcels he could not possibly carry anything more.'

'Then allow me to be of service,' said the Colonel, bowing again. 'I am free for the moment and would be delighted to carry your purchases for you.'

'Oh, how kind,' exclaimed Anne. 'Although we have now finished all our shopping and are about to make our way back to the carriage.'

'Then pray allow me to escort you,' he said, gently removing the packages from Anne's grasp and tucking them under his arm.

There was nothing the ladies could do but accept gratefully and the little party set off, retracing their steps through the busy streets. Much to Madeleine's relief, Anne continued to chatter as the three of them made their way back to the coach, where the Colonel gallantly handed them in, and it was Anne who leaned forward to bid him farewell.

'Goodbye, Colonel Rutter, and thank you, you have been most kind.'

'It was a pleasure, Miss McBinnie. And I will not say goodbye, because I feel sure our paths will cross again.' He put his hand to the carriage door, but did not immediately close it. Instead, he looked at Madeleine for a long moment, his face unreadable. 'And I hope *you* will not disappear before I have had the opportunity to meet your father, Mademoiselle d'Evremont.'

With that he shut the door and stepped back, waving to the coachman to drive on. As one, Maddie and Anne sat back against the squabs and closed their eyes.

'Oh, dear, how unfortunate!' muttered Anne. 'Of all the people to meet in town.'

'And he is not on leave,' added Madeleine. 'With his record of service in Scotland, I fear he can only be investigating the latest threats from across the water.'

'Then thank heaven Papa has distanced himself from such matters! But what about you, Maddie? What did you tell him about yourself?'

'What could I say? I did not dare lie, I had to tell him Grant and I had parted.' Maddie clasped her hands together, frowning. 'Grant must be warned and as soon as possible.'

'He is dining with us this evening so I could tell him then,' Anne suggested. 'He is accompanying us to the theatre this evening.'

Again, Madeleine was aware of the prickle of jealousy. It was irrational, but it was there, gnawing away at her, although now it was overridden by the need to protect Grant.

'I shall be there, too, with my father.' She sat forward, saying earnestly, 'Pray impress upon Grant that on no account must he approach me. In fact, if you could persuade him to quit London altogether, that would be even better.'

'I do not think he will do that. Not until he is sure you are in no danger.'

Maddie did not know if she was most alarmed or comforted by Anne's statement. The web of intrigue and deceit was being woven tighter around her every day. Grant had risked everything for her once before, but that had been four years ago, when they were very much in love. Before the tragedies of lost babies and his father's death had come between them.

Chapter Eighteen

After Anne had dropped her at Surrey Street, Madeleine ran upstairs to change for dinner. She would have given a king's ransom not to go to Drury Lane that night, but her father had demanded her attendance. *Mr Smith* was to dine with them first, along with Lord Froome and his lady. Madeleine knew what would be required of her at the theatre. She would sit at the front of their box and during the interval any number of gentlemen would appear. Ostensibly they came to pay court to Mademoiselle d'Evremont, but while she laughed and chattered and flirted, the Comte and his guest would be in the shadows at the back of the box, exchanging a word with each of the gentlemen, passing messages, weaving plans.

Papa might always maintain that suspicions were more easily aroused if one avoided crowds and public places, but Madeleine was afraid her father had gone too far this time. True, no one would be expecting to see Charles Edward Stuart in Drury Lane, but the risks were enormous and the consequences, if the Prince were discovered, did not bear thinking about.

Dinner was a trial. Her father and his guests were in high spirits, but although she smiled and entertained her guests with her usual cheerfulness, Madeleine could not be easy. The theatre was bustling, as expected, and she tarried in the foyer with Lord and Lady Froome, greeting acquaintances and admirers, drawing all the attention while her father and his guest slipped quietly upstairs to their box.

When eventually Madeleine did take her seat, her eyes raked the crowd for familiar faces while she waited for the performance to begin. She recognised Sir William Maxton, but quickly shifted her gaze away from him. She knew he would be coming to their box during the interval, but she refused to offer him any encouragement. She would have liked to give him the cut direct, but the knowledge that he held some power over her father made it impossible to repulse him completely.

However, when Madeleine's searching gaze

reached the box opposite her own, Sir William and even the Prince were forgotten. Grant was there, placing a chair for Anne McBinnie and hovering attentively while she made herself comfortable. As if aware of her gaze, Grant looked across at Madeleine and she saw his smile disappear. He acknowledged her with no more than a distant nod, to which she responded in a similar vein, anxious that no one should guess that the lively Mademoiselle d'Evremont and the Laird of Ardvarrick were anything more than the merest acquaintances.

It was a relief when the play began and Madeleine could fix her gaze upon the stage, but the actors could not hold her attention. Knowing Grant was in the box opposite and that she was in full view, she braced herself for a most trying evening.

Grant tried to concentrate on the stage, but his eyes and his thoughts constantly returned to his wife. She was sitting at her ease between the Comte and an older lady, whom Sir Edmund informed him was Lady Froome. Maddie was watching the play with every appearance of delight and he could not deny she made a charming picture. Her lustrous black curls were swept back and held in place with a diamond comb.

More diamonds sparkled at her ears and throat. She was dressed to attract attention, there was no doubt about that, and she would do so. She looked ravishingly beautiful.

Anne had warned him that Madeleine would be present this evening, but it was sheer misfortune that their boxes were directly opposite one another. He would have preferred to ignore her, but when he felt her eyes upon him it was impossible not to look up and meet her gaze. He had hoped to give her a polite nod, but feared his face gave him away, the anger, the sense of betrayal he felt that she had fled from him, from Ardvarrick.

Anne had described their meeting with Colonel Rutter that afternoon and passed on Madeleine's warning that he should keep his distance. A sensible precaution, he knew that, but there was no sign of the Colonel in the auditorium and Grant could not help thinking that Maddie was merely ensuring she was free to flirt tonight with whomsoever she wished.

The play finally came to an end and the McBinnies decided to remain in their seats while they waited for the musical entertainment to begin. A number of their acquaintances came in and Grant made way for them, moving to the back of the box, from where he could watch what was going on in the auditorium.

The box opposite was soon full and mainly with gentlemen, Grant noticed. Lady Froome was presumably there in the role of chaperon, but she had moved to a chair at one side while Madeleine remained in her seat at the front of the box, plying her fan adroitly as she talked—nay, flirted!—with each gentleman who sat down beside her. His lip curled. Fops, all of them, in their elegantly curled and powdered wigs and every one of them sporting an overabundance of fine lace and ruffles.

His gaze returned to Madeleine. Could it be that this was her natural milieu, enjoying the company of wits and dilettantes, mixing with the crème of society? He had first met her during the terrible aftermath of Culloden and she had proved herself to be brave, intelligent and resourceful. They had been through a great deal together and supported one another during their flight through the Highlands, but he had little knowledge of her life before that.

She had always seemed happy enough at Ardvarrick, but now he felt a new frisson of doubt. Perhaps she did miss it, the balls and parties. The excitement and intrigue. After all, she had not denied it when he had accused her of wanting to

return to her old life. Perhaps that was the real
reason she had left Ardvarrick. She was bored
with his world. With him.

It was an effort to thrust those thoughts aside,
but Grant did his best to observe dispassion-
ately what was happening in the box opposite.
To those who were not acquainted with Yves
d'Evremont it would appear that Madeleine was
the attraction, that the gentlemen were there
solely to court her, but Grant was convinced this
was a charade of the Comte's making. It was
the reason he wanted his daughter with him, to
deflect attention away from the true purpose of
the evening, which was the discussions taking
place between the little knot of men at the back
of the box.

His eyes went back to Madeleine. She looked
so happy, so natural and animated. It was hard to
believe she was not enjoying herself. The thought
tormented him, but he squashed it and turned
his attention to the gentlemen in the shadows
behind her.

They were barely more than shapes in the
gloom, nothing to arouse suspicion, but Grant
began to see a pattern emerging as indistinct figures appeared briefly, then slipped away again.
A few of the visitors stepped forward and were
momentarily illuminated by the lamps blazing

around the auditorium. They included Lord Elibank, Grant's neighbour from Henrietta Street whom he knew to be a well-known supporter of the Stuarts.

There was another person Grant recognised, a gentleman in a coat of mulberry damask, lavishly embroidered with gold thread. Sir William Maxton. Sir Edmund had pointed him out earlier.

'A particularly powerful and dangerous man, according to Colonel Rutter,' Sir Edmund had told him. 'He warned me against Maxton when Anne mentioned that we had been introduced to Sir William.'

'You have seen Colonel Rutter?' Grant replied, momentarily diverted.

'Why, yes. He arrived at Broadwick Street shortly after Anne returned this afternoon. Apparently, they met earlier and he had carried Anne's shopping back to the carriage for her.' A faint smile tugged at Sir Edmund's lips. 'It appears the Colonel, er, forgot to hand over one of the smaller packages and called to return it.'

Grant could not prevent himself from laughing at that. 'It sounds to me like the fellow is smitten!'

'I thought that, too, and Anne does appear to like him very well. But it is early days yet. We shall see what comes of it. An English soldier is not what I would have chosen for her, but I have to say I like the fellow.'

'Aye, he's a good man, I am sure. But to get back to Maxton,' said Grant, growing serious again, 'what did Rutter say of him?'

'He would not go into detail, but I made a few enquiries of my own and discovered that Sir William is a good friend of the Secretary at War.'

'The devil he is! If that is so, then what is he doing in the company of the Comte de Vaucluse? Unless he is gathering information against him for the government.'

'Or he has a foot in both camps.'

Sir Edmund's final remark returned to Grant as he watched Maxton and the Comte with their heads together. He had taken an immediate dislike to Sir William, angered by his possessive attitude towards Madeleine. Watching him now, he did not believe it was merely his aversion to Maxton that made him think the man was playing some deep and dangerous game.

The music for the burletta struck up and the visitors began to leave the Comte's box, but Grant noted that Maxton remained. He slipped into the seat previously occupied by the Comte. The seat next to Madeleine.

* * *

Grant did not enjoy the remainder of the evening. He found nothing entertaining in the comic opera and his eyes kept wandering across to the opposite box. Madeleine's gaze was fixed upon the stage, but Sir William Maxton was leaning close and whispering in her ear. She was making good use of her *brisé* fan to cover her mouth, but Grant knew she was talking. Were they discussing another of the Comte's schemes, or was she responding to the scoundrel's whispered endearments? Grant could only guess, but either way, he could not be easy.

Never had an evening been so fraught for Madeleine. She could not forget that Charles Stuart was sitting in the shadows at the back of the box. She expected at any moment that the door would burst open and they would all be arrested. The interval was particularly trying. She kept up her carefree chatter, ignoring the whispered conversations behind her, and the uneasy feeling that Grant was watching her, even though she could not see him.

She waited impatiently for the entertainment to begin again, hoping that she might then relax, but, alas, Sir William Maxton sat down beside her. Her heart sank as he pulled his chair closer,

until it was almost touching hers. What would
Grant make of that, if he was watching? The
knot of unhappiness inside her tightened. Would
he even care?

'How did you enjoy the play?' Sir William
asked her.

'It was *très amusante.*'

She replied coolly and without looking at him.
Perhaps if she showed an interest in the perform-
ers, her companion would remain silent.

'For myself, I thought it most appropriate,' he
drawled, dashing her hopes.

'Oh?' She raised her fan to cover the lower
part of her face and kept her eyes upon the stage.

'The Provok'd Husband.' He leaned closer
and muttered, 'I know your game, madam. It
did not take much investigation to discover you
are the wife of Sir Grant Rathmore!'

Maddie's blood turned to ice in her veins. She
continued to fan herself slowly and gave no out-
ward sign of agitation.

'We met in the aftermath of Culloden,' she
said with a shrug. 'Our marriage was a mistake
and it is over. He is nothing to me, nor I to him.'

'Then why is he in London?'

'I neither know nor care.'

'Yet you danced with him.'

'I did not wish to do so, but to refuse would

have incurred much talk.' She flicked a scornful glance at him. 'You more than anyone should know my father would not want to attract any undue attention at this time.'

Had Sir William seen Grant here tonight? She fought down the impulse to let her eyes wander to the box opposite.

'Perhaps Rathmore wants to win you back.'

'No, that is not so. We are nothing to one another, *je vous assure.*'

'You relieve my mind, madam, because it means there is nothing to prevent you accepting an offer from *me.*'

She felt a kick of alarm at his words, but managed to keep the fan waving steadily and her eyes fixed on the singers, as if enraptured by the music.

'I am sorry to disappoint you, Sir William, but I have no intention of accepting any offers. I shall be returning to France with my father.'

'I think not. At least,' he continued, as her eyes flew to his face, 'not before we have enjoyed a little…dalliance.'

'No, sir. That is absurd. You would do well to put the idea from your mind.'

She shifted in her chair, turning away from him to indicate their conversation was over. Undaunted, he leaned closer, his lips almost touching her ear. She heard his next words quite clearly, despite the duet taking place on stage.

'I advise you to reconsider, my dear Madeleine. Your father has much to lose should his French paymasters discover that his daughter is married to a supporter of Hanover. They would not like that.'

She gave a little huff of disdain. 'Then it is very remiss of them not to have discovered it already. Perhaps they have and think it irrelevant. After all, I have returned to my father and I challenge anyone to deny *his* loyalty to the cause.'

'Mayhap you are right,' he continued, his voice silky with menace. 'However, let us not forget the very real danger to the Laird of Ardvarrick.'

Her heart was pounding heavily against her ribs, but she replied as if bored with the conversation, 'I have told you, Grant Rathmore is nothing to me.'

'No? Can you look at me and say you do not care what will happen to him when the British learn that his wife is actively working for the Stuarts?'

'And how should they learn that, pray?' Her voice dripped scorn, despite the icy fear clutching at her heart.

'From me, my dear, from me. He will face

certain disgrace, possibly even indictment as a traitor, once I have submitted my evidence against him.'

'There is no evidence!'

'Oh, but there is,' he purred. 'A statement from myself, signed and sealed, denouncing Sir Grant Rathmore and the Comte de Vaucluse.'

'Then you are lying!'

'But who would believe that?' he said to her, his brows raised. 'I have powerful friends, you see. Men in the highest positions on both sides of the water, who trust me completely. A whisper from me is enough to see any man disgraced. Imagine what my signed deposition will achieve. It will spell disaster for them both.' He added thoughtfully, 'And for you, too, my dear.'

On the stage, the duet ended in a joyous crescendo of orchestra and voices. The audience applauded wildly and Madeleine joined in, giving herself time to quell her panic.

'I do not believe you,' she muttered at last, her voice low and angry. 'You cannot speak out without endangering your own position.'

Sir William was leaning back on his chair, clapping lazily.

'There are hazards, certainly, but the British will forgive much and reward me well if I deliver the Stuart into their hands,' he said. 'On the other hand, I *could* do nothing, which would please those foreign powers who will be very happy if the Young Pretender continues to irritate the British a little longer. Either way, you see, I will win. Make your choice, madam: refuse me and you and all you hold dear will be lost. Accept and you shall have every luxury.' He sat up, smiling at her. 'You are a very beautiful woman, Madeleine. I have attended the French court and I believe, with a little effort, you might even rival the Pompadour herself. Assuredly you are a prize worth the fight, don't you think?'

When Madeleine made no reply, he gave a little laugh.

'But I am not a monster. There is no reason why anyone should suffer from this, my dear. If you become my mistress, then I shall allow your father to complete his…er…*business* successfully and return to France.'

'And my husband?'

'So, you do still care for him.'

'As I would care about the fate of any innocent man,' she retorted.

His knowing smile showed he did not believe her.

'Grant Rathmore may return to Scotland a free man, as long as he does not interfere in my plans. Well, what do you say? It is a very small price to pay, after all. You will live in luxury in my house and share my bed, and your men will go free.'

She swallowed. 'What if I do not please you?'

'You must make sure you do, madam.'

The leer that accompanied his reply sent a shiver of revulsion running through her, but Madeleine knew she must remain calm.

'It is not a decision I can make lightly,' she replied. 'I need time to consider.'

'I can give you until Sunday evening. You must come away with me then, or I shall inform the authorities. The Comte and his, er, *guest* will be arrested. As will all the other conspirators.'

She stared at him. 'You would give them all up? But they are your friends.'

His lips curled. 'They are fools, chasing a spent cause. However, I am willing to let them go free and allow the Stuart to leave England without hindrance. Once I have made sure of you.'

He put his hand out to touch her knee and she slapped it away with her closed fan.

'I *will* agree to your demands,' she said slowly, 'but I will not leave the house Sunday night. I will not quit Surrey Street until I am assured my father is safely on his way to France.'

'Is that so, madam?'

He gave her a long, considering look and her chin came up.

'I shall not back down on this point, Sir William. Those are my terms.'

'Your terms?' He raised his brows. 'And if I refuse, what will you do, run to your father?' He glanced back towards the shadowy figures behind them. 'He cannot save you and I believe he knows better than to cross me. Or do you mean to have me murdered within the next day or so and escape your fate? You would be ill advised to attempt anything so rash. My deposition is safe and will be passed to the authorities should anything happen to me. I assure you it is more than enough to secure a verdict of treason against each and every one of you.'

The opera was coming to an end. Lively music was playing, but Madeleine barely heard it as she tried to think what to do. An invisible, silken web was closing about her, cutting off every avenue of escape.

Something of her thoughts must have showed in her face, for Sir William laughed suddenly.

'But it need not come to such a pass. I am prepared to be generous. If you give me your word now, it shall be as you wish. It is only a matter of a few hours, after all.'

His last words were uttered softly, as if to

himself, but Madeleine seized upon them. Could it be true, was Papa planning to leave England under cover of darkness on Sunday night? He had told her to be ready, but she had not thought he meant to leave England quite so soon. Sir William might be bluffing, he might know nothing of Papa's plans, but she could not be sure. She was obliged to fight down the sudden tightness in her throat.

'Very well,' she said, 'then you have my word. Once my father is safe, I will come with you. I will be your mistress.'

As if to mock her words, the audience burst into life as the operetta ended. The theatre rang with catcalls and cheers from the rowdy audience in the pit as the singers took their bows. Sir William rose from his chair.

'An excellent evening's work,' he declared, taking her hand and raising it to his lips. 'I always intended to have you,' he went on with a predatory smile. 'You will be in my bed by Monday night. Do not think of betraying me, Madeleine. If you do, your father may escape, but you may be sure that Ardvarrick and Clan Rathmore will pay the price.'

Chapter Nineteen

'A most successful evening,' declared the Comte, as he handed Madeleine into the carriage. 'The charming *Mr Smith* has gone off with Lord Froome and we are free to enjoy ourselves!' He called out his orders to the driver and climbed in beside her.

'Must we attend another party, Papa? Can we not go back to Surrey Street?'

'Not yet, *ma fille*. We go to Lady Thanet's.'

She hunched a shoulder and said somewhat pettishly, 'I do not even know the lady.'

'*Non*, you were not with me when I dined with her, but she told me she would very much like to meet you. We were great friends once, when she was young. When we were *both* so much younger!' He gave a gusty sigh. 'Ah, *La Belle Marie*, as she was then. I believe we will be in good time—'

'Oh, how much more of this?' Madeleine broke in, her voice weary.

'It will be but a few hours, *ma fille*, no more. I have given my word that we would look in at my lady's rout tonight.'

'Not that,' she said impatiently. 'This whole escapade. When do you return to France? I want the truth now, Papa, if you please.'

Perhaps it was her serious tone, or her obvious agitation, but for once he did not prevaricate.

'The ship sails with the morning tide on Monday.'

So, Sir William did know what was going on. *You will be in my bed by Monday night.*

His words echoed in her head, taunting her, and her hand came up, an involuntary gesture of alarm. The Comte caught it and gave it a little squeeze.

'*Tiens,* you look so serious, Madeleine! I thought you enjoyed a little excitement.'

'I have never liked your games, Papa.'

'Then you will be pleased to know that this will be the last of them. I grow too old for intrigues. A few more days, then we will be in France and I shall deliver you to my Comtesse, who will cosset you like a daughter and keep you in luxury. You will like that, *hein*?'

Madeleine nodded and tried to smile, but it

was an effort. The knowledge that Sir William knew of Papa's plans only tightened the chains binding her to her fate.

Upon their arrival at Thanet House, the Countess greeted them warmly and it was clear that she still held the Comte in great affection. Feeling decidedly *de trop*, Madeleine went off, leaving her father and the lady ensconced in a window embrasure, flirting outrageously. There were one or two familiar faces in the assembly, but no one Madeleine recognised as a Jacobite. That was a comfort. It was refreshing not to be constantly guarding her speech or looking over her shoulder. She began to relax.

She was enjoying a lively discussion on the merits of Mr Richardson's novels when something caused her to look up. Grant was standing across the room, watching her. She quickly turned back to the little group around her, but the arguments she had been about to make withered and her brain ceased to function properly. She took refuge behind her fluttering fan and said nothing more.

Grant made no move to approach, but Madeleine was painfully aware of his presence. She mingled with the crowd, trying her best to evade him. When she thought she had succeeded, she slipped away to the supper room, but as she was filling her plate from the buffet table he suddenly appeared at her side.

'I did not expect to see you here,' she muttered, startled.

'I heard the Comte tell your driver the direction.'

'How dare you follow me!'

Maddie turned and made her way from the cold meats towards the large punchbowl at the far end of the table. Annoyingly, he remained at her side. She filled a cup with punch and when he still did not move away, she succumbed to temptation and asked him the question that had been bothering her all day.

'Why did you tear up my statement?'

'I did not want it. For better or worse, you are my wife.'

'Hush!'

She glanced about her, alarmed, but no one was standing close enough to hear them. Yet.

'Stay away from me,' she muttered. 'We must not arouse suspicion.'

'Apart from your father, no one else in this house knows we are married.' He exhaled. 'Sometimes I wish everyone knew it, then we might put an end to this charade!'

Madeleine felt a sudden rush of fear for him.

With a look that she hoped said 'follow me', she set down her cup and walked across the room to the doors leading out to the terrace. They had been thrown wide and a few guests had already spilled out. She did not need to look back to know Grant was behind her and she walked on, looking for a quieter spot. Around the corner of the house was a deserted terrace. No doors stood open and the windows were dark. There was only the moon bathing everything in a soft grey light. They were unlikely to be observed here, or overheard.

She stopped and turned to Grant.

'Someone *has* discovered our secret,' she told him. 'Sir William Maxton. He has threatened to denounce you as a Jacobite.'

He laughed. 'On what grounds?'

'Just your being in London at this time is sufficient. At the very least you should leave town immediately.'

'You know I cannot do that. Besides, I have done nothing wrong.'

Maddie wanted to scream at his insouciance. Could he not see the danger?

'That is not the point.' She put out a hand to touch his arm. 'Maxton has many powerful friends who will support him, even if he chooses to fabricate the evidence against you. It is not safe for you here.'

'What do you care for that?'

'I care too much!' The words were out before she could stop them and she hastily took a step away. 'That is, I promised you I would not cause a scandal for your family. I cannot keep that promise if you remain in London.'

He looked down at her. 'Do you really want me to leave you here, Maddie?'

His face was in shadow, but she could imagine the smile in his eyes that accompanied those soft words.

'Yes, I do.' She ran her tongue across her dry lips. 'We are agreed we cannot live together.'

'Are we? Do you not think we were a little hasty? I should like us to try again.'

He was coming closer, towering over her and filling her senses. She could feel the heat from him and when she breathed in, she inhaled the mix of spicy soap and fresh linen that was so familiar. It was intoxicating. She wanted to step closer, to fill her head, her lungs with the scent of him. How easy it would be to lean against that solid chest, to have his arms wrapped around her, his lips on hers, making her forget everything but this moment.

No! Maddie backed away until she felt the

rough wall of the house against her shoulders. Unable to retreat further, she put her hands out to keep him at bay.

Grant stopped when he felt her dainty palms pressed against his chest. She was looking up at him, her eyes shining like stars in the moonlight, bewitching him. Her tongue grazed for a second time across her lips and his heart kicked, as if she had been skimming them over his skin.

'No, Grant,' she warned him, her voice soft, breathless. 'Not again.'

'Why not?' He put his hands on her shoulders and saw the involuntary flicker of her eyelids as he ran his thumbs gently over the delicate collar bones. 'We are man and wife,' he murmured, lowering his head so he could place featherlight kisses on her cheeks. 'How can this be wrong?'

She melted into him without a sound and his arms tightened. It felt so good to be holding her again, breathing in her sweet perfume. He heard a soft sigh as she turned her face up, her lips seeking his, and when they met it sent a shudder through Grant. His heart was thudding a tattoo, the blood roaring in his ears as his body responded to the kiss.

Her tongue darted and teased, tangling with his, sending the heat coursing through his aroused body. He ran his hands over the bodice of her gown, wanting to rip away the padded silk and expose the soft flesh beneath, but he resisted. Instead, he caressed her neck, his fingers gently stroking the smooth skin.

She moaned against his mouth, pushing her breasts hard against him as if begging for his touch. He obliged, his fingers gliding over the smooth swell and slipping beneath the lacy edge of her chemise. He felt the slam of desire when they reached one hard, erect nub. He was overwhelmed with memories of lying together, their naked bodies writhing, mouths exploring, teasing, the passion mounting between them until they were both riding high on a cresting wave of passion. He pulled her even closer and deepened the kiss.

'No. I cannot do this, Grant!' She struggled against him. 'Please, let me go.'

Her sudden, anguished cry broke the spell and brought him back to the present. He released her quickly, the distress in her voice overriding desire and rousing a strong protective instinct.

'What is it, sweeting?'

He held on to her hands, aware of how tightly she clung to his fingers, as if afraid she would collapse if she let go. His body was screaming for him to drag her back into his arms and he fought against it. She had not repulsed him, but she might still do so, for she looked truly distraught. He tried hard to speak gently.

'There is no sin in what we are doing, Maddie. Although…' he looked about him and gave a shaky laugh, trying to lighten the mood '… Lady Thanet's terrace is perhaps not the place I would have chosen for our reunion.'

She did not even smile.

'There will be no reunion, Grant,' she said, disengaging her hands. 'It is too late for that. You must forget about me.'

'Forget—!' Her words made no sense. He was still on fire. He could still feel her body pressing against him, hear the soft moan of longing when he kissed her. 'How can I forget you after such an embrace?' he demanded. 'You responded. You wanted it as much as I!'

She said in a broken voice, 'That was just a…a memory from a time when we thought we could be happy together.'

'No!' Desire was giving way to frustration. He shook his head. 'You know that is not true. There is a strong bond between us, there always has been. You feel it just as much as I!'

'There is nothing binding us together save bitter memories.' She moved away from him. 'We should never have married. I know that now. I have failed you.'

'Failed me—?'

'You need someone who can provide you with a child. An heir.'

He suddenly remembered that day in the park, when the little boy had charged against his legs. He recalled her stricken look, the hurt and despair in her eyes. Why had he not realised it before?

He reached out and took her hands again. 'Oh, Maddie, you have not failed me. You could never fail me. As for an heir, I have cousins enough for that, if needs be. But there is time yet. We are not old—there may still be children of our own.'

'No.' She sighed. 'You do not love me. You are piqued, because I ran away, but you do not really want me any longer.'

He stared at her. 'How could you think I no longer love you? Especially after that kiss. And the one before, at Lady Elizabeth's firework party. How can you think I do not want you? Surely you must know how much you mean to me.'

'Lust is not the same thing as love, Grant. You only want me now because I am unobtainable.'

He couldn't prevent an angry growl escaping

him. 'You are wilfully misunderstanding me, madam.'

'It is the truth, Grant. Why else have you shunned my bed for so long?'

'*I* shunned *your…*' He raked a hand through his hair. 'It was *you* who kept me at a distance.'

'After the stillbirth, yes. I needed time to recover.' There were tears on her cheeks now. 'But later, once you became Laird, it was clear you no longer wanted me.'

Grant stared at her.

'I left you alone, *as you had asked me*!' he ground out.

Grant turned away. Confound it, had he not suffered, too? But he had hidden his pain, thrown himself into the work of the estate, given her space and time to grieve. And this was how she repaid him! Running back to the glittering salons and luxurious lifestyle she had known before they met. The life he could not give her.

His hurt and bewilderment was replaced by an all-consuming rage. He swung back to face her.

'Do not try to play the saint, madam! We both know why you kept me from your bed. A child would have tied you to Ardvarrick for ever and you decided that was not what you wanted, didn't you?'

'No! That's not true, Grant. I admit that after

we l-lost the baby I was anxious and frightened. And the doctor advised complete rest—'

'Oh, yes, the doctor! He would have said anything for his fee! I gave you time, left you alone, but you remained as cold as ice.'

'You shut *me* out!' she cried. 'I tried to talk to you, after Logan died, but you did not want me. You were always too busy.'

'*Of course* I was busy,' he retorted. 'I was the new Laird of Ardvarrick. Everyone needed me. They all looked to me to guide them, to take care of them. I could not allow myself to be distracted from my duty!'

She seemed to shrink into herself before his eyes.

'Then do your duty now and return to Ardvarrick,' she said quietly. 'It is what I have been urging you to do since you first came to town.' She looked about her. 'I want to leave here, but I dare not go back into the house until I have composed myself, it would cause too much comment.'

He gave a savage laugh. 'And we must avoid gossip at all costs, must we not?'

She waved him away. 'You have said quite enough. Please, I beg you will leave me now.'

'Oh, I will, madam, I will. I have given you enough of my time. Enough of my *life*. The sooner you return to France with your father the better it will be for all of us!'

With that he strode off across the lawn. He did not go towards the house, but headed for the deep shadows of the moonlit gardens. No more than Madeleine did he want to appear before the other guests until his temper had cooled. He was burning up with rage and mortification.

How dare she turn the blame on him! He had paced the floor throughout the night while the doctor and nurse attended the birth. When he learned that the baby had not survived, he had been devastated. Not just at the death of his child, his heir, but the fact that he felt so help-less, so out of place.

Madeleine had been left very weak and dis-tressed, beyond his comfort. The doctor and Mama had told him it would take time for her to recover from such a blow and he had under-stood that. He had been all kindness, all consid-eration, had he not? He had ordered the prettiest guest room to be put at her disposal, a separate bedchamber where she might be private.

Even when Father had died, three months later, he had kept away from her, afraid to get too close, lest his need for her should overwhelm him. He had never burdened her with his grief—

even though he had been desperate for the comfort of her arms, he had kept away.

You never asked if that was what she *wanted.*

His pace slowed and he allowed the memories of those lonely months to come back, sifting through them as he had never done before. Logan's sudden death had been a shock to them all. His mother had been distraught, but as the new Laird it was his duty to take charge, to look after his household and his people. Not for him the luxury of sharing his misery with anyone.

Looking back, Grant realised now it was not duty that kept him silent, but fear. He had been afraid that if he acknowledged the grief he felt at the loss of the father he had loved and revered, it would overwhelm him and he would not be able to go on. He had thrown himself into his work, keeping his hands busy and his mind occupied. Speaking to no one of his pain.

But was Maddie to blame for that?

He remembered her coming up to him after the funeral. She had touched his arm and asked him if there was anything she could do. He had wanted to hold her then, to take comfort and support from the feel of her arms around him. But she was so pale, so fragile in her black mourning robes, that he feared his grief would crush her beyond recovery. He had stayed strong and walked away with barely a word.

He came to a low stone wall and sat down while the confusion of his thoughts and feelings settled. Was it really Madeleine who had kept him at arm's length during those grim times, or had he distanced himself from her? They had never spoken of it.

Face the truth, man. You never gave her a chance to talk of it!

Closing his eyes, Grant forced himself to look back, recalling the pain of those long, bleak months of mourning. Apart from the first few weeks while she recovered from the stillbirth, Madeleine had continued to run his household with her usual efficiency. She had also helped him to comfort his mother, but while Madeleine had wept with Ailsa, not one tear had Grant shed. He had kept his own anguish buried deep inside, afraid that if he once lowered his defences he would crumble. He would no longer be the man they needed him to be.

You shut me out!

No. He shook his head, refuting the charge. Arranging the funeral had kept him busy, then there had been the business of taking over as Laird, stepping into his father's shoes. By heaven, did she not realise how much work that entailed?

It was not as if he had locked himself away, for they had met at dinner every evening, had they not? And if conversation was sparse, was it any wonder, when he was exhausted with the effort of looking after everything and everyone. There had been no time to think, let alone talk. As for sharing his thoughts and feelings, how could he inflict his burdens upon anyone else?

With a groan he dropped his head in his hands. Fear had kept him aloof. Fear of showing weakness when Maddie needed him to be strong for her. But did she? Had it been a mistake not to confide in her? They might have comforted one another. But he had kept silent, he had not allowed anyone to come close. Looking back, he thought it was as if he had been imprisoned by a spell, held captive in a little bubble, living and working but detached from everyone else.

With a sigh he looked up. The half-moon was gliding high above, serene, untroubled by the doubts that now tormented him. When was the last time he and Madeleine had really talked? Ailsa had suggested that he should take his wife away for a while and spend some time alone together, but he had put it off. There was always too much work to be done. He realised now that his mother had recognised they were struggling, but he had been too blind to see it. Just as he had been too blind to notice Madeleine's efforts to help him.

She had always been present when he returned to the house of an evening. She had never left him waiting for his dinner, nor grumbled if he was late. When Ailsa was prostrate with grief, Maddie had looked after her and taken on the extra duties without a word of complaint. In the evenings she would sit in the drawing room with her embroidery or a book. Even on the nights when he remained at the dining table with his brandy until the early hours she rarely retired before him.

She had always been there. Always ready to talk, waiting for him to reach out to her...

'By heaven, Rathmore, what a crass fool you have been!'

Grant jumped to his feet, berating himself soundly. He needed to find her, to put this right, and as soon as possible. He hurried back towards the terrace and the lighted room, which was still crowded and buzzing with lively chatter. He soon spotted the Comte de Vaucluse at the centre of an animated group of guests, but of Madeleine there was no sign and after a quiet enquiry to his hostess he discovered to his chagrin that he was too late. She had gone.

Chapter Twenty

'A masquerade at Vauxhall. How delightful this is!'

Lady Molton's exclamation found no echo in Madeleine, sitting with her pink domino pulled closely around her. She and her father had taken a boat across the river to join Sir Evelyn and Lady Molton in the pleasure gardens and they were now all taking supper together in one of the painted boxes in the Grove, facing the orchestra and listening to the music that filled the darkness.

There was a time when Madeleine would have relished such a visit to Vauxhall, with its twinkling lamps, the mysterious Dark Walk and the delicious excitement of not knowing whether it was a prince or a pauper behind each mask. But after a day of intense worry, the gardens held no charm for her at all. Even wearing the black velvet mask studded with diamonds failed to rouse a spark of excitement. Sir William's ultimatum, issued at the theatre last night, hung over and around her, like a shroud.

When she and her father were alone at breakfast that morning, she had tried to warn him about Sir William. She had told him the man was not to be trusted, but Papa brushed aside her concerns before sailing off about his business, which she very much suspected was connected with the affairs of Charles Edward Stuart.

Papa had merely reminded her that she must be in readiness to leave London the following night. His response only confirmed what Madeleine had always known, deep in her heart: that he considered her no more than another pawn in his games. In his world, women were of little value other than as an ornament. However, as his daughter, she hoped she was worth slightly more and she had made one final push to confide in him.

'I fear, Papa, Sir William means no good by me.'

'You are an attractive woman,' he had replied, smiling at her. 'No man means well by you.'

With that he had left her and now, as she sat beside her father in the supper booth with their chattering companions, she felt very cold and alone.

No man means well by you.

The words kept ringing in her head.

'It isn't true,' a small voice whispered in her heart. 'You know there is one man who does not wish you harm.'

But Grant Rathmore was the one person she could not turn to. Maddie felt bruised and battered from their encounter at Lady Thanet's. She could no longer deny the attraction she felt. He had the power to turn her into a quivering mass of desire even though he no longer loved her. However much he denied it, she knew she had disappointed him. After nearly four years together she had been unable to give him the heir he needed. Or any child, for that matter.

Those last months at Ardvarrick he had barely looked at her and, when he had, it was with a cold, stony gaze that seemed to go right through her. He had avoided even being in the same room with her, yet he had had the audacity to say it was her fault!

Was it not?

A bothersome little voice in her head refused to be silent.

Were you not a little afraid to let him back

*into your bed, afraid to face the pain and dis-
appointment of losing another baby?*

Maddie pushed the food about her plate, her
appetite gone. If only they had talked. If they
had been honest with one another...

'Ah, but see who is here!'

She looked up at her father's genial exclamation, her spirits leaping, but the gentleman
approaching their box had neither Grant's bear-
ing nor his agile stride.

'Sir William, welcome, sir!' cried the Comte.
'Pray join us.'

How foolish of her to think Papa would welcome Grant so effusively! Madeleine was silent
while greetings were exchanged, but she could
not avoid Sir William for long and was obliged
to give him her hand to kiss.

'Miss d'Evremont,' he purred, his eyes glittering through the slits of his mask. 'I am minded
to walk a little. Perhaps you would care to join
me?' He continued, clearly anticipating her refusal, 'You appear to have no appetite, the ex-
ercise might help.'

'Yes, yes, off you go, *ma chère*, you appear
to be in low spirits this evening and I am sure a
little stroll will be beneficial!'

Her father was nodding at her and Madeleine
knew she had little choice but to go. She adjusted

her bejewelled mask and allowed Sir William to escort her out of the box.

'You have been out of sorts, my dear?' he enquired as he led her away from the Grove.

'It is nothing serious.'

'I trust you are not working up an excuse to go back on your word.'

She lifted her head a little higher. 'I would never do that, Sir William. Unless I have cause to believe you will break *yours*.'

'I have no need to do so. I am not vindictive and wish no ill to anyone.' He squeezed her fingers and leaned a little closer. 'I am, however, eager to sample the delights in store for me.'

She covered her reluctance with a laugh and fluttered her fan, saying playfully, 'It is anticipation that makes these things even more delightful, sir. I must advise you to be patient.'

'M-Madeleine?'

The sound of a surprised female voice caught her attention. Anne McBinnie was on the path in front of them. With her hood pushed back and only a thin wisp of satin masking her eyes there was no mistaking her. She was accompanied by a thin, tall gentleman who, it had to be said, looked a little uncomfortable in his black domino and plain mask.

Madeleine recognised Colonel Rutter immediately and, despite her own worries, she felt a wave of relief that he was Anne's escort and not Grant. She also hoped she might turn the meeting to her own advantage.

'Anne!' she cried, giving her friend a wide smile. 'How delightful to see you here. You know Sir William Maxton, of course?'

'We have met.' Anne smiled and dipped a slight curtsy, but there was a flicker of doubt in her eyes as she regarded Maddie's companion.

'And Colonel Rutter,' Maddie went on. 'I do not believe you are acquainted with Sir William…'

She performed the introduction and both men bowed. They spent a few moments exchanging pleasantries, but any hopes she had of persuading Anne and her companion to turn and walk with them were soon dashed. Neither man seemed inclined to tarry and the couples soon went on their separate ways.

The encounter made Madeleine quite forget her own predicament for a moment. Her mind was prey to the liveliest conjecture. Colonel Rutter was far too much the gentleman to escort a lady to Vauxhall on a whim. Neither would Anne be strolling through these dark walks with a man she did not trust. What could this mean, other than that they had formed an attachment? The idea made Maddie smile inwardly. It would be an excellent match, for Anne was at heart quite a serious young woman. The Colonel would suit her friend very well, she thought, although perhaps she was jumping too far ahead.

'Would you not agree, Miss d'Evremont?'

Madeleine started. 'I beg your pardon, Sir William, what was that?'

'Fie, madam. you have not been listening to a word I have said to you.'

Sir William sounded irritable. They had wandered some way from the lamplit walks now and although the moon provided plenty of light, their path was quite deserted. It was lined on each side with rather dilapidated ornamental walls, broken by the occasional pillared entrance that gave on to a secluded alcove. Maddie's senses were on the alert and she knew she must tread carefully.

'I admit my mind was wandering, sir, I apologise.' She gave him an encouraging smile. 'Tell me again what you were saying.'

'No, I do not think I shall.' He stopped and looked down at her. 'I would rather kiss you.'

He went to pull her into his arms and she held him off. 'Patience, sir. A few more days and there will be all the time in the world for that.'

'Patience be damned, I want you now!'

Ignoring her outraged cry, Sir William bun-

dled Madeleine into the nearest alcove and
began to cover her face with kisses. She tried
to fight him off, but he was too strong and held
her fast. Pinning her against a tree, he pushed
aside her domino and began to tear away the
fichu she had tucked into the low neckline of
her gown.

'Stop, stop, I pray you! I am not ready for
this. *Let me go!*'

But her assailant was beyond reason. Maddie
struggled, but her resistance only seemed to in-
flame him more. His arm tightened in a vice-like
grip and she felt the panic rising. Then suddenly
she heard a shout and a rough voice calling.

'Hah, sirrah! Did you not hear the lady?'

The stifling hold on Madeleine slackened. The
next moment she was free and Sir William was
sprawled on the floor with a large, menacing
figure standing over him.

'Away with you,' barked the stranger. 'Get ye
gone, scoundrel, and let the lady be.'

Madeleine stared at her rescuer. His large
frame was outlined quite clearly in the moonlight. A coachman, she thought, taking in the
caped greatcoat and serviceable top boots. His
face was shadowed by the brim of his tricorn,
but the deeper black around the eyes hinted at
a mask, which made her question her first im-

pression, but his voice was gruff and jocular, very like the drivers of the hackney coaches that plied their trade throughout the capital. Perhaps he was here waiting for a customer.

She was still pondering these irrelevances when Sir William picked himself up off the floor, spluttering and viciously cursing his opponent.

'How dare you attack your betters!'

'Betters?' The coachman laughed. 'You're no better than I, sirrah, for all your fine clothes.'

'We'll see about that!'

With a roar Sir William drew his sword and flew at the stranger. As the man jumped back, the slashing blade sliced across his sleeve. Madeleine heard a grunt and saw the coachman drag a small-sword from beneath his greatcoat, just in time to parry a second blow from Sir William.

It was soon clear to her that the stranger was the better swordsman. Despite his heavy coat he showed surprising skill and dexterity, forcing his opponent to defend himself. Sir William took a hasty step backwards, lost his balance and crashed to the ground where he remained, motionless.

Breathing heavily, the victor scooped up his opponent's sword and tossed it into the bushes before turning back and nudging the lifeless form with one booted foot.

'Unconscious. Good,' he said, in a completely altered voice. He pulled off his mask as he turned to face her. 'I did not want to kill him.'

Chapter Twenty-One

'*G-Grant?*' Maddie took a couple of steps forward, straining to see his face beneath the wide brim of the hat, which had miraculously remained jammed on his head. 'It *is* you! But what are you doing here? And why are you dressed like that?'

'I came here to keep an eye on you. As for my clothes…' she saw the sudden flash of white '… I knew Colonel Rutter was joining Sir Edmund's party tonight and thought it prudent to disguise myself.' His laugh ended in a hiss and he clutched at his left arm. 'Damnation, that went deep.'

'Let me see.' Remembering Sir William's wild attack, Madeleine hurried across to him. Even in the dim light she could make out the long gash in the coat sleeve. 'You are wounded! We must bind it up.' She was already easing the coat from his shoulder when a noise made her look up. 'Grant, look out!'

Sir William had risen to his feet and was lunging towards them. Grant pushed her out of the way just before Maxton crashed into him and she watched in horror as the two men grappled. This time Sir William had the advantage, for Grant was taken unawares and the wound in his arm made it too painful to be of use. It could only be a matter of time before he was overpowered.

Madeleine dashed out of the alcove, desperate to find help, but there was no one in sight. As she turned back, her eyes fell on the lion's head finials that topped the entrance pillars to the recess. She grasped one and it came away easily, the mortar having long since crumbled, and she ran back to the two men.

Grant was losing ground. She heard his grunt of pain as Sir William's fist pounded into his stomach and she did not hesitate. Stepping closer, she swung the stone with all her might at Sir William's head and he fell without a sound. For a moment there was silence, then she became aware of Grant standing beside her, his breathing ragged.

'Thank you. I am in your debt,' he muttered.

'I was merely returning the favour.' She stared down at Sir William. 'Have—have I killed him?'

She felt sick with fear. If so, then all was lost. Sir William's damning statement would be released and it would most certainly result in her father's plans being exposed. All three of them would be arrested for treason. She watched as Grant dropped to one knee beside the body.

'No, he breathes.' He pulled off Sir William's powdered wig to inspect the skull. 'Maxton should thank his perruquier for his good fortune, your blow hasn't even broken the skin.' Grant replaced his mask and rose to his feet. 'Come. Let us get away from here.'

'But you are bleeding!'

'We must deal with that later,' he said, hurrying her away. 'I am almost sure he did not recognise me and he won't know it was you who hit him, so we should go now, before he regains consciousness.'

They walked away, Madeleine with her arm around Grant, who was decidedly unsteady. She wanted to bandage his arm, but dare not stop until she was confident Sir William would not easily find them. They changed direction several times before she guided Grant into a small rose-covered arbour where one of the myriad lamps was shining directly on to the bench. She guessed that was the reason it was not already occupied, but it made the place ideal for her purpose.

Once she had persuaded Grant to sit down, it was the work of a moment to remove the great-coat. The wool riding jacket beneath proved more difficult, for the finely tailored sleeves were much tighter and one of them was already soaked with blood. Grant's shirtsleeve was also heavily stained, but she was relieved to see the cut beneath was quite a shallow one.

'I feared he might have cut you to the bone,' she told him, rolling up the sleeve. 'Thankfully, the thickness of your coats took the force of the blow.'

The fichu she had defended so hard against Sir William's predations was now torn off without a second thought and used to bind Grant's own handkerchief tightly over the wound.

'There, that seems to have staunched the bleeding.'

'Thank you,' said Grant. 'Now help me back into my coat and let us be gone.'

'Not yet,' she said. 'Do you have a dirk?'

'Not with me.'

'Then give me your sword and I will cut off

the shirtsleeve. It is quite ruined and will only be uncomfortable for you.'

He waved towards his sword belt. 'Pray, help yourself.'

Grant watched her as she used the small-sword to pierce the fine linen just below the shoulder and proceeded to tear away the sleeve, being careful not to disturb the injured arm. He smiled a little as he remembered how she had tended him once before.

'History repeating itself,' he murmured. 'I shall have another scar on that arm now, to go with the old wound made by the redcoat's bullet.'

Her hands stilled for a moment, then she continued to cut the bloodied cloth away.

'Which reminds me,' Grant continued, 'you were used to carry a silver *sgian* to protect yourself from men such as Sir William Maxton. Do you no longer have it?'

'It is in my trunk, in Surrey Street. The gowns Papa had made for me are not designed to conceal a knife. And I did not think it would be necessary to carry a weapon in London.'

'You were wrong then.' He scowled for a moment, before another thought struck him. 'You say your father arranged for all your new gowns?'

'Yes.' She paused. 'Did you think I would

leave you and then spend your money upon my finery?'

'I knew that was not the case but...' he shrugged '...a lover might have paid for them.'

She did not respond to that, but her lips tightened, as if she did not appreciate the suggestion. She thrust the bloodied sleeve deep into a bush before making a final inspection of the makeshift bandage.

'It will hold, at least for a while. You should go back to your lodgings.'

'I will, but you must come with me.'

She shook her head. 'I cannot. Papa—'

'Damnation, Maddie, you cannot go back to your party now! Maxton will be sure to look for you. We will find a servant to carry a message to your father to inform him that you have gone back to Surrey Street.' She hesitated and he pressed home his advantage. 'You must see that I need someone to accompany me, lest I faint on the way back to Henrietta Street.'

Madeleine looked up suspiciously, but he met her glance with an innocent look and finally she nodded.

'Very well. I suppose there is a possibility that you might collapse, if you go alone.'

'Oh, I think it very likely,' he replied gravely, then was obliged to smother a laugh at the look she threw at him. Even though half her face was concealed by a mask, he could tell she was deeply suspicious.

No one spared a second glance for a pair of masked lovers, arms about one another, making their way through the crowds. As they skirted around the Grove, Madeleine sought out one of the waiters to deliver a message to her father.

'I also think we must send someone to find Sir William and render him assistance,' she suggested to Grant. 'Much as I hate the man, I do not want him to die.'

'Sadly, that outcome is not at all likely,' Grant assured her, 'Although you are right, we should send help. We could make it work to our advantage. The message to your father will say no more than that you have gone home. For a few extra coins, the servant might be persuaded to tell Sir William that he was attacked by a group of rich young bucks.'

'Will he believe that?'

'Oh, I should think so. I have seen a few such groups roaming through the gardens tonight. They drink to excess, behave abominably and generally cause mayhem.'

'Then that might well throw him off the scent,' she replied, her brow clearing a little.

Maddie wondered if she should tell Grant about the hold Maxton had over her, but decided that information was too dangerous to share with him. After all, there was little he could do. Any attempt to help would only make things worse.

Their messages sent and the servant amply rewarded for his trouble, Maddie and Grant walked on to the jetty and soon found a waterman to take them across the Thames. The moon was shining down from a cloudless sky and, once safely aboard the boat, Madeleine checked Grant's wound again. She was relieved to see it had stopped bleeding.

By the time they were in the cab hired to take them back to Henrietta Street, he appeared to have recovered a little of his strength.

However, when they arrived at his door Grant insisted he needed her help to reach his rooms on the upper floor and Madeleine helped him up the narrow stairs. Hearing a noise above them, she looked up to see a man holding a lantern and looking down at them from the landing.

'Robert, thank heavens!' Her voice was low but urgent as they climbed the last few steps. 'The Laird is injured. We need water, to clean his arm, and clean bandages.'

'Immediately, madam.'

'Whisht, quit your fussin', lassie, 'tis not so bad,' muttered Grant, addressing her in a fond manner that she had not heard for a long time.

'It is bad enough,' she insisted, helping him through the open door and into a large room. 'Sit down at the table and let Robert inspect the wound. I must go.'

'No.' He put out his good hand. 'Please stay.'

She stepped away from him. 'The coach is waiting…'

'No, it isn't. I paid him off and told him to leave. While you were unlocking the street door,' he explained, when she stared at him.

Madeleine ran across to the window and opened one of the shutters sufficiently to peep out. The street was empty.

'Oh. You had no right to do that!'

'I beg your pardon, but I need you here, Maddie. Robert is very good, but he lacks your gentle touch. Is that not so?'

Grant addressed his man as he came back into the room with a bowl of water and a selection of cloths over his arm.

'Indeed, it is, Sir Grant. My lady has no equal when it comes to dressing wounds.'

Maddie scowled at Robert, knowing full well he would always agree with his master, but she could not deny that the urge to tend Grant herself was strong. After a few moments, she capitulated.

'Very well.' She unfastened her domino and threw it over the sofa. 'Light more candles, if you please, Robert.'

She set to work on the injured arm. Once it was cleaned and bound she helped the valet to ease Grant out of his clothes and into his silk banyan. By the time the clock chimed the hour, he was sitting on the sofa, his arm propped up by cushions and with a fortifying glass of wine on a table at his elbow.

'You look far better now,' declared Madeleine, smiling slightly. She glanced at the clock and picked up her domino. 'It is past one and I must go. I believe you will be fully recovered in a few days.'

Grant waved towards the sideboard. 'Will you not take a glass of wine with me first? Robert has left the bottle and an extra glass.'

'I must not.' She hesitated, then looked up, saying impatiently, 'Where *is* Robert? I need him to find a cab for me.'

'He will be disposing of the washing cloths and damaged clothes,' said Grant, picking up his wine in his good hand. 'He will not come back unless we ring for him. Do not leave me just yet.'

Maddie was sorely tempted. She told herself it was because she wanted to be sure Grant would not relapse, but in truth she was reluctant to go, knowing this was likely to be their last goodbye.

'Please, Madeleine,' Grant's voice was low, gentle. 'Stay and talk to me.'

She could not resist. Silently, she laid down her cloak again.

Grant was filled with a huge sense of relief. He watched as she poured herself a glass of wine and sat down in a chair opposite.

'This is quite like old times,' he murmured. 'Before we married, I mean. Those weeks we spent together, after Culloden, although we were often in far less comfortable surroundings than these.'

'Enough, Grant. Please do not go on.'

She looked down at her glass, turning it restlessly between her fingers. He leaned back on the sofa and continued as if she had not spoken.

'Remember when that dashed redcoat put the bullet through my arm? You bound me up and brought us safe to Calder House and the McBinnies. I should never had made it that far without you.'

'I would not have survived that time unscathed, without *you*,' she said, not looking up.

'Then Sir Edmund hid me until I had recovered, while *you* lived with the family and enchanted the British officers with your wit and charm!'

'I did what was necessary,' she replied, sipping at her wine.

'But with such aplomb!' Grant laughed. 'We made a good team, did we not, Maddie?'

The clock on the mantel ticked, the only sound in the room. Grant watched her, pleased to see the slight upward curve of her lips and hoping that she, too, was remembering those early days. Not the danger or the hardship of their journey, but the laughter they had shared and the friendship that had grown between them. The love that had blossomed as they faced danger together.

He put down his glass and rose to his feet.

'Don't go back to Surrey Street tonight, Maddie.' He held out his hand to her. 'Stay here, with me.'

Chapter Twenty-Two

Madeleine did not move. Her throat was dry and the pounding of her heart was so loud she thought Grant must surely hear it. There was nothing she wanted more than to take his hand and go with him into the bedroom, but that was impossible. If she allowed herself to take comfort in his arms, if she gave herself up to his kisses and caresses, how would she ever be able to leave?

As leave she must, if she was to save him.

Tonight's escapade at Vauxhall had almost ruined everything and she knew it might already be too late. If Sir William had recognised Grant, or if he did not believe the story they had bribed the servant to tell him, then his vengeance would be swift and brutal. But Madeleine knew that if Maxton wanted her badly enough, he might yet be persuaded to spare Grant and his family. If there was the slightest chance of that, then she must take it. She should go now, while it was still possible to return to Surrey Street before her absence was noticed.

And yet...

Grant was looking down at her, his dark eyes gleaming with the familiar fire that ignited her very soul.

Why not enjoy one last night with him? You might never see him again.

The siren voice was too strong for Madeleine. It echoed the desires of her own body. She put her hand in Grant's and he pulled her to her feet. Looking up into his face, she expected him to find him exultant, but instead what she read there only strengthened her love for the man. True, there was a glow of desire in his dark eyes, but there was no triumph, only a look of profound relief. It almost broke her heart.

'Don't be afraid, Maddie.' Grant squeezed her fingers. 'I know it has been a long time, but I will not rush you.'

'Those fears are quite gone,' she murmured truthfully. 'But your arm...'

'Another reason for taking it slowly,' he teased her. 'Well then, madam. Will you come to my bed?'

Smiling, she nodded. If this was to be their last night together, she would give her all, wholeheartedly, to Grant.

* * *

In the bedroom, a pair of candlesticks on the mantelshelf provided the only light. Grant closed the door.

'I thought we should never do this again,' he murmured, pulling Madeleine into his arms and tilting her face up to his.

When he kissed her it was everything she had hoped. All her doubts and fears disappeared. She forgot everything but the joy of being in his arms. She slipped her hands about his neck and pulled off the ribbon that confined his hair, then she drove her fingers through his auburn mane, revelling in the sensuous feel of the silky locks on her skin.

His kiss deepened. She felt the tug of it through her body, not only between her thighs, but in the tingling of her breasts. They felt full and heavy and they strained against the confines of her bodice. She was impatient to shed her restrictive clothing and when Grant finally broke off the kiss she began to fumble with the ribbons of her stomacher.

'Here, let me help.' His voice might be unsteady, but his fingers quickly dealt with the ribbons. The bodice was tossed aside and he turned his attention to the heavy skirts, which soon sank with a whisper to the floor.

'Ah, your armour,' he murmured, regarding her whalebone stays. 'Let us see if I remember how this is done.'

His fingers moved tantalisingly close to her breasts as he began to unlace her. Maddie kept still, watching his hands as they slowly pulled out the laces. The faint vibration sent little shivers of anticipation running through her body. Her senses were heightened, the air around them positively thrumming with energy and excitement. Her mouth went dry as Grant dragged the lace from the final eyelets and tossed the stays aside. She was standing before him clad only in a gossamer thin shift and she trembled at the thought of what was to come.

When he reached for her, she stopped him.

'Now it is my turn.'

Trying to work slowly, as he had done, Madeleine carefully loosened the knotted tie at his waist and the silk banyan fell open to reveal his naked body. The sight of it made her take a step back, her gaze fixed on the hard, muscled body. How many times had she run her fingers through the dark shadowing of hair that covered his chest and tapered like a shield between his hips? He stood before her, hard and aroused, and her mouth went dry at the sight of him.

Memories flooded in. Wonderful memories of

the glorious nights they had shared, their bodies entwined, moving together with no thought of anything but pleasing one another. The heartache of the past long months vanished like mist before the sun.

She reached out her hand and rested it gently against his chest.

'I had forgotten,' she breathed, trailing her fingers downwards over his honed body.

He caught her hand. 'Not yet.'

He shrugged off the banyan and drew her close for another kiss, teasing her lips apart and plundering her mouth with his tongue. Maddie responded eagerly. A familiar excitement was building deep within her, melting her very bones. As one, and without breaking off the kiss, they moved towards the bed, then she was lying on her back on the cool sheets while Grant's mouth roamed over her face and neck, teasing her heated skin with soft, languorous kisses that made her quiver with delight.

He began to gather up the chemise and she raised her arms so he could ease it over her head, but instead of removing it completely he caught her hands in the soft folds. Her breath hitched. She was held, a willing prisoner, as his mouth fastened over one breast.

Madeleine's body arched in response to the

double pleasure of his tongue circling one hard nub while he caressed the other with his free hand. He worked slowly until she was close to fainting and she groaned softly. The exquisite torture ended, only to begin again as his mouth began to move down over her belly, planting kisses that set her skin on fire and sent the heat searing through her body.

His fingers caressed her hips, smoothed across the soft skin of her stomach, then they moved down to slip between her thighs. Her hands were free now and she clutched at the sheet beneath her as he gently stroked her very core. The pressure was mounting inside, little waves of it, slowly, relentlessly growing stronger and making her shift restlessly beneath him.

Maddie clutched at his shoulders as he changed his position and settled himself between her thighs. She felt his mouth on the hot, enflamed skin and moaned in pleasure as he began to lick and tease her. He slipped his fingers into her and she gave a little gasp at the double delight he was inflicting. She was only half conscious, her body liquifying under the onslaught of such pleasure. It was too much— she cried out for him to stop, then immediately begged him to go on.

He raised his head and gave a ragged laugh,

but a gasp at the end of it brought Maddie quickly to her senses. She realised his injured arm would not support his weight.

'No, no, Grant, let me!'

Swiftly but gently, she pushed him on to his back and straddled him. When she looked down into his dark eyes, almost black now and lustrous with desire, a glorious sense of power came over her. She could and would restrain her own satisfaction a little longer.

'Do not think you can finish this yet,' she purred. 'I am going to give you some of your own medicine!'

She ran her hands over his chest and across nipples that were as hard and aroused as her own. He threw his head back and groaned.

'I don't…think…there is time!' he gasped.

With an exultant laugh she eased herself on to him and as he slid inside her she felt the waves of pleasure beginning to build again. She moved against him, her body clenching, tightening around him as he pushed into her, hard, again and again. They were as one, moving together, flying. She heard Grant shout even as her own mind was splintering, her body beyond her control. She threw back her head, gasping and shuddering against him as he made the final thrusts and her body bucked for one final, exquisite, soaring moment before they both collapsed on to the bed, sated and exhausted.

Grant lay back, his eyes closed, exulting in what they had just shared. He felt dazzled, as if he had finally dug his way out of the dark earth and into bright sunshine. Maddie completed him; he could see that so clearly now. How could he ever have thought that he was the strong one in their partnership?

He should have confided in her, accepted her comfort and worked with her rather than trying to shoulder everything alone. When his father had died Grant had thought she was still coming to terms with the tragedy of the stillbirth and he had wanted to spare her additional pain. He had kept his distance, withheld his comfort and, in so doing, denied himself hers.

He knew now he was wrong. He must tell her that. And how long was it since he had told her he loved her? He should have told her every day, every hour, that he could not live without her. And so he would, in future, but not now. If he said it now, after all this time, she would think it was merely because he had bedded her. That it was passion making him say it rather than cool reason. No, it must wait, he thought drowsily, pulling Madeleine against him with his good arm. Now they needed to rest.

Grant woke up to find the candles had guttered and died, but there was sufficient light coming in above the window shutters to indicate that it was almost dawn. Someone was lying close beside him. Madeleine. He became aware that she was placing light, butterfly kisses on his shoulder and his neck. His mind and his body jumped to attention, but when he reached out for her, she held him off.

'I must go,' she whispered.

'Not yet,' he said, kissing her.

She sighed. 'Oh, pray do not make this more difficult for me.'

In response he drew her closer, his mouth seeking hers and finding it for a long, languorous kiss. She trembled and melted against him, but only for an instant, then she disengaged herself and slipped out of the bed. She began to don her clothes, little more than a moving shadow in the twilight of the room.

'Are you in such a hurry to leave me?'

'I must,' she said, fastening her skirts about her waist. 'I have to return to Surrey Street before the housemaids set about their duties.'

She picked up her bodice and he waited for

her to ask him to help, but she managed very well, fixing the lace through only a few of the eyelets and fastening it loosely in place. Why should that surprise him? he wondered idly. She had always been self-sufficient, able to cope without a maid.

Without a husband.

He pushed himself up with his good arm, suddenly uneasy.

'Is it so important that the housemaids think you slept in your own bed?'

'Servants will always gossip. You know that.'

'Then tell them the truth, that we are reunited.'

'But we are not.'

'What?' He laughed, but his disquiet was beginning to grow. 'After what we have done this night?'

'It should never have happened. I am sorry for it.'

The words hit Grant like a blow to the gut. He sat up and stared at her.

'You are serious.'

The air suddenly struck cold. He slipped off the bed and scooped the banyan from where it had fallen on the floor. Pain shot through his injured arm as he eased it into the sleeve, but it was only a momentary distraction. What was going on here? Last night had been like old times. Not just the hours they had spent in bed, but their camaraderie at Vauxhall. The exhilaration of working together, of facing and overcoming a common danger.

'I am,' said Madeleine, walking away from him. 'It is over between us,'

'No, that cannot be.'

He followed her through to the other room, where she picked up her cloak and swung it around her shoulders.

'Alas, it is true, Grant,' she told him. 'We can never be happy together.'

He shook his head.

'I do not believe that,' he said. 'I will never believe it.'

'You must.' She did not look at him, too busy fastening the strings of the domino. 'I am going back to France with my father. You will be free to find another wife.'

'I do not *want* another wife!'

Grant took a few hasty strides about the room before turning towards her again.

'Why are you doing this?' he demanded. 'I don't understand'

'What we had between us is gone. We cannot bring it back. Let us not prolong the agony of parting.

She stepped around him and made for the door, but he was quicker, putting his hand out to prevent her from opening it.

'No, you cannot leave like this. Do I not deserve an explanation, at the very least?'

She shook her head. 'Please, Grant. You must let me go now.'

'Say it, then,' he challenged her. 'Tell me that this night meant nothing to you. That you no longer love me.'

'No. There is nothing more to be said. It is over between us.'

She was standing very straight, eyes fixed on the wooden panels of the door and a stubborn set to her mouth. Strong, determined. He wanted to drag her back to bed, to kiss her into submission, but he knew that would not work. Brute force would not win her back.

He sighed. 'Very well, go now. But I will not give up hope, Madeleine.'

He stepped away from the door. She flicked the hood of her domino over her head and swept out, leaving him alone.

Chapter Twenty-Three

Grant stared at the door, wondering if he had somehow tumbled into a nightmare. How could she leave him like this, after the night they had spent together? At Vauxhall they had been allies, fighting together, protecting one another and afterwards, here in his lodgings, she had tended his wound with loving care and then they had fallen into bed. They had rediscovered the joy of exploring each other's bodies through the long, dark hours before dawn. Like true lovers. Surely it was not merely conceit that made him think that they belonged together. Last night he had thought—believed—that they were as one again. Standing together against the world. Was he wrong?

The thud of the heavy outer door closing roused him. He swung about and strode over to the window, but by the time he had unfastened the shutters and looked out, the street below was deserted.

Madeleine blinked away hot tears as she hurried through the early-morning streets. She felt quite wretched. Foolish, foolish girl. Why on earth had she allowed herself to succumb to Grant's charms again? She should have known that another night with him would only make the inevitable parting that much more painful. She had convinced herself that it would be a good memory to squirrel away, to help her through the difficult times ahead, but now she knew it would only make her more aware of what she had lost.

'It is all my fault,' she muttered. 'All those weeks after the stillbirth I would not let him near me, when we might have comforted one another. I denied him my bed, but never told him why. He thought, he thought…'

She dashed away a rogue tear that had escaped and trickled down her cheek. She had been morbidly frightened of losing another child, of disappointing Grant even more. Because of that she had denied herself the comfort of his arms, until it was too late. Until Grant himself was in mourning and, instead of turning to her in his grief, he kept it all to himself. To spare her. She had thought him uncaring and accused him of pushing her away, but she was equally to blame.

'And now it is too late to tell him. Even if I could explain and beg his forgiveness, what point would there be in it? There can be no future for us now. If I go back to him, he will be branded a traitor. We would have to flee abroad and Grant would be heartbroken to leave his beloved Scotland.' She turned her anguished gaze towards the sky, where the clouds were tinged blush pink by the first rays of the sun. 'Oh, why could he not let me go?' she cried, the words bursting from her. 'Why did he have to follow me to London?'

But in her heart she knew the reason and a sob choked her throat. He had been trying to protect her. Damned chivalrous Highlander that he was, that he had always been.

'You are home in one piece, I see,' remarked the Comte, when Madeleine joined him at the breakfast table some hours later.

'As you see, Papa.' She sat down opposite him, praying her attempts to disguise a prolonged bout of weeping had been successful. 'I had a servant carry a message to you. I hope you received it?'

'I did, but that did not prevent my being anxious about you.'

She stretched her lips into a smile. 'Not anxious enough to wait up for me, I hope.'

He spread his hands. 'What good would that have done?'

'None,' Maddie acknowledged, reaching for the coffee pot.

'*Mais,* your message, it was not clear. It did not tell me why you had gone off so precipitately. Sir William, when we saw him, was not at all forthcoming. He appeared to think you had been abducted, until I told him of your note.'

'I beg your pardon if I caused you any uneasiness, Papa.'

He shrugged. '*Un peu.* The servant who delivered your message, he told me you showed little distress, but that means nothing. You are my daughter, after all.'

'I am indeed.' The smile faded. 'I was a trifle shaken, but nothing more. It was a party of young gentlemen, all the worse for drink, who attacked Sir William, but since he had been molesting *me* at the time, I took advantage of the situation to slip away from him.' She filled both their coffee cups before asking, 'I trust he was not seriously hurt?'

'He appeared not to be. But why did you not return to our supper booth? You would have been quite safe with me.'

She was able to reply to that quite truthfully.

'After the mauling I had received I was in no mood for company. Also, you wish to keep Sir William sweet. I thought a confrontation might not suit you.'

'That is true, *ma chère*, it would suit me *pas du tout*. But my work here is almost done. By tomorrow, Sir William, he becomes an irrelevance.' He regarded her as he slowly stirred sugar into his coffee. 'You did not come in until sunrise. Why was that, *ma fille*?'

Maddie's thoughts raced. She had hoped the footman who answered her soft knock would be too sleepy to remark upon her arrival, but it was clear her father had learned of it. The truth, or part of it, would serve her best now.

'I went to Henrietta Street,' she said at last. 'To see my husband.'

His painted brows went up. 'A reconciliation?'

'Perhaps.' Her eyes slid away from his astute gaze. She could guard her secrets as well as Papa, but it was best not to take chances. Especially when she had now to prepare her father for what must happen. 'I may well decide to remain in England.'

'*Vraiment?* With Rathmore?'

'Who else?' She managed to look at him this

time. After all, it was not quite a lie. 'Grant is my husband and a good man.'

She knew her father would not question her decision too closely if he thought she was returning to Ardvarrick.

'That surprises me, *chérie*.'

'It should not do so, Papa. However, let us not speak any more about it, if you please. I have not yet fully made up my mind and would prefer it if my plans were not discussed outside this room.'

'As you wish.'

'There is one final thing.' She tried to sound cool, rational. 'If I should change my mind, in the future, would there be a home for me in France?'

'You will always be welcome in my household, *ma fille*, you know that.'

There was not only sympathy but also understanding in his grey eyes and Madeleine felt a momentary alarm. Papa could not know of Sir William's threats, it was impossible. She willed herself not to blush, not to confess the whole sorry business.

'Thank you, Papa.' She gave him a bright smile. 'I am glad to know that, although I doubt it will be necessary.'

Unless I plunge my dirk through Maxton's black heart and have to fly for my life.

Her father nodded and turned his attention back to his breakfast, signalling quite clearly that the matter was of little importance to him. Madeleine knew that she, too, would be an irrelevance once he had returned to France. He did not need her there. An unmarried daughter might be an asset to the Comte and Comtesse de Vaucluse. A woman estranged from her husband, and one who had vowed often that she would be no man's mistress, would be nothing but a burden.

Madeleine finished her own scant breakfast of bread and butter and pushed aside her plate.

'Do we drive in the park today, Papa?'

'Later. First I have matters to set in order.'

'So, too, do I,' she replied, her thoughts already moving to how best she could organise the house for their departure. She would have to leave money with the housekeeper to pay any outstanding bills and to reimburse the servants. Then there would be references to write for her English maid and the senior staff…

'I have invited a few of our friends to join us this evening.'

His casual announcement caught her attention and she looked at him with suspicion.

'How many?

'Eleven of us will sit down to dinner and afterwards, *peut-être,* another dozen will call. We must have music, too. Lord Froome has kindly arranged for musicians to play for us. He says they are the finest Italian artists in London, but he has also assured me they can be trusted to be…discreet.' He spread his hands. 'You look surprised, Madeleine, but why? It is to be my last night in London, *ma chère.* I have decided we should celebrate with a little party.'

'A *little party* and no word of it to me?' She almost stamped her foot in annoyance. '*Mon Dieu,* you are impossible!'

'No, no,' he said soothingly. 'You have arranged soirées such as this for me countless times before.'

Maddie glared at her father for a few more moments, resisting the urge to protest further, knowing it would be pointless. She pushed back her chair and rose.

'Then if you will excuse me, I must prepare. There will be a great deal to do. It may have escaped your notice, sir, but it is a Sunday. A rest day for many of our staff.'

'A half-day only, my dear. I was most explicit about that when I employed them. I am sure you will be able to arrange things satisfactorily.'

'But they need direction, Papa,' she replied crossly, 'And they will look to me for that!'

'And you will direct them excellently,' he replied. 'Go, Madeleine, go and give your orders, but you must be ready to drive out with me at three of the clock. Lady McBinnie invites us to take tea with her.'

'Indeed!' She gave him a scathing look. 'And when did you learn of this?'

'Yesterday, but it, ah, slipped my mind.'

'And if I am too busy to go with you?'

His smile was undimmed by her ill humour. 'But I have complete faith in you, *chérie*. You will not fail me.'

Madeleine went off, her anger against her father soon fading into wry amusement. It had always been thus with Yves d'Evremont and it was too late now for her to take umbrage at his high-handed ways. She must placate Cook, who would be in high dudgeon at having to prepare food for the company at such short notice, and goodness knew there would be nothing fit to buy on a Sunday! Then the rest of the staff would be required to clear rooms and rearrange the furniture in preparation for such a crowd, while chairs would need to be hired, as well as linkboys to light the homeward journey for their guests.

She would arrange the whole, of course, as she had done in the years before her marriage, when she had run her father's chaotic and peripatetic household. And since she was not predisposed to be miserable, she welcomed the challenge: it would keep her mind off her heartache as well as other, more pressing, matters.

Grant was in a foul temper and not only because he had overslept and his head was pounding. He did not want to believe Madeleine's assertion that it was over between them. After the way they had worked together at Vauxhall, the passion they had shared in his bed, he could not comprehend how she could leave him of her own volition. Yet she had done so.

Face the truth, Grant Rathmore. She no longer loves you.

That small, stubborn voice had been whispering in his ear ever since she had walked out of his lodgings in the grey light of dawn. He had tried to drown it out with brandy, but it had been his last thought before falling asleep and his first when he opened his eyes, shortly before noon. He refused to believe it. He could not allow himself to believe it, because without Maddie, life would not be worth living.

He needed to think, to work out how he could make her change her mind, but by the afternoon he was no nearer an answer. When Robert came in, dressed in his oldest coat and with a muffler about his neck, Grant vented his frustration by demanding furiously where the devil he had been all morning and why he had not been there to wake him.

'And if that wasn't enough,' he railed, 'I was obliged to dress myself and with one arm all but useless, too!'

'I beg your pardon, sir,' said his long-suffering manservant, not noticeably cowed by his master's ill humour. 'When I realised you were alone this morning, and saw the empty brandy bottle on the table, I…er…thought you would be the better for being left to sleep.'

'Damnation, man, that is not your decision to make!' Grant shut his eyes and rubbed a hand across his eyes. 'Forgive me, Robert, I should not shout at you. You are right, I would have cursed you roundly if you had disturbed me. But you have not yet answered my question. Where were you?'

'I have been visiting a drinking establishment in Devereux Court. A tavern, to be exact.'

'Is that so?' Grant threw himself into a chair, wincing as the action jarred his wounded arm. 'Since you are not in the habit of drinking in taverns, I assume you have been busy on my behalf. In which case I apologise for my devilish temper this morning.'

'Apology accepted.'

Grant looked suspiciously at his man, whose innocent gaze caused him to utter a crack of laughter.

'The devil it is! Very well, man, tell me what you have learned.'

'You may recall a certain coffee house, sir. A frequent haunt of the Comte de Vaucluse. I have been calling in regularly, even though the Comte has not been there much of late.'

'And they would notice such a colourful character,' muttered Grant. 'Hard to miss.'

'Precisely, sir. Well, yesterday I fell into conversation there with a gentleman who is acquainted with the Comte de Vaucluse, although he has not seen him for some time. The fellow is a gossipy type, which might explain it.'

'Aye, I imagine the Comte would wish to avoid such a man.' Grant waved an impatient hand. 'But go on. How is this supposed to help us?'

'It appears this gentleman's servants mix with those from the houses in Surrey Street, including several from the Comte's residence. Not the upper servants, of course, but the grooms and one or two of the under footmen. Those engaged through a Register Office. They are in the habit of gathering at the Running Man of a Sunday morning rather than attending church.' Robert allowed himself a slight smile 'The pies there are exceptionally good.'

'And no sermons to upset the appetite.' Grant laughed, feeling his mood easing a little. 'Go on, Robert.'

'I thought I might learn something. These fellows are paid well to keep silent about their master's business, but I hoped they might be prone to a little harmless gossip, as they see it. And I was fortunate, because they were very amenable to my joining them.'

'And who did they think you were?' asked Grant, folding his arms.

'I said I was manservant to a gentleman stopping in London for a few weeks, but that our landlady's abilities in the kitchen were a little lacking. They accepted that readily enough. And the jugs of porter I ordered,' he added. 'They soon relaxed and, as I was too busy enjoying my meat pie to join in, they continued to talk among themselves. I learned that the Comte's staff were uneasy because they had heard, although not directly, you understand, that their master will be leaving very soon.'

That caught Grant's attention. 'Will he, by Gad? Do we know how soon?'

'They have been given no firm date, but they were complaining that they had been ordered to return within the hour today to prepare the house for a party. One of them had overheard the Comte say it would be their last and another had noticed the Comte's man was packing his bags. From that they surmised that his departure is imminent.'

'Interesting. Well done, Robert.' Grant pushed himself to his feet. 'You must tell your men to be vigilant in their watch on Surrey Street. Promise them extra payment, if necessary. I shall visit Sir Edmund. He may have heard something. Also, if Madeleine is planning to leave London so soon, I feel sure she will have informed Anne, regardless of any plans her father might be hatching.' He rubbed a hand over his chin and glanced at the clock. 'But before I can see anyone, I must shave!

The afternoon was well advanced when Grant finally reached Broadwick Street. The footman who opened the door to him looked a little flustered as Grant stepped into the hall and stammered that he would have to ascertain if Her Ladyship was at home. At that moment Lady

McBinnie appeared at the top of the handsome staircase and, although she gave a little start of surprise when she saw who was at the door, she recovered quickly and invited Grant to join the family in the drawing room.

'Thank you,' he said, coming up the stairs to meet her. 'I hope I am not interrupting anything?'

'N-no, just a small tea party.'

Her smile was a little strained and when he followed her into the drawing room, Grant realised the reason for it. There were three guests present, including the Comte de Vaucluse and his daughter, but almost as soon as he had entered the room Grant knew it was not Madeleine's presence that had caused Lady McBinnie to look so uneasy. It was the third guest, who had been sitting beside Anne McBinnie but now rose to his feet.

'Sir Grant Rathmore.' Colonel Rutter gave a punctilious bow. 'A pleasure to meet you again, sir.'

Chapter Twenty-Four

Madeleine thought she might faint. She was standing by one of the windows when Grant came in and she put one hand against the folded shutter to steady herself. Why did he have to appear now, of all the inopportune moments? In her careful planning she had not allowed for her father and her husband meeting again.

Lady McBinnie came over to join her, a look of apology on her kind face as she murmured to Madeleine, 'I wish with all my heart this had not happened! He was in the hallway—what could I do but invite him to step upstairs?'

'Nothing.' Maddie clutched her cup and saucer with both hands to prevent the fine porcelain from rattling. 'Please do not make yourself anxious, ma'am.'

My lady sighed. 'Oh, dear, could anything be worse than Grant's turning up today?'

'Indeed not.' Maddie's answer was hushed but heartfelt and Lady McBinnie continued, biting her lip in concern.

'Anne was insistent that I should invite the Colonel to take tea with us. You will see how close they have grown. Oh, Madeleine, I do believe they will make a match of it!'

'Then I wish them both very happy, ma'am.'

Madeleine managed a smile, but her eyes were still on the two men. She noticed how little Grant was using his left arm, but he disguised it well—no one would guess he was injured. Then, to her consternation, she saw her father leave his chair and make his way over to join them, his jovial tones carrying easily across the room.

'Good day to you, my boy. My daughter told me you and she are on better terms now, eh? I am very glad to hear it!'

Oh, please, do not say anything more!

Madeleine uttered the cry silently as she watched the little group. The Colonel was looking politely interested, but Grant refused to be drawn into a conversation. He bowed and turned to talk to Anne, who had brought a cup of tea across to him. They moved away a little, leaving the Colonel to engage her father in conversation.

Maddie looked at her hostess. 'Did Papa

know Colonel Rutter would be here today, Lady McBinnie?'

'Oh, yes. That is what made him so eager to come. I would have thought it would be safer *not* to have come…but there, Yves d'Evremont has always gone his own way. I am so sorry, Madeleine, this must be very uncomfortable for you.'

'It is not your fault, ma'am. If I know my father, he will argue that by meeting Colonel Rutter he will allay any suspicions.'

'Perhaps. But it is a great risk.'

'Papa thrives on risk,' replied Madeleine, her gaze moving back to where he was standing with the Colonel.

Her father was exerting his considerable charm, but she had no idea from the officer's unreadable countenance just how much he was taken in by the Comte's bonhomie. Then she saw Grant coming towards her and all other thoughts were driven from her mind.

Lady McBinnie quickly reached out and took Madeleine's cup from her unresisting grasp, saying, 'You have finished your tea, my dear. I will fetch you some more.'

She hurried away as Grant came up and Maddie was left alone with her husband. He stood close, effectively trapping her in the shallow window embrasure.

'What are you doing here?' she demanded in an angry whisper.

'Is it so unnatural that I should want to talk with my wife?'

'And I have told you I have no wish to see you again! Oh, *why* will you not leave me be?'

He did not appear the least bit put out by her angry response. His eyes glinted down at her. 'Your father is very pleased to see me.'

'He should not be.' She eyed him resentfully. 'I was obliged to tell him that I was with you last night.'

'Ah. No doubt, then, he thinks we have re-solved our differences.' He paused. 'I wish you would come back to Ardvarrick with me, Mad-die.'

'Impossible! You know that.' Those golden flecks in his deep brown eyes were very dis-tracting. She crossed her arms, as if to shield herself from his charm. 'Please go away, Grant. You can do no good here. In fact, you will only make the Colonel suspicious.'

'Why, because I am talking with you? Per-haps he will think I am plotting with you and your father.'

She shivered. 'Do not joke about such mat-ters.'

'I want to keep you safe.'

Oh, Grant, no one can do that, least of all you.

Aloud, she said, 'It will be over soon.'

'By the morning, in fact.' Her eyes flew to his face and he gave a little nod of satisfaction. 'A lucky guess, but I can see from your expression that I am right. You are leaving tonight.'

'No, that is not the case at all,' she insisted, fanning herself rapidly as she tried to recover. 'La, how absurd you are! As a matter of fact, we are entertaining this evening.'

'What better time to slip off than from your own party? From what I have learned of your father that is precisely the sort of thing he would do.'

Grant was smiling and Maddie silently railed against her own foolishness. How could she have given herself away like that? It would be useless now to try to persuade him otherwise. She glanced around her desperately.

'Where is Lady McBinnie? She said she would bring me more tea...'

'She is leaving us alone to talk, like the good friend she is.' Grant leaned closer. 'Last night convinced me there is still hope for us. Who, or what, is preventing you from coming back to me?'

'Why, no one, nothing,' she protested, afraid to look up at him.

'I cannot believe it is what you truly want, is it, Maddie?' When she did not answer, he went on, 'Perhaps I should execute my right, as your husband, and *take* you back—'

'No! You know I would never forgive you if you forced me to go with you.' Another deep breath, another battle royal to appear calm before she went on in a low voice, 'Please, Grant, if you have any love left for me at all, you will go away. Go back to Ardvarrick and leave me in peace.' Her voice broke a little on the last words and she turned her face away from him, struggling for composure.

'Even after last night?' he said softly. 'Are you sure that is what you want me to do?'

'Yes.' Madeleine knew she must do this and do it convincingly. She put up her chin and looked him in the eye. 'Truly, I never want to see you again.'

Afterwards she could never say how she managed to sound so calm and keep her cool poise while he held her eyes for what seemed like a lifetime, challenging her to blink, to give the lie to her statement. Her willpower was being tested to the limit. With every moment the temptation was growing to throw herself on his chest and admit how much she loved him. The only thing that kept her strong was the knowledge that if she did so, she would condemn him to a traitor's fate.

Somehow, Madeleine held firm, finally seeing the warm, glinting challenge fade. When his eyes darkened to near obsidian, she knew she had convinced him. The thought gave her no pleasure. In fact, she felt quite sick with misery.

'Very well,' he said at last. 'You shall have your wish, madam. I wish you a fair wind and a safe passage to France.'

With that he gave her a nod and walked away. Maddie remained by the window, unable to move lest her legs collapse beneath her. She watched him stop and exchange a few words with Anne McBinnie, then, with a bow and a word of farewell to his hostess, he left the room.

It was over. She stared at the closed door, trying to convince herself it was for the best. Grant would recover. If he truly loved her, he could not have talked so reasonably, argued so calmly. Now all she had to do was to pretend that neither did she care a jot.

Like an automaton she walked across to Lady McBinnie and accepted another cup of tea. It revived her and she knew she must do what she could to improve the situation. When she saw the Colonel momentarily alone she took the opportunity to approach him.

'Your husband did not remain very long,' he observed.

'No.' His direct manner encouraged her to respond in the same vein. 'Colonel Rutter, I must tell you, despite anything you may have seen or heard here today, I will not be returning to Sir Grant, or to Ardvarrick.'

'I am most sorry to hear that.'

'So, too, am I.' It was impossible not to admit it. But now she must try to avert the threat posed by the Colonel. She said, 'Sir Grant's loyalties lie in a very different direction to mine own.'

'Oh?' He raised his brows. 'In what way?'

How far dare she go? Maddie resorted to her fan, fluttering it playfully, as if this were a matter of little importance to her.

'My husband's allegiance is very much to the Crown, as you witnessed for yourself four years ago, Colonel.'

'I did. He saved my life.' His steady gaze rested upon her. 'Are you saying your own loyalty lies elsewhere, ma'am?'

She responded with a careless laugh and a roguish look. 'I am too much my father's daughter, *tu sais*. Which is why I have chosen to return to France with him.'

With a little smile she walked away, praying she had done enough to save her husband, but hopefully without further incriminating her father.

Chapter Twenty-Five

They stayed another hour in Broadwick Street and Madeleine was relieved her father's conversation had moved to unexceptional subjects, light chit chat and anecdotes. Nothing to cause her any concern. She sat down and talked with Anne, making light of Grant's leaving and assuring her friend that, although Papa could not be brought to believe it, they were as far apart as ever. Then she turned the subject and laughed and chattered, convincing everyone but herself that she was very happy to be with Papa, enjoying a busy life of parties and balls, breakfasts and routs, as his hostess.

'Which reminds me, Anne,' she said, putting a hand on her friend's arm. 'I have been meaning to ask you, what is your maid's trick for smoothing your hair? I particularly like the way she dresses it. The girl I employ here has tried to straighten my curls, but she just has no notion of how to do it. I should have looked for another maid, I suppose, but it is not worth it now, when we will soon be leaving the country. However, I was very much hoping I might wear it smooth this evening, because I particularly wanted to look my best for Papa's party. Alas…' She trailed off, giving a sigh, and was soon rewarded.

'I could send Eilidh around to dress your hair for you, if you wish,' Anne offered.

'Would you really give up your maid for me?' Maddie beamed at her. 'I should so like to have Eilidh attend me. And, would it be too much to ask you to let me keep her until the morning? My hair is so thick and unruly I know it will need to be redressed after a few hours and my poor maid is not one to learn tricks quickly. She would be sure to make a hash of it.' When her friend looked a little surprised, she went on quickly, 'It would only be for tonight. I will have her driven back to you first thing tomorrow.'

'Why, yes, then, if you think it necessary,' said Anne. 'I am sure I can manage without her for one evening.' She smiled. 'I shall prepare early, that she may come to you in good time!'

Madeleine thanked her and rose to join her father at the door, where he was taking his leave of his hostess with assurances that they would all meet again in Surrey Street later.

'And of course, we would be delighted to have you join us too, Colonel Rutter,' he said, setting Madeleine's already frayed nerves even further on edge.

The Colonel declined politely, much to Madeleine's relief, only to give her another anxious moment when he turned to address Anne.

'However, my duties lie in the Strand this evening, so I shall be able to accompany you to Surrey Street, Miss McBinnie.'

The Comte laughed. 'How delightful to have your *chevalier* escort you to my door, *mademoiselle*! I think it not impossible that we might persuade him to step inside and join us after all, *non?*'

Colonel Rutter bowed and shook his head. 'Alas, Comte, I only wish I could.'

Madeleine recognised the game; her father's confidence made him appear quite innocent. No one with anything to hide would invite a British officer into their house. However, she was not convinced that the Colonel was taken in by her father's guileless chatter, as she warned him on the short carriage ride back to Surrey Street.

'You think him dangerous, *my petite?*'

'I do not think him a fool, Papa.'

'*Mais non*, the good Colonel is not a fool,' he agreed. 'I thought him a little stiff, but then, your husband is very much the same with me. It is because they do not know me, *hélas*. I am full of sadness that the Colonel will not join us tonight.'

'And *I* am very thankful he will not!' retorted Maddie. 'It is bad enough that you have invited the McBinnies, let alone an officer of the Crown!'

'But they are especial friends of yours. It would have looked most odd if we had not invited them. *Certes*, I was a little surprised that Sir Edmund accepted the invitation, but he is very fond of you, Madeleine.' He turned to gaze out of the window, saying, 'He is under the impression that you are coming to France with me.'

'Is he, Papa? How…how strange.' Madeleine held her breath.

'As you say, *ma chère*, it is indeed strange. I understood you had decided to return to your husband once I have left the country, yet neither of you mentioned this fact today. Indeed, there was very little sign that you had made up your differences.'

'We agreed we should not talk of it in company. Neither Grant nor I want our affairs to be the subject of gossip.'

'Truly?' He looked at her for a long moment and when she did not reply he gave a little laugh.

'You have secrets of your own, Madeleine, but then, you are my daughter, *non*? You will know your own business best.'

She smiled, glad that he did not question her further, but her relief was short-lived when he went on, 'I did, however, tell your charming husband that we would be happy to see him tonight.'

'What?'

He said innocently, 'I thought it would please you, since you are, ah, reconciled.'

'Y-yes. Yes, of course,' said Maddie, quickly recollecting herself. 'But I do not wish to see him until tonight's arrangements are concluded!'

He looked at her for a moment, then he flicked her cheek with a careless finger.

'Poor Madeleine, you are truly not happy, are you?'

He sounded genuinely concerned and for a moment she was flustered, thinking he could see into her heart. But that foolishness lasted only a moment. Yves d'Evremont was only interested in his own plans.

'How can I be happy, Papa?' she replied. 'Your schemes put us all in danger.'

'By dawn you will be free of your troublesome parent, *ma chère*. All this will be over and then you may rest easy.'

If only that were true, she thought sadly.

There was little time for Madeleine to fret when they reached Surrey Street. By the time she had assured herself that the house was in readiness for their guests, Anne's maid had arrived and Maddie took the young woman upstairs with her when she went up to change for dinner. She had decided to wear the golden robe *à la Française* again, knowing Papa expected her to impress as well as entertain their guests tonight. Especially so since this was to be the last time they would see him, although they did not know that yet. The Comte de Vaucluse would not want the occasion to pass unremarked.

In the seclusion of her bedchamber Madeleine told her own maid she would not be required again until the morning, then explained to Eilidh just how she wanted her to arrange her hair. She sat down at her dressing table and watched in her mirror as the maid set to work, smoothing out the dark, unruly curls and arranging them in an elaborate coil at the back of Maddie's head.

'You have been with the McBinnies a long time, Eilidh,' she remarked, as if to make idle conversation.

'Aye, my lady, that I have,' replied the maid in her soft Highland voice 'My mother, too, was in service at Calder House before I was born.'

'And now you are a lady's maid.' Madeleine smiled at her in the mirror. 'You have done very well. You were a housemaid when I first met you, do you remember?'

'I do that, my lady, very well!' A reminiscent smile lit the young woman's face. 'What times they were, poor Master Rathmore wi' a bullet hole in his arm and hidin' away frae the Dragoons.'

'In the attic, yes, I remember that! Those were dark times, after the defeat at Culloden.'

'Aye, ma'am that they were. And the poor Prince Charlie forced to flee. Wanderin' the Highlands for months, he was, until he could be carried safe away to France.'

'You followed his progress, then?' asked Maddie, carefully watching the maid's reflection in the glass.

'Aye, that we did. Och, the stories we have heard, in the years since, about how the bonnie young man went back and forth to avoid the redcoats and they pursuin' him like a thief until the wee MacDonald lassie helped him escape across the water to Skye!' Eilidh's face took on a faraway look and she gave a gusty sigh before returning to her task. 'We still talk of him now, ye ken, when we hear any news. Although not in the master's presence, of course. He's not one to hold wi' gossip.'

'No, of course not.'

Eilidh threaded a gold ribbon through the knot of curls at the back of Madeleine's head. She fixed the final pin in place, gave a tweak to the ribbon and stepped back.

'There, my lady, I am done.'

'That is very pretty, Eilidh, thank you.'

'Will ye no' be having the hair powdered, ma'am?'

'No. I never wear powder,' said Madeleine, rising and shaking out her skirts. 'Thank you, Eilidh, there is nothing for you to do now.' She turned to look the maid in the eye. 'Although later I shall need your help with a *very* important matter, if I can trust you...'

Madeleine joined the Comte in the drawing room a little before the dinner hour. He was overseeing the servants as they lit the candles and fastened the shutters across the windows, but once they had completed their tasks and filed out, he turned and studied Madeleine through his quizzing glass.

'You look *magnifique* tonight, *ma fille*,' he said, nodding in approval. 'Enchanting.'

'Thank you, Papa. I hope the dinner will be acceptable. You gave me such short notice.'

'I am aware, but on this occasion it was unavoidable,' he told her. 'I make plans for someone other than myself.'

'And will this *someone* be present tonight?' she asked him.

'That is not my intention, but his movements are not in my control. If I had had the arranging of the whole it would have been different. Very different.' An uncharacteristic furrow creased his brow, but the next moment it was gone and he was smiling again. 'I have had word that the musicians will arrive while we are at dinner. I have given instructions that they are to be shown in here and to commence immediately, even if we have not yet left the dining room.

'They will entertain us very well, I hope. I have ordered also that the windows be left open behind the shutters. The music will be a fitting distraction for those who watch the house. Indeed, I hope it will entertain them! They will see nothing amiss. Tonight will be a grand occasion, but it will be *une fête très innocente*.'

She replied mechanically, 'Of course. I would expect nothing less of you.'

'But you are pale, *ma petite*, and you do not look happy. How can this be, when you are returning to your husband? Is that not an occasion for celebration?'

'Why, yes, Papa, but the joy of it is tempered by knowing that, by dawn, you will be gone.'

'Ah, I understand that! But it will not be for ever, *ma chère*. And you love this man, Grant Rathmore, *non*?'

'Oh, I do, Papa. I love him so very much.' She felt the hot tears stinging her eyes and was obliged to blink rapidly.

'Then all will be well. I shall see to it.'

He regarded her for a long moment, his face serious. It was as if debating with himself, then he stepped back and clapped his hands.

'But this will not do, Madeleine! I cannot have the sadness tonight; it is to be our last party in London and we must enjoy these final hours together.'

'I shall do my best, Papa.'

He nodded, smiling with satisfaction. *'Bon.* With the exception of Sir William, our guests know nothing of my plans, although, as ever, there will be speculation. They must not think there is anything afoot this evening.' The sound of voices in the hall caught his attention and he raised his head, listening. 'Ah, our guests, they arrive. Remember, *ma fille*, you must smile!'

Chapter Twenty-Six

For the next hour the servants were kept busy announcing the favoured guests who had been invited to take dinner at Surrey Street. The Froomes and the Moltons were first to arrive, followed swiftly by Sir Edmund and his family. Anne immediately went over to Madeleine, taking her hands and regarding her critically.

'Let me look at you,' she cried. 'You really do look very well tonight.'

'Thank you. Eilidh certainly has worked a miracle with my hair. It has never been so smooth.'

'It looks very elegant, although I do like your curls, too, Maddie!'

With a laugh, Madeleine moved on. She would have liked to spend more time with her friend, but she knew her duty as hostess. The remainder of the dinner guests had now appeared and she made her way around the room, a word for everyone, but all the while skilfully avoiding Sir William Maxton. There was an extra frisson of excitement in the air and it was not long before Lady Thanet, an old flame of the Comte's, dared to voice the question Madeleine suspected many of them wanted to ask.

'Are we to expect *Mr Smith* to join us this evening, Monsieur le Comte?'

Her father laughed gently. '*C'est possible*, my dear lady, as ever, but one cannot be sure. Let me help you to a little more wine. A particularly fine example from a part of France that I know well…'

Madeleine went across to Sir Edmund, who was regarding the Comte and looking grave, his lips pressed tightly together.

'I beg your pardon,' she said, smiling for the sake of anyone who might be watching them. 'Papa should have warned you, although I believe if the gentleman in question does appear, it will not be until the early hours of the morning.'

'I very much hope that is the case and that we shall be gone before he does so. If I had known—' He broke off. 'I thought I had made my sentiments clear to your father. It was only consideration for you that persuaded me to accept the invitation to come here tonight. And…'

He trailed off, as if he had said too much and she raised her brows.

'And?' she prompted him.

'I gave my word to Grant that I would look out for you this evening,' he said at last and reluctantly. He lowered his voice, 'I wish you would reconsider your decision to return to France, Madeleine. We should all like to see you back where you belong, with your husband.'

She could not quite prevent a spasm of pain flickering across her face.

'I wish that were possible, Sir Edmund. Very much.'

'I beg you to think well about what you are doing,' he said earnestly. 'The Comte's associates are not all trustworthy.'

He raised his eyes, briefly looking over her head before excusing himself. As he walked away, she turned and with a sinking heart saw Sir William approaching.

'You escaped harm at Vauxhall, I see,' he murmured. 'I was perturbed when I came around to discover you were gone. Quite *désolé*, as the Comte might say.'

She could not tell from his tone if he suspected she had been involved in the attack, but she was too much her father's daughter to show weakness.

'I cannot deny, I wish they had murdered you,' she replied with brutal frankness.

He laughed.

'Always such spirit, my dear Madeleine. It is irresistible.' He took her hand, twisting it over to place a kiss upon her wrist. 'I wish I might carry you away this very moment but, alas, I suppose we must wait. I am on fire to make you my own!'

She pulled her hand free. 'I have given you my word. Is that not enough?'

'I doubt I could ever have enough of you, Madeleine.'

She shuddered inwardly, but when she would have turned away from him he caught her arm.

'Do not think you can defy me, Madeleine. If you are not in my carriage by midnight, the Comte and his visitor will be arrested before they have even left Surrey Street.'

'No. I do not trust you. I want proof before I will leave this house.'

'Proof?'

'That my father and his companion have reached their ship safely.'

He looked pained. 'What reason have I for betraying them, other than to secure you for my mistress? You have seen for yourself that I support the cause.' He caught her look of disbelief and added, 'When it does not conflict with my own interest, of course.'

'Then you will be as eager as I to know they reach the ship. My maid will go with them. Only when she has returned and tells me they are safely on board will I go with you. Not a moment earlier.' His eyes narrowed and she repeated stubbornly, 'I must know my father and his guest are free. Then I shall be yours to command.'

It was a battle of wills, but one she was not prepared to lose. She needed to be sure Sir William would not do anything to prevent her father and the Prince from sailing. Once they were out of harm's way, she would go with Sir William. She would do whatever was necessary to save Grant.

Madeleine remained calm and composed during dinner. She kept up a flow of conversation and consumed her meal with every appearance of enjoyment. She had no doubt the dishes were excellent, but worry over what the future had in store had quite destroyed her appetite and she might as well have been eating ashes. Sir William hovered about her with a proprietorial air that frayed her nerves, although she tried to ignore it.

She felt some relief when she carried the ladies away and left the gentlemen to their cognac. The double doors had been opened between the drawing room and the salon beyond to make one large reception room and the musicians were already installed and playing something soft and soothing to the empty room. The ladies exclaimed at this extravagance as they all disposed themselves in the chairs to listen. Madeleine was glad of the respite, but it was over all too soon. The gentlemen appeared and everyone settled down to await the guests the Comte had invited to join them for his *petite soirée*.

It was not long before the first arrivals came in. Madeleine was glad to be distracted as she exchanged a few words with each of them. With the exception of the McBinnies, everyone present was an avowed Jacobite and she was more thankful than ever that Colonel Rutter had refused her father's invitation. It crossed her mind that his 'duty' that evening might well be to keep watch on Surrey Street and a little chill of apprehension ran down her spine at the thought. Her only solace was that she believed him to be genuinely fond of Anne. She was sure he would not have allowed the McBinnies to come tonight if he thought they would be in any danger.

* * *

Sir Edmund was the first to leave, citing the excuse that the chairmen charged double after midnight. Madeleine went with them to the hall, where she struggled not to show her true feelings as she bade them a fond farewell. She turned to Anne last, pulling her into a close embrace.

'Goodbye, my very good friend.'

'Will we not meet again before you go?' asked Anne, holding on to her hands. 'Surely you are not leaving the country for a few days yet.'

'No, I am not,' said Maddie, with perfect truth. 'But, alas, it will not be possible to see you.'

'Then I shall miss you, Maddie.' Tears sparkled in Anne's soft grey eyes. 'You will write to me?'

'I promise,' Maddie assured her, although she thought it would be some time before she was free to write to anyone. She squeezed her friend's hands and said, with a little smile, 'But *you* will have no time to miss me, I think. I believe Sir Edmund hopes to make a happy announcement before you leave London.'

Anne blushed. 'Oh, Maddie, is it not wonderful? Who would have thought, back in those dark days after the Rising, that I should end up marrying an English soldier?'

'I am truly pleased for you,' Maddie told her sincerely. 'You and the Colonel are very well suited. And that is all the more reason why you must be gone from here. It would not do for your family to be implicated in anything to do with me or my father now.' She kissed Anne's cheek and stepped back. 'Goodbye, dear friend. And thank you again for sending Eilidh to me, she has proved herself to be most valuable. I shall arrange for a carriage to bring her back to you in the morning.'

'Thank you, that is very kind.'

'No kinder than you to allow her to help me tonight,' she responded, hoping the maid would come to no harm in the escapade that was yet to take place.

Madeleine remained in the doorway while Anne and her mother stepped into the waiting chairs and set off with Sir Edmund walking beside them. She watched until they reached the end of Surrey Street and were lost to sight then, with a barely concealed sigh, she stepped back and allowed the footman to close the door.

From the upper rooms she could hear the music, mixed with laughing chatter of the guests. Maddie felt suddenly tired and in need of a few moments alone to recover her energy before resuming her duties as hostess. She made her way to the little room at the back of the house that her father had set aside as his study. It was no surprise to find the room already glowing with candlelight, but Madeleine was startled to discover her father there. He was standing before the empty hearth with two other men. Mr Alexander Murray was one; the other was Charles Edward Stuart.

Chapter Twenty-Seven

Madeleine quickly shut the door and sank into a low curtsy. 'Your Highness!'

'Mademoiselle d'Evremont.' The Prince came forward to take her hand and raise her up. '*Ravissante*, as always. A thousand pardons for intruding upon you so early.'

She had seen the glances that passed between the three men when she came in and said quickly, 'I trust nothing is amiss, sir?'

'Nothing to concern you, my dear,' her father assured her. 'A meeting was cancelled and it was not safe for His Highness to remain in his current quarters. Murray thought it best to bring him here.'

'But I have just come from the street. How—?' She broke off, frowning.

'They arrived the same way we shall later

depart,' murmured her father, glancing towards the door that led out to the garden. *'En bateau.'*

'If we have finished here, Comte,' said the Prince, who was still holding Madeleine's hand, 'I suggest we go upstairs and join your guests.'

Mr Murray stepped forward. 'Sir, I do not think that is wise!'

Madeleine heard the man beside her utter a merry laugh.

'Wise, my friend? Possibly not, but the Comte has assured me there are only friends gathered here this evening and I will not skulk away like a villain. Also, I have heard music.'

'Why, yes, Your Highness.' The Comte nodded. 'A small ensemble from Italy.'

'If there is music and beautiful women,' declared the Prince, smiling at Madeleine, 'then it is my duty to dance!'

She was moved to protest, but he silenced her with one finger upraised.

'My business in London is concluded, *mademoiselle*. I am now free to enjoy myself until it is time for my departure.' He drew her hand on to his arm and looked at the others. 'Well, gentleman, shall we go upstairs?'

It was like a dream, thought Madeleine as she walked into the crowded room on the Prince's arm with her father following behind them and beaming proudly. In truth, she decided, it more nearly resembled a nightmare. A sudden hush fell over the assembled company, quickly followed by an excited murmuring, and people began to move closer, eager to exchange a word with her escort.

Madeleine disengaged herself and slipped away to the side of the room. She watched the guests crowding around the Comte and his companion. Tonight there was no dissembling, they openly acknowledged Charles Stuart as their Prince and he accepted their obeisance with regal dignity. There was no doubt he was charming, she thought, and her father looked very pleased with himself, but Madeleine was fearful for them both. She would not rest now until they were safely away from Surrey Street.

She remained in her corner, listening to the pledges of support. The chatter grew louder, the company was in the highest of spirits. Then His Highness called for dancing and as if by magic the room was cleared, the carpet rolled away and the musicians began to play a series of country dances.

The Prince summoned Madeleine to perform the first dance with him and after that she was free to stand aside while he gratified some of the other ladies who were clamouring to be his partner. It was quite unreal, she thought. Everyone was enjoying themselves, as if they had not a care in the world, but they all knew that at any minute there might be a knock at the door and they would all be arrested for treason.

At two o'clock, the Comte touched Madeleine's arm. 'It is time.'

She nodded and slipped away to her bedchamber. Eilidh was already there, as instructed, clutching the voluminous cloak that Maddie had insisted she should wear to keep off the chill of the night air.

'Am I to go now, ma'am?'

'Yes.' Madeleine threw the cloak about the maid's shoulders and tied the ribbons. 'You have the money for the ferryman?'

'Aye, that I have.'

The maid held up a small purse. Her eyes were sparkling with excitement and Madeleine was suddenly filled with doubts.

'I should not be involving you in this, Eilidh. It is dangerous.'

'Whisht, now my lady, 'tis Prince Charles himself that I shall be helping tonight. I wouldna' miss it for the world!'

'If you are sure, then. Come along.'

Maddie went out to check that the stairs and hall were deserted before leading the way to the study, where her father and Charles Stuart were waiting, both wearing greatcoats and mufflers over their fine clothes. The Comte's valet was there, too, two large portmanteaux at his feet.

'Your maid is coming in your place?' asked the Prince, raising his brows.

'Only to see you safely aboard ship and then she will report back to me,' Madeleine explained.

'I see. Then I shall bid you adieu, *mademoiselle*.' He kissed her fingers. 'I am sorry you do not accompany us. The journey would have been far more enjoyable with you as my companion.'

'You are very kind, sir, but it cannot be.' Madeleine curtsied low, then turned to her father. 'Goodbye, Papa.'

'Farewell, Madeleine.' He stepped up and drew her into his arms. 'I doubt we shall meet again for some time. I hope you will be happy with your Scottish Laird.'

She felt his lips kissing the top of her head, but her heart was too full to answer him. He released her and put a finger under her chin, turning her head a little, so the candlelight fell on her face. She saw his eyes narrow and for a moment she feared he would remark upon the tears in her eyes, but instead he merely leaned forward to kiss her cheek.

'*Courage, ma fille,*' he whispered in her ear. 'All will be well; you must trust your papa for this.'

With that, he turned and followed the others out into the darkness.

Madeleine watched them all vanish into the shadows and stayed by the door until they appeared again, dark shapes scrambling over the garden wall. She counted them, waiting until the fourth figure had disappeared before going back inside. Closing the door, she stood for a while, acutely aware of the stillness around her in the room. Then she took a steadying breath and returned to her guests.

There was no doubt that the Comte's soirée was well attended, Grant thought, as he and Robert sauntered into Surrey Street soon after nine o'clock that evening. Torches blazed outside the house and the street was bustling with carriages lining up to deposit finely dressed ladies and gentlemen at the black door.

Grant recognised many of the guests as the wealthy and well-connected supporters of Charles Edward Stuart. He was also aware that he and Robert were not the only ones watching the house. The street sweeper was in evidence, but also there were a couple of men loitering on the corner of the street, a street trader plying his wares, despite the late hour, and a beggar was sitting against the railings of an empty house.

There was also an abundance of link boys and chairmen, and Grant could not be sure if they were all genuine. He feared some of them might be Government men. There could be foreign spies, too. It was impossible to believe the Comte's activities this past week had gone unnoticed.

Music issued from the open windows of the reception room on the first floor, even though the shutters were in place and all that could be seen was the blaze of golden light above the wooden panels. Grant imagined Madeleine up there, making her way around the room, greeting her guests, talking and laughing. Was she taking her leave of each and every one of them? Or perhaps she and her father were acting as if nothing out of the ordinary was going on, until the moment that they slipped out of the house, and out of England.

Just before midnight Sir Edmund and his ladies came out of the Comte's house. Grant watched as they descended the steps to the waiting chairs and he saw Madeleine standing in the open doorway to see them off. The flaming torches illuminated her features as she smiled and waved goodbye to her friends, but once they were out of sight her smile faded and Grant's heart lurched when he saw how unhappy she looked.

Leaving Robert to watch the front of the house Grant slipped off through the gate to the jetty. Thankfully, it was deserted and there was no one to question his presence there. The river gleamed in the light from the half-moon, a pewter ribbon. The Thames was busy with ferrymen plying their trade on the water, although none of the vessels approached the Surrey Street stairs.

Their passengers would be revellers, thought Grant, returning from the inns and pleasure houses of Southwark. He cradled his left arm, remembering how Maddie had inspected the wound as they were being ferried back from Vauxhall. He was fortunate, the cut did not trouble him as long as he did not use the arm too much.

A small craft was heading downstream towards him and he moved back to the stairs, pulling his hat lower over his face. Watching from the shadows, he could see figures seated in the boat and a single waterman standing in the bow, using his oar to propel the little boat. Grant tensed, ready to retreat quickly if the waterman pulled up alongside the jetty, but the boat glided past him and stopped at the Arundel Stairs. Two cloaked figures scrambled out and stood on the jetty, watching the ferryman move off. Grant expected them to walk up the steps and into Arundel Street, but instead, they began to make their way along the narrow stretch of riverbank, heading back towards him.

Grant watched as they came closer. When they reached the wall separating the river from the garden of the Comte's residence, he saw one of the figures bend and pick up the ladder, which he propped against the wall. Moments later the two men had scrambled over the wall and disappeared, leaving the ladder in place.

With a quiet grunt of satisfaction Grant sat on the steps. He settled down to wait, thankful for his greatcoat which kept off the chill now coming from the river. Time moved slowly. A church clock in the distance chimed the hours: one, two. Occasionally the slight breeze off the water dropped and he could hear the faint sounds of music playing. It was coming from the open windows of the Comte's house, he guessed.

The half-moon was sailing high above him now, but the clear sky induced a chill that began to seep through his coat. He got to his feet. Perhaps he had been wrong after all. Perhaps they were not leaving tonight. Then, just as he was thinking of going back to see if Robert was having more luck watching the street, a movement on the water caught his eye. A boat was approaching. No ferryman, this. It was larger, with several oarsmen. More like the launch of a sailing ship.

On the alert now, Grant watched closely as the oarsmen rowed directly towards the embankment and drove the boat on to it. He could hear the murmur of their voices and a smothered laugh, but no one made any move to step ashore. They were waiting for someone and very content to do so. Keeping deep within the shadows, Grant sat down again, the cold air forgotten.

At last, he saw a movement on the top of the wall. A man in a greatcoat scrambled over and on to the ladder. Grant saw him turn back and reach down for something. The next moment he was hefting a bag over the wall and dropping it on to the narrow strip of ground at the foot of the ladder. Another bag followed, then the fellow clambered down just as another dark shape appeared atop the wall.

Grant strained his eyes against the dark. There was something different about this one.

He finally realised that this figure was wearing a cloak and encumbered by skirts. After that, two more men followed and from their shape and size Grant was sure one of them was the Comte de Vaucluse. The other, tall and somewhat leaner, he thought was one of the men he had seen earlier, alighting at the Arundel Stairs.

Grant watched all four climb into the launch and felt a sickening heaviness in his stomach. Until that moment, he had not realised how much he had been hoping Madeleine would change her mind. He had not really believed that she would leave him.

Now he had to face the truth.

The launch moved quietly away from the embankment. Grant watched until it was making steady progress downriver, then he ran back up the stairs to join Robert. He prayed Maddie and her father would get away safely. As for the Stuart and his supporters, they might do as they pleased, he did not care. He would collect Robert and they would go back to Henrietta Street. The watchers could be paid off now, Grant had no further interest in Surrey Street. He had no interest in anything save getting very, very drunk.

Chapter Twenty-Eight

The final dance was coming to an end when Madeleine walked back into the salon. Sir William was standing to one side and raised one brow at her. She nodded slightly and went to pass, but he detained her.

'How long until your maid returns?'

She gave him a stony look. 'That is impossible for me to say, since I know not where their ship may be waiting. You should come back at dawn.'

'And give you the opportunity to slip away from me? Oh, no, madam, I will stay in this house and my chaise will remain in the street until you are ready to travel.'

With no more than a nod of assent she moved away from him and went to the window. A peep through a crack in the shutters showed her that the street was busy with link boys and servants, milling around the chairs and carriages that were lined up and waiting to carry their precious charges away to their beds.

The musicians were packing up and some of the guests began to drift towards the door. Madeleine moved among them, speaking to each one, smiling and explaining that her father was engaged elsewhere and she must be his proxy and take leave of them. All the time she was aware of Sir William hovering in the background, a constant reminder of what was to come.

It was almost an hour before all the guests had departed. All except Sir William. Madeleine ignored him as she directed the servants to tidy the rooms and snuff the candles. Another hour passed. For Madeleine, time dragged while she waited for the maid to return and yet, when Eilidh did appear in the dark hours just before dawn, it did not seem nearly long enough.

'They had no trouble getting away?' she asked, carrying the maid off to her bedchamber.

'None at all, my lady. They rowed us a fair way downriver to where the ship was waiting, then the Comte exchanged passwords with the captain and made certain all was well before he and His Highness went aboard. And all in the moonlight, like a story!' exclaimed Eilidh, her eyes shining. 'The captain now, he was all for setting sail immediately and leaving me to make my own way back. He didna' want to be sending his launch out again, which he said would delay their departure another two hours at least. But His Highness, Lord bless the bonnie man, he insisted they find a ferryman to bring me back. It was a little while before they could arrange that and when I finally left, they were ready to set sail. Och, what an adventure it has been, helping the Prince to escape!' The maid clasped her hands together and added, earnestly, 'I prayed all the way back that they have a safe passage to France, my lady!'

'That was very good of you,' said Maddie, smiling a little. 'I very much hope your prayers are answered. Now, get you off to your bed and rest while you can. I have arranged for a coach to take you back to your mistress. You should be there before she rises.'

'Thank you, ma'am.' The maid's shrewd gaze moved towards the bed, where Madeleine's new riding habit with its silver trimming was spread out upon the covers. 'But are ye no' going to bed yourself, ma'am?'

'No.' Maddie turned away, trying to keep her tone light. 'I am leaving here very shortly.'

'Ah, ye'll be setting off to join your man,

then?' Eilidh's smile widened. 'Would you like me to help you to change, before I go, ma'am?'

Almost an hour later Madeleine left her room, the teal-blue camlet skirts of her new habit rustling as she descended the stairs. A cravat of finest Brussels lace frothed beneath her chin and a little beaver hat edged with silver was pinned on her head. She reached the hall to find Sir William waiting for her.

He said impatiently, 'About time, madam. Shall we go?'

Without a word she accompanied him out to the street. The first grey fingers of dawn had been obliterated by heavy cloud and it was beginning to rain steadily as she climbed into Sir William's travelling chaise.

As soon as he opened his eyes, Grant felt it, the heavy weight of oppression on his spirits, and it had nothing to do with the leaden skies he could see in the gap above the shutters. Madeleine was gone and this time there was no hope of her returning. At least his head was clear: by the time he had reached Henrietta Street he had been too tired to do more than drink one glass of brandy before collapsing into bed. Stifling a groan, he sat up and rubbed his eyes just as Robert came in.

'Good morning, sir. Awake already? You must have smelled the coffee!

Grant swung his legs over the edge of the bed and glared at him. 'Do you have to be so damned cheerful?'

His man glanced at him, then carefully put the tray down on the table beside the bed.

'You will feel more the thing once you have broken your fast.'

'I doubt it.' Grant's mouth turned down in a grimace as he looked at the ham and bread and butter lying on the plate. He reached for the cup. 'What time is it?'

'Seven o'clock, sir. As we agreed.'

'The devil we did!' he muttered, but the coffee was having its effect. He now recalled telling his man he wanted to quit London with all speed.

'Once I have fetched your hot water, sir, I shall go and arrange for the hire of a post chaise.'

'Bring the water up now, if you please,' said Grant, reaching for his banyan. 'As soon as I am washed and dressed I will come with you.'

Robert hesitated. 'I will need to look at your arm first, sir.'

'Yes, yes, you shall do so. Now go!'

Perhaps it was the coffee, but Grant suddenly

found he was indeed hungry. By the time his man returned with the can of hot water he had cleared his plate. After that it did not take long before he was washed and shaved.

Grant was just easing his freshly bandaged arm into his coat when there was a sharp knock at the door.

'See who that is, Robert, if you please.'

He straightened his coat, listening to the rumble of voices from the other room. Who could be calling at this ungodly hour? He made a final adjustment to the lace at his neck and went to find out. His brows rose when he saw his visitor.

'Colonel Rutter! To what do we owe this pleasure?'

'I am on my way to apprehend a traitor, Sir Grant, and I thought you might like to come with me.

'Alas, Colonel, much as I should like to assist you, I am leaving for Ardvarrick today.'

'My quarry is Sir William Maxton.'

'Really, Colonel, I have no interest—'

'He has left town and taken your wife with him.'

Grant froze. 'That cannot be. She has gone to France with her father.'

'You are mistaken, sir, Maxton carried the lady off from Surrey Street at dawn this morning.'

Frowning, Grant shook his head. 'But I saw her myself, getting into the boat and being rowed out to the ship.'

'That was a lady's maid, sent to report back that the Comte and his…er…companion, had got safely away.'

'No. I don't believe it.' Grant pushed a hand through his hair and threw an accusing look at the Colonel. 'How can you possibly know that?'

'It was Miss McBinnie's maid. She arrived back at Broadwick Street while I was…' For the first time, Colonel Rutter looked a little disconcerted. 'While I was taking breakfast with the family.'

'Breakfast with the—' Grant was incredulous. He glanced at the clock. 'It is barely eight now!'

The Colonel said, stiffly, 'I met Sir Edmund in the Strand, on his way back from the Comte's soirée, and I escorted the family home. He invited me to stay and use the guest room last night and, when I told him I must be away early, they all decided to break their fast with me.'

'You appear to be mighty friendly with the family, Colonel,' observed Grant with a grin.

'I have always held Sir Edmund in esteem,' replied the soldier, a tinge of red colouring his cheeks, then he straightened his shoulders and returned diligently to the matter in hand. 'As

I was saying, Miss McBinnie's maid had just come back from Surrey Street, where she had been sent last evening, supposedly to dress your wife's hair. She returned full of such an outrageous story that Anne—Miss McBinnie—persuaded the woman to come down and tell it to me herself.'

The Colonel broke off, his mouth twisting slightly and a disapproving frown creasing his brow.

'She informed me that the Comte's companion was Charles Edward Stuart. She was not a whit perturbed about it, either. Kept likening herself to some female who had helped the Pretender to escape in 'Forty-six.'

'So, Madeleine is still in England?'

Grant drove his fingers through his hair as he tried to make sense of all he had just heard. Had she played both him and the Comte for fools? That thought was instantly discarded. Whatever else Madeleine might do, she would not willingly go off with Maxton. He would stake his life on that. He voiced the only other solution through his clenched jaws.

'He has abducted her.'

'I believe so,' replied the Colonel. He pulled out his watch. 'He is taking her to his hunting lodge in Hainault Forest. They are travelling by carriage, or I could not have spared you so much time. As it is, it will take them at least another hour to reach the hunting lodge. We are not that far behind them and with good horses we should be able to make it in two.' He paused. 'Will you come?'

Madeleine huddled in the corner and pretended to sleep as the chaise rattled through the streets of London. In reality, she was very much awake and keeping as far away from Sir William as possible. He had handed her into the chaise and climbed in beside her, but when he attempted to take her hand as they set off from Surrey Street she snatched it away, informing him that she was a very bad traveller and, if he did not wish her to be extremely ill, he should leave her to rest undisturbed.

At first she tried to see which way they were going, but soon realised that was futile. The torrential rain and her scant knowledge of London made it impossible for her to recognise any of the landmarks. As the carriage rumbled on, she considered her position. Her father was safely out of England now. She could do no more for him, but Grant was still in danger.

Sir William had told her his damning indictment against Grant was written and lodged with his attorney. She needed to find a way to recover it. The thought of what she might have to do before that, to gain her captor's trust, made her feel quite sick. She could only hope she did not end up killing the villain before she had found a way out of this mess.

They stopped once to change horses, but Madeleine refused Sir William's invitation to step down and take refreshment with him in the coffee room.

'I am feeling very unwell,' she told him, adopting a weak and woebegone voice, quite at variance with the steely resolve inside her.

There was no possibility of anyone coming after them, so the sooner they reached their destination and she faced the coming ordeal, the better.

Chapter Twenty-Nine

Grant was in a fever of impatience for the first part of the journey, his feelings shifting constantly between fury at Madeleine for putting herself in Maxton's power and fear for her safety. He was eager to catch up with the villain, but although the rain had stopped and the horse Colonel Rutter had provided for him was in excellent condition, the traffic of the city streets meant it was impossible to travel at more than a trot.

The road was clearer once they had passed through Whitechapel and he found some relief in a gallop before they settled down to a steady canter until they reached Stratford, where the Colonel's Dragoons were waiting for him.

'Our quarry passed through here just under an hour ago,' he told Grant, after conferring with his sergeant. 'The rain has slowed them down.

They will not reach the lodge very much before us.'

They set off again, walking the horses to rest them, and Grant took the opportunity to ask a question that had been nagging at him all morning.

'Why did you ask me to come with you, Colonel?'

'To rescue your wife. I thought you would want to be there.'

'Of course, but there must be more to it,' Grant insisted. 'I am sure it is not usual to invite a husband to come along in such cases. And you have men enough with you to arrest Maxton without my help.'

The Colonel was silent for a moment to consider his reply.

'Four years ago, you saved my life. Lady Rathmore reminded me of the fact yesterday, when we met at Sir Edmund's house. I believe her reason for doing so was to ensure I did not think of you as a traitor, but it also reminded me of my obligation, to both of you. I thought this might go some way to repaying that debt.' His shoulders lifted slightly in a shrug. 'Perhaps my own impending nuptials had something to do with it, too.'

'Anne McBinnie?' Momentarily diverted,

Grant swung around in the saddle to stare at him, then he laughed. 'Well, I cannot say it comes as a complete surprise! I wish you both joy, Colonel. When is it to be announced?'

'Sir Edmund is dealing with that today and the wedding will be arranged as soon as maybe. There is no reason for us to wait. Anne and I had hoped that you and your lady would…'

The Colonel's words trailed off and Grant felt another sickening kick of apprehension.

'Aye, well, let us see how we get on today.' Grant's nerves caused him to doubt his earlier certainties and he added bitterly, 'We have no proof yet that the lady did not go willingly with Maxton.'

Colonel Rutter reached inside his jacket and pulled out a sealed paper. 'I was asked to give this to you.'

Grant took the letter and stared at it.

'From the Comte de Vaucluse?' he demanded, his brows rising.

'It is.'

Tearing open the seal, Grant unfolded the letter and quickly scanned the elegant script.

My son,
    You will not offended be if I call you that,
I hope, as we are by marriage related.

Madeleine informed me she would be returning with you to Ardvarrick. If that is so, then pray do not regard this letter. But allow me to know something of my own daughter, sir. To me it is impossible she could look so unhappy if she was to be re-united with her beloved Laird. It is my be-lief Sir William Maxton intends to make her his mistress. She, I think—I believe— is gone with him in some ridiculous plan to protect us both.

I have given the good Colonel Rutter all the information he needs to convict Maxton of high treason and Madeleine will be free to return to you. Treat her well, mon fils.

There is no time for more. The tide does not wait and I have a person the most im-portant to escort safely out of the country.

Je suis, mon cher fils, &c
*Yves d'Evremont
Comte de Vaucluse*

It was signed with a flourish, but this extrav-agant gesture was lost on Grant, who cursed roundly.

'Once again, the damned scoundrel has gone off and left his daughter to fend for herself!' He waved the paper angrily. '"Treat her well," he says. As if he had left her safe in my care!'

'The Comte does appear to be an indifferent parent,' replied the Colonel in disapproving accents. 'Apart from attesting that you and your wife had no knowledge of his plans, he shows very little regard for his own child.'

'Wait, wait!' Grant pushed up the front of his tricorn and frowned at the paper again. 'I do not understand. You *met* with the Comte, *talked* to him?'

'No. He wrote to me, but arranged that the despatch should not be delivered until after he had departed from Surrey Street this morning. It finally reached me at Sir Edmund's house. I had hardly finished reading it when the maid returned and gave us her account of the evening's events.'

Despite the gravity of the situation, Grant felt a smile tugging at his lips. 'A rare morning you have had of it, then, Colonel. And the Comte's letter to me?'

'Included within the sealed despatch to myself.'

'But what did you know of its contents?'

'Nothing, but I guessed some of it, having received word that Maxton had left Surrey Street in a travelling chaise and with a lady fitting

Lady Rathmore's description.' The Colonel shot a quick glance across at Grant. 'That is why I thought you might like to join us.'

He urged his horse to a canter and Grant followed suit. The small troop travelled on in silence, save for the noise of the hoofbeats and jangle of harness. Grant kept pace, hands steady on the reins and his eyes fixed ahead of him, but his thoughts were going over everything Rutter had told him.

'But I still do not understand,' he said at last, when they slowed to cross the river at Woodford Bridge. 'You had the Young Pretender within your grasp. Why did you not detain him?'

'My orders were to watch the house and report back. It would appear that Whitehall has always known about this visit,' said the Colonel, staring straight ahead. He added, his voice wooden, 'They did not consider it in the country's interests to make an arrest.'

'How can that be? Surely Charles Stuart is a very real threat to the King.'

Rutter shrugged. 'I understand foreign support for his cause is waning. If he were arrested, the British government would have no alternative but to put Charles Edward Stuart on trial and an execution would surely follow. That would not be viewed favourably by our neighbours.'

'And, as a martyr, he would be far more dangerous than a weak and ageing Pretender.'

'Precisely.' The Colonel turned away to speak to his sergeant, who had ridden up beside him, then he glanced across at Grant. 'We are only a few miles away from Hainault Forest,' he said. 'Shall we press on?'

'Aye, gladly.' Grant gathered up his reins. He was as eager as his companion to catch up with Maxton and as quickly as possible. He tried not to think what the villain might do to Madeleine before they could reach her.

They soon arrived at a fork in the road and took the southern track, which wound its way through the forest. The trees grew close and thick on each side, making a canopy over their heads that was still dripping from the recent rains. The little party slowed to a trot and they rode on in silence while the forest seemed to close in upon them, still and silent.

'We do not know the exact location of the lodge,' said the Colonel, 'It might take us some time to locate it.'

Grant pointed to the ground ahead of them 'There are tracks from something that passed this way recently. A travelling carriage, perhaps.'

'Yes, I see them.'

They continued along the forest road, following the wheel marks until the tracks veered off into a narrower lane. The Colonel glanced across at Grant, who nodded.

'Let's try this. It's our best hope.'

Chapter Thirty

Madeleine's nerves were stretched to the full by the time the carriage came to a halt at the hunting lodge, built in the style of a small, Jacobean mansion with a warm redbrick façade, latticed windows and tall chimneys. A charming prospect, in other circumstances, but now Madeleine viewed it with apprehension. They had travelled for miles through dense forest with no sign of any other habitation. She had seen no one she might call upon to help her.

A wooden-faced footman opened the chaise door and Sir William jumped out. He turned back to Madeleine and held out his hand.

'Come, my dear. Welcome to your new home.'

'You mean to keep me here?' she asked, allowing him to help her alight.

'For the moment. While we get to know one another.' He paused, listening to the frantic barking of dogs that could be heard coming from behind the stable block. 'My hounds,' he explained. 'They are kept half-starved, ready to track down man or beast. Or woman,' he added, giving her a look that made the hairs rise on the back of her neck.

Madeleine suppressed a shudder and walked quickly to the house. There were servants waiting inside, but they showed no surprise at her arrival. They looked sullen and incurious, which made her heart sink even more.

'And here is Evans, my valet,' said Sir William with a false affability that put her teeth on edge.

A rough-looking figure in brown fustian stepped closer and bowed. He looked more of a prize fighter than manservant, thought Maddie, as she untied the strings of her cloak. She cast a quick glance about her. The hall was darkly panelled, the wood so dull that even on a sunny day it would be gloomy.

'Let me take your cloak.'

Sir William's hands were on her shoulders. They lingered a moment longer than necessary before he lifted the woollen mantle. She wanted to shrug him off, but she knew she must be careful. It was important she did not show how much he repulsed her. Not yet.

He had passed the cloak to a waiting footman and she felt his hand upon her back.

'Shall we go into the parlour?'

'I should first like to go up to my room,' she said. 'I need to remove my bonnet and perhaps wash away the dirt from the journey.'

'You may go and wash your face and hands, but I shall expect you to join me in the parlour as soon as you have done so. Do not keep me waiting.' He lifted one hand and a dour-faced woman appeared. She wore a white apron over her black gown and a white cap covered her iron-grey hair. 'This is Mrs Jenkins, my housekeeper. She will show you to your room.'

The woman made a grudging curtsy and turned her basilisk stare upon Madeleine. 'If madam would like to follow me.'

As they moved towards the stairs, Sir William called out, 'Remember, Jenkins. I want her back downstairs again in half an hour.'

Maddie accompanied the housekeeper up the grand staircase. Her attempts at conversation were met with silence and she realised she had found no ally there. She was shown into a small bedchamber with faded blue silk decorating the walls. There were matching hangings at the windows and around the bed, all equally worn. Everything looked insipid and not particularly clean.

The housekeeper pointed to the jug of water on the washstand. 'That should be hot enough for your needs. There's no lady's maid here. If you're needing help, I will send up one of the housemaids to you.'

'I can manage very well for myself, thank you.'

'Then I will come back to escort you to Sir William shortly.' She went out and Madeleine breathed a sigh of relief to be alone, if only for a while.

She made a quick tour of the room, noting the door to a small closet and the window, its opening too small to allow anyone larger than a child to escape. Not that there could be any escape for her; Sir William had made it quite clear he would not hesitate to publicly accuse both her and Grant of treason if she tried to get away. She squared her shoulders and prepared to meet her fate.

Madeleine washed her face and hands, then removed her bonnet and regarded herself in the spotted looking glass standing on the dressing table. Her hair was already escaping from its elaborate knot and, once she had combed it out, she knew there was no possibility of pinning it up again as smoothly as Eilidh had done. Instead she pulled it back into a tail and secured it with the gold ribbon that had earlier nestled among her curls.

Looking down, Madeleine saw the skirts of her blue camlet were sadly crushed from the journey. She shook them out, almost as an act of defiance, then slipped one hand through the folds and into the pocket she had instructed the tailor to insert. Her fingers touched the handle of the little dagger she had secreted there. It had served her well in the past and now the small silver weapon gave her some comfort.

When Mrs Jenkins returned, Madeleine followed her downstairs to the parlour. The room smelled stale and musty. A large bay at one end of the room was filled with tall leaded windows that reached from the ceiling almost to the floor, but none of the casements were open, and a series of coloured glass panels across the top cut down the light. Dark, wainscoted walls and a low, heavily plastered ceiling added to the oppressive atmosphere.

Sir William was waiting for her, standing before the ornate carved chimneypiece. He had removed his coat and replaced his boots with Moroccan leather slippers.

'Please forgive my state of undress,' he said, when they were alone. 'I like to be comfortable when I come here. This is a house that was built for pleasure. As are you.' She suppressed a shudder as his lascivious glance ran over her. He went on, 'I gave orders that a dressing gown should be laid out for you in your room. Did you not see it?'

'You ordered me to return within the half-hour,' she retorted. 'There was no time to change.'

She did not add that she had no desire to put on the filmy lace robe she had seen lying on the bed.

He shrugged. 'No matter, I shall enjoy undressing you myself. Later.'

He walked over to a heavily carved buffet and poured two glasses of wine from a decanter.

'Well, what think you of my little hunting lodge?' he asked, holding out a glass to her.

'It is well enough,' said Madeleine coolly. 'The wainscotting would be better for being polished.'

He laughed at that. 'I did not bring you here to keep house for me.' As she took the glass from him, his fingers skimmed her skin. 'Mmm. I am tempted to carry you off to bed without further ado.'

Her reply was deliberately prosaic. 'I think it

would be wise to eat first. The morning is already well advanced and we have had nothing since supper last night.'

'A practical woman, how refreshing.' He raised his glass to her. 'It would appear my cook was not informed I would be arriving so early and there is nothing prepared. I have sent word to the kitchens that we will eat in an hour.' He patted the sofa. 'In the meantime, come and sit down with me and drink your wine. It will relax you.'

His predatory smile did nothing to put her at her ease and instead Maddie began to walk around the room, showing a spurious interest in the paintings. Most were hunting scenes, but there were one or two badly executed portraits displayed between them. After a few moments Sir William gave an impatient sigh.

'Come and sit down with me,' he repeated, more sharply this time. 'Here, on the sofa. I want to kiss you.'

Her lip curled. 'Can you not wait until we retire for that?'

'No, madam. I have been patient long enough. I will not wait another moment.'

A chill ran down Madeleine's spine.

'It is very hot in here,' she said, trying to put

off the inevitable. 'Do you object if I open a window?

'If you wish, why not?'

He watched her walk across the room, but made no move to come to her aid as she struggled with the window catches, which were stiff from lack of use. Eventually she managed to open two of the casements and pushed them wide on their creaking hinges.

The air outside was fresh after the recent rain and patches of blue sky that were appearing only seemed to mock her predicament.

'Come over here.'

This time it was an order. Reluctantly Maddie turned away from the window and walked slowly back into the centre of the room. She kept her head up and was outwardly calm, but her resolution was faltering. She was not sure if she could do this.

Sir William reached out and caught her hand, but when he pulled her into his arms to kiss her, she was swamped with a mixture of anger and revulsion and instinctively pushed him away. She stepped back, driving her hand into the folds of her skirt until she found the pocket. Her fingers curled around the little silver dagger.

'Stay away from me or I swear I will kill you!'

He had his back to the window, but she could still see the gloating look on his face.

'Fine words, my dear, but quite futile, you know. I will have you.' He saw her glare of revulsion and laughed. 'You look as if you would like to murder me, but think, madam, what would that achieve? My servants here are very loyal and they have orders to set the dogs loose if you tried to escape. Besides, where could you go? We are surrounded by forest and you may be sure the hounds would find you before you were a half-mile from here.'

'But if I had killed you I would have the satisfaction of knowing you could do no more harm!'

'Ah, but you know that is not true.' The hateful complacency in his voice made her skin crawl. He went on, 'I have already told you; my deposition against you, your father and your husband is signed, sealed and ready to be delivered to Henry Fox. The Secretary at War himself, my dear, and a close acquaintance of mine.' His mouth widened into an arrogant smile. 'No, you will not harm me, my beautiful Madeleine. Nor will you kill yourself, rather than submit to my attentions. Think what would become of your beloved Grant Rathmore in either case. He will die a traitor's death, but only after he has suffered horribly. His body would first be torn apart in the most hideous and painful manner. Is that what you want?'

His argument fell on her like a heavy net, weighing her down. There was no escape. At least not until she could find a way out of this coil. Her grip slackened on the little knife. It must stay hidden for now, however much she would like to plunge it into Maxton's black heart.

He came closer, the shadow of his powerful frame falling over her.

'Very well, madam. Enough of this procrastination. It is time for you to demonstrate how well you can please me.' His hand came up and she had to steel herself not to flinch as he touched her cheek. 'Who knows, you may even enjoy it? I know I shall.'

'I think not,' drawled a smooth familiar voice.

Chapter Thirty-One

It couldn't be true. Madeleine thought she must have imagined it, but Sir William was cursing and swinging around to see who had spoken. His bulk still blocked her view and she quickly stepped to one side. Only when she saw the speaker with her own eyes did she allow herself to believe.

Grant was sitting on the window seat, a caped greatcoat hanging open to display his riding attire of coat, boots and buckskins. A black tricorn was set at a rakish angle on his head and he was holding a cocked pistol in one hand. She thought, for one absurd, happy moment, that he looked very much like a highwayman, come to steal her away.

Then the black fear of the threat hanging over him came flooding back. She quickly put herself between Sir William and that deadly pistol.

'You cannot kill him, Grant' she said urgently. 'You must go, now.'

Maxton laughed. 'You see how she protects me, Rathmore? You should accept defeat. Crawl back to your Scottish lair and leave the lovely Madeleine to enjoy herself, with me.'

Grant looked amused. 'As your mistress? Never. Move out of the way, Maddie.'

'She won't do that.' Maxton's arm slipped around her waist and she could feel his breath on her ear. 'You want to stay here with me, is that not so, my dear?'

Madeleine heard that hateful voice, so smooth, so confident, and it filled her with repugnance, but she dare not show it. She had to send Grant away, to keep him safe.

'Yes,' she said quietly, forcing herself to meet his eyes. 'I *want* to stay.'

Sheltering like a coward behind Madeleine, Maxton's smile was triumphant, but Grant was not fooled by her lie. He had not missed that glow of happiness that lit up her face when she had first seen him. It was fleeting and swiftly suppressed, but it had told him all he wanted to know. Heart soaring with relief, he smiled at her and softly repeated his words.

'Move aside, my love.'

Almost before he had finished speaking Grant realised his mistake. Sir William's arm tightened around Maddie, pulling her back against him.

'You cannot shoot me, Rathmore,' he snarled. 'The moment your lovely wife leaves here you will both be hunted down as traitors. I have made sure that will happen, even if I am not alive to do it myself. Tell him, my dear.'

'He is right, Grant. Your only hope is to escape. To go now.'

Madeleine was looking at him, her eyes beseeching. Grant could not risk firing and hitting her. He must think and quickly. Carefully he un-cocked the pistol and dropped it into the capacious pocket of his greatcoat.

'So that is how you persuaded her to come with you,' he remarked casually. 'I wondered how you had achieved that.'

'She was already lost to you, Rathmore,' Maxton hissed. 'Or do you hope to win her back with your heroism? You cannot have her love, so you would settle for her gratitude, is that it?'

Maddie could see the words had caught Grant on the raw. She wanted to deny it, but it was impossible to speak. Sir William's left arm had tightened painfully around her, forcing the breath from her lungs. He grabbed her hair and pulled her head back, that hateful voice purring in her ear.

'Look your last upon him, my dear, before I call my servants to tie the cur to the whipping post and flay him alive. Evans! *Evans!*'

Sir William was shouting for his manservant and Maddie knew she must act. Slipping her hand back into the pocket, she pulled out the little knife and swung it up. She grasped the handle with both hands and drove it into Maxton's forearm, as hard and deep as she could. He screamed with pain and she wrenched herself free, twisting away just as Grant hurtled past and cannoned into him.

Both men crashed to the floor. Grant's fist drove into his opponent's jaw and Maxton's head snapped back. He remained on the ground, stunned, while Grant struggled to his feet.

'Fortunate to catch him with that blow,' he muttered. 'Had to overpower him quickly.'

Maddie saw that he was clutching his left arm, but she had no time to worry about that.

She said urgently, 'Quickly, Grant, you must leave while you can!' She heard sounds of a commotion in the hall and stepped closer. 'Go now! They must not find you here. I will delay them as long as I can—'

The door burst open and Madeleine moved in

front of Grant, but it was not servants who came into the room. She uttered a little cry surprise.

'Colonel Rutter!' Brandishing the knife in front of her, Maddie glared at the Colonel and the redcoats at his shoulder. 'Stand back. I will not let you take him!'

Behind her, Grant laughed. 'Put your *sgian* away, Maddie. Colonel Rutter is here to rescue you.'

'Rescue be damned!' snarled Maxton, climbing to his feet. 'Arrest them. She tried to kill me. Look!'

He held out his arm. The white linen sleeve of his shirt was already heavily stained with blood. Grant turned on him, looking murderous.

'You attacked *her*,' he retorted. 'The lady was merely defending her honour.'

'It will all be added to the charges laid against him,' stated Colonel Rutter. 'Come along, Sir William. You are under arrest and we are taking you back to London. Now.'

Maxton stared, his face almost puce with rage.

'How dare you!' he shrieked. 'I am a friend of Henry Fox. I demand to see him!'

'Oh, you will see him, sir, no doubt of that. After you have answered the charges that have been brought against you.' The Colonel gestured to his men. 'Take him away and bind up his arm.'

Madeleine watched in shocked silence as Sir William was escorted out of the room.

'No, no!' She ran across to the Colonel. 'You cannot arrest him, you must not!'

'Indeed I must, ma'am. He has been passing intelligence to foreign governments.'

Maddie pressed a hand against her temple. 'I do not understand. I thought he—' She broke off and started again. 'Are you sure this is wise, Colonel? Sir William is a dangerous man to cross. He has very powerful friends.'

'I doubt he will have so many allies once the evidence against him is made known,' said the Colonel.

The door had closed, but Madeleine could still hear Sir William protesting vehemently as he was led away. What if he accused Grant?

She said anxiously, 'I should not wish you to jeopardise your career, sir.'

'Thank you for your concern, ma'am, but I am confident the charges will be upheld. We have all the evidence.'

'Not quite all,' put in Grant, amusement in his voice. 'I doubt your informant told you of his own part in all this.'

'It would appear the Comte had very little to do with any of it,' replied Colonel Rutter, in his measured way. 'Certainly not sufficient to warrant seeking him out in France.'

'The Comte!' Madeleine pounced on the words. 'Papa—my *father* gave you this information?'

Colonel Rutter nodded. 'Aye, ma'am. He sent me a very detailed report with names and dates, as well as witness statements and letters. There can be no doubt that Sir William has been selling our military plans to France and to Prussia for some time now.'

'But Maxton has information, lodged with his attorney.' She looked at Grant, desperate to make him understand. 'It is sufficient to c-convict you of treason. You will have to fly the country!'

'I will disprove any fabricated lies, have no fear about that, Madeleine. I have done nothing wrong.'

'No, no, I *know* you are innocent!' She turned back to the Colonel and said wretchedly, 'This is all my fault, *I* am the guilty one, it was I who c-carried messages for Papa, arranged his meetings and parties. Grant had nothing to do with it at all. Sir William's testimony is all lies!'

Colonel Rutter nodded. 'I have no doubt it is.'

'But he, Sir William, he said the Secretary at War...'

'You may be sure that Mr Fox will be very

eager to distance himself from such a rogue,' the Colonel reassured her. 'Maxton's word will carry no weight with the government now.'

'Then—then Grant is safe?'

'He is, my lady,' affirmed Colonel Rutter with a faint smile. 'You are both quite safe.'

Dazed, and still clutching the *sgian* in front of her, Maddie tried to take it all in.

'So...' she passed her tongue across her dry lips '...you...you will not be arresting us?'

'Quite the opposite, Lady Rathmore. You are free to go wherever you wish.'

Free. The word meant little to her. She had told Grant she no longer loved him, that she wanted to go to France with her father. She had told him too many lies and destroyed his trust; how could he want her back when she had deceived him so? True, he had taken her to his bed, they had enjoyed a night of pleasure, but he had not uttered one word of love.

She had seen the bond between Ailsa and Logan, it had been something far more precious than mere physical lust. There were stark facts that must be faced. Grant might want her for a few years yet, but later, when her bloom had gone, when she could no longer entice him into

her bed, what would they have left then but an
empty shell of a marriage?

Watching her, Grant read the doubts and distress crossing Madeleine's beautiful face. He saw
how she glanced at him, uncertain, anxious. She
reminded him of a wounded animal, frightened
and ready to flee. He was not even sure she had
noticed that the Colonel had withdrawn and left
them alone.

'Here.' He pulled out his handkerchief. 'Clean
that blade and put it away before you do some
mischief.'

She started and glanced up at him, then silently took the linen square and began to wipe
the knife. Her hands were shaking, an echo of
his own nerves, although his were under better
control. Or so he thought.

'The Colonel is right. You are perfectly free
to do what you wish now, Madeleine. A chaise
is on its way here for you even now and I will
go with you—'

He sounded officious and stern, even to his
own ears. Her eyes flew to his, such fear in their
blue depths that it shook him to the core. Did she
think he was trying to coerce her? He made an
effort to speak more gently.

'I will escort you back to London, what you
do from there is quite your own concern.' Con-

found it, that sounded as if he didn't care! And his voice was still too harsh. He drew in a long, steadying breath and tried again. 'What I mean is, this is your decision, Madeleine. Yours alone.' He turned away, not wanting her to see in his face the hunger and need that he felt for her. 'If you wish to join your father, then we will arrange safe passage on a ship to France. I will not force you to return with me.'

Madeleine's heart sank. The words were polite, impersonal. His tone was the same he had used with her at Ardvarrick for the past year or more. There was no warmth in his voice. He was merely being kind, chivalrous. Trying to do his duty by her, nothing more. She pushed back the tears that threatened to spill over. Surely it was better to end this doomed union now. He would find happiness with another woman and she could make a life for herself with Papa, in France. She slipped the little knife back into her pocket and held out his handkerchief.

'I gave you my decision, before we left London, Grant. I think it is best that we part, do not you?'

She paused, giving him the chance to argue, to tell her she was wrong, to beg her to return with him and try again, but he remained obstinately silent. So be it. She meant no more to him that that bloodied square of linen that he had thrown into the fireplace. Calling upon every ounce of willpower, she turned away and walked towards the door.

'I must collect my cloak and my bag,' she said, her voice surprisingly calm. 'Then I should like to quit this house with all speed.'

Chapter Thirty-Two

Grant stood on the drive, watching Colonel Rutter and his party of Dragoons ride off, Sir William a prisoner in their midst. Rutter was also carrying with him a number of incriminating papers that had been found and claimed for the Crown.

Several of the servants, such as Evans, who had put up a fight when the soldiers had burst in, were being taken away in shackles and the remainder were all huddled in the kitchen, wondering what was to become of them. Grant guessed they would eventually slip away, taking some of their master's valuables with them as recompense for the wages they had lost. Good luck to them; it would keep them from starving until Martinmas, when they could get work at the next hiring fair.

He had not seen Madeleine since she had gone

off to fetch her bag and he had remained in that gloomy drawing room, cursing himself for a fool. That was an hour ago and he had now resigned himself to losing her. How could he ever have thought he could keep such an exotic creature hidden away in the Highlands?

Having seen her in the glittering salons of London, he knew that was where she belonged, dressed in fine silks and mixing with the cream of society. In France, as the daughter of the Comte de Vaucluse, Madeleine would be appreciated as she deserved. She would be fêted and acknowledged for her wit, her charm and her beauty. She would not have to worry about rents or harvests or cattle prices and with only the rare occasion to wear a ballgown. She would have every luxury, move in the highest circles. In comparison, he had nothing to offer.

The travelling chariot he had hired came into view, bowling along the drive towards him. Grant went back into the house to fetch Madeleine, but she was already descending the stairs.

'I saw the chaise from the window,' she explained, not looking at him.

She walked past him with her bag in her hand and he followed her to the waiting carriage. When she climbed in without his help he silently took his seat beside her, regretting that he had not asked Rutter to leave him a horse.

The Colonel had assumed he would want to travel back in the chaise with Madeleine, probably imagining they would spend the journey locked in each other's arms. Instead, the carriage rattled away along the drive with Madeleine's stiff little figure huddled in the corner, her back to him. He thought grimly that the Colonel was very far off the mark.

It wasn't until they reached Woodford Bridge that Grant made any effort to break the stony silence.

'No doubt you wish to return to Surrey Street. I presume the rest of your trunks are still there?'

'What? Oh, yes.' She kept her eyes fixed on the passing landscape. 'I left instructions that my trunks were to be forwarded on to me, but now I shall be able to collect them myself and take them to France.'

Was he imagining that bleak note in her voice?

'Your father will be very glad to have you with him.'

'Yes.'

'You do not sound very sure of that.'

'I am no longer sure of anything.'

She sounded so forlorn that his heart missed a

beat. He said carefully, 'You could always come back to Ardvarrick.'

'No.' She gave the tiniest shake of her head. 'It is too late for that.'

'I confess that is what I thought, when I first came to London,' he said slowly. 'But these last few days, when we were facing the danger together at Vauxhall, and later, in my lodgings—'

'Ah, no.' Her hand fluttered upwards, as if to ward him off. 'Please say no more!'

He lapsed into silence. Looking out of the window, he noticed it had started to rain again. The cloud-covered sky cast a pall over everything, dulling the colours, but in his head images of Madeleine blazed in jewel-bright detail. Her red lips and dazzling smile, her sapphire eyes flirting with him over the top of her fan, those same eyes sparkling with rage when she confronted Maxton. Her dusky hair like a stormy cloud on his pillow when he took her to his bed…

'I had forgotten,' he said suddenly. 'I had forgotten how strong you are. How resourceful. The first time I ever saw you, you had broken a pitcher over the head of a drunken rogue who had had the temerity to attack you!'

She did not respond and he continued reflectively.

'Do you remember how we criss-crossed the Highlands, trying to get you to the coast? You spoke not a word of the Gaelic then, yet you won the hearts of those desperate Scots we met in the hills. Do you remember, they were hiding out from the redcoats and gave us shelter?' He laughed. 'And your disguises! One day you were a young lady, charming everyone who saw you, the next I was accompanied by a bold young lad who played cards so well he could fleece a British officer of his ill-gotten gains.'

'And you almost died because of it.'

She still had her back to him, but she had replied. That encouraged him to continue.

'It was only a flesh wound and you bound it up expertly before leading me to safety. You were brave and resourceful, as always! We have been through so much together, Maddie, will you not come home with me, and let us try again?'

She shook her head.

'I am not the wife for you, Grant. I shall go to France and leave you to find a bride who can give you the family you deserve. The heir that you need.'

'I want no other wife, Madeleine. And as for an heir, the doctor was confident that in time—'

'No! I cannot do it,' she said, the words wrenched from her. 'I—I am neither so brave nor so strong as you think, Grant. I could not bear to go through it all again. To see the hope in your eyes fade and be replaced by bitter disappointment. To know how much I have failed you.'

'Failed me?' His brow creased. 'How could you think that?'

'It was quite clear to me,' she said, dashing a hand across her eyes. 'I knew the doctor had told you I needed time, but when the months turned into a full year and you had still not come back to my bed…' She closed her eyes, as if to keep out the painful memories.

'Oh, Maddie, I am sorrier than you can ever—'

'No, the fault was as much mine,' she interrupted him. 'How can I blame you for not confiding in *me* when I had not told you how I felt, after I lost another baby?'

Madeleine saw his eyes darken and her heart clenched with guilt. Hers might have been the physical pain of childbirth and the previous miscarriage, but Grant had suffered too. She should have acknowledged that. Was it any wonder he had withdrawn from her? She had killed his love.

She said now, 'It is over between us. We should both accept it.'

Grant looked at the dejected figure beside him and knew this was his last chance. He drew a breath and braced himself to tell her what he had not been able to say these past twelve months and more.

'After our son was stillborn, I felt so *helpless*, Maddie. You had the nurse and the doctor in attendance. Even my mother was there to help you, but I could only watch from a distance. The weeks passed, I saw your distress and could do nothing to help. I wanted to comfort you, but I was so frightened I would only hurt you more. Everyone told me you needed time to recover, I was afraid even to touch you! Then my father died and I did not know what to do, except to continue to be strong. I had to carry on and do my duty. For you, for my mother, everyone.'

'Duty!' The sob that was wrenched from her tore at his heart. 'After Logan died, I tried to talk to you, truly I did, but you were always too busy, or too tired. You avoided my company.'

'Yes. Yes, I did, and I am sorry for it now. At the time I thought it was the right thing to do, to keep you safe. I had forgotten how resilient you could be.' He drove his fingers through his hair. 'Believe me, Maddie, I wanted you so much. I was desperate for your comfort, but I saw that as my weakness. That is the reason I could not allow myself to be near you. I thought if I gave in and told you how I felt, I would be adding to your woes. I believed it would only cause you more pain if I came to you for comfort, when you were dealing with your own heartache at losing the baby.'

'I was mourning for your father, too,' she muttered, for the first time turning a little towards him.

'I knew that, but I could not give you the sympathy you deserved without acknowledging my own grief and I could not do that. I had convinced myself the only way to get through it all was to keep busy. Not to depend upon anyone. As the new Laird of Ardvarrick, there was much for me to do and I welcomed it. I threw myself into my duties, working on the ledgers with the factor, labouring in the fields, helping to build the new barn and gather in the harvest. I did anything and everything, except the one thing I should have done. Confide in you.'

'Ailsa was distraught and grieved hard, for months,' said Maddie, jerking her handkerchief through her fingers, 'But I was there, Grant. I was ready to help you, even if it was only to talk, or to listen.'

'Yes, you were. I realise that now and I am sorry I did not turn to you, but I could not. It was impossible. It was as if I was trapped in a dark tunnel, alone with my grief. I thought that if I just kept working, taking it all on my shoulders and not sharing my burden, then I was protecting you and Mama. I wanted to give you both time to mourn and recover.

'But it was more than that,' he went on, determined to tell her everything. 'I was afraid. Afraid to let you see how much I wanted you to comfort me. I thought you would think me a useless, pitiable creature. I feared you would reject me.'

'Oh, Grant…' she looked at him then, her eyes glistening with tears '…if only you could have told me! I did pity you, because I guessed what you were suffering, but I did not love you any the less for it.'

Madeleine turned away to wipe her eyes. If only he had come to her, shared his feelings, how different things might have been. Perhaps if she had not been so reticent, if she had spoken earlier, there might have been some chance for them.

But she had spoken now. She had laid her soul bare to him and still he'd uttered no words of love. She stared out of the window as the carriage rattled on and her last hopes died. She blew her nose and put her handkerchief away, despising such a display of weakness.

'Is it really too late for us, Maddie?' Grant said at last. 'Do you no longer need me?'

'Of course I do not need you. La, what a sad creature you must think me!'

She resolutely quashed an urge to weep and lifted her head a little higher as she turned to look him in the eye.

She said, as haughtily as she could, 'You need not worry about me. I can manage very well without you.'

His lips quirked upwards and she saw the glint of a smile in his eyes.

'And I you. But my life will be far less colourful, and much less exciting, if you are not in it.' He took a breath. 'I love you, Madeleine. I have never stopped loving you, although I was a fool not to tell you so more often, especially during those long dark months of grief.'

Could it be true? Madeleine wanted so much to believe him. She had waited so long to hear him say those words and now her heart was so full that at first she could not reply, then she was afraid to speak. He reached over and took her hands.

'You know how we live at Ardvarrick,' he said. 'There are no magnificent balls to attend, no paved walkways or well-tended parks, but we used to enjoy ourselves, did we not? We danced at the gatherings and rode out over the hills together. And we spent hours discussing the estate and what we could do to improve it.' He squeezed her fingers. 'I thought you were as interested in Ardvarrick as I, even if the society is nothing compared to London or Paris.'

'Oh, I would much rather be discussing the crops and the cattle than exchanging drawing room gossip,' she confessed. 'And I would infinitely prefer to be riding through the glens with you than promenading in a park!'

'Then will you not come home with me?' He gazed down at her hands, held tightly between his own. 'I cannot give you the riches and luxury you will have in your father's household. All I have to offer you is my heart and all my love. Every last ounce of it, until the day I die.'

'Oh, Grant.' Tears brimmed in her eyes again, 'Oh, that is all I have ever wanted!'

'Then come with me, my darling. Come back to Ardvarrick.' He pulled her close, tilting up her chin 'I want you beside me as my partner, my friend. My mistress and lover, now and for ever. What do you say, my dearest love?'

'Yes,' she smiled up at him mistily. 'Oh, yes, my darling!'

His lips closed on hers and Madeleine surrendered herself up to his kiss. As his arms came around her she knew, without a shadow of doubt, that she had come home.

Epilogue

Ten years later...

Grant was in the drawing room, sitting in a chair by the window and making the most of the evening light to read, but when Madeleine came in he put aside his book and rose.

'Are the children asleep now?'

'Baby Hector has settled in his crib and your mother is now singing lullabies to Morag and Catriona. They are a little over-excited, having had Anne's children here as playmates for the past two weeks.'

'I thought the visit passed off very well,' he remarked, taking her hand and leading her across to the sofa. 'Anne seems very happy with her Colonel.'

'Yes, they are very well suited. And their little

girls are quite delightful, although I think Anne is hoping the next baby will be a boy.'

He sat down and pulled her on to his lap. 'Talking of boys, how is my heir, is he asleep yet?'

'Logan is in his room, reading,' she replied. 'He is waiting for his grandmother to go in and say goodnight. She has promised to tell him one of her stories.'

'She spoils them all,' he muttered, with a mock frown.

Maddie chuckled. 'She dotes on them, as any grandmama should. Which is excellent, since their grandfather shows no interest in them.'

'The Comte de Vaucluse certainly does not appear to be enamoured of his grandchildren.'

'My father is only enamoured of one person—himself!'

'Does it upset you?' Grant asked her. 'Are you disappointed that Yves has never come here to see us?'

'No, or at least, not very much,' she confessed. 'I am content for him to remain in France with his Comtesse, who is proving a very good influence. From her letters I have gleaned that she was never in favour of his involvement with the Stuarts.'

'She must be pleased, then, that the French

government no longer supports the Young Pretender.'

'I imagine she is,' said Maddie, snuggling closer. 'She keeps Yves very much at home now and has severely restricted his activities. The only things she allows him to plan are the chateau's winter ball and the village fête!'

'But would you not like our children to meet their grandpapa?'

'One day, perhaps. But to be truthful I have no desire to have him here, disrupting our life.'

'Well, I know you have said he is a most unnatural parent,' he replied mildly, 'but the fact remains that Yves *is* your father. He would be very welcome at Ardvarrick, should he wish to come.'

Maddie sat up and stared at him, her eyes twinkling. 'Grant Rathmore, I do believe you are mellowing with age!'

'Can you blame me, when I have such a lovely wife and family? Which puts me in mind of something. Logan is growing rapidly and I have promised him a new pony for his birthday.'

'And you say your mother spoils them!'

'He must ride and he has outgrown his little pony. Besides, Catriona and Morag will be needing it.'

'I am surprised you do not say we must buy a second small pony, since the girls are twins.'

'Och, well, that was going to be my next suggestion,' he said, grinning and pulling her back into his arms.

Maddie laughed and with a happy sigh she rested her head on his shoulder.

'It is ten years since you fetched me home from London, my love. Where has the time gone?'

'We have been busy improving the house and the land. Bringing up our children.' He turned his head so he could look at her. 'Has Anne's visit unsettled you with all her talk of London? I know it is some time since we last went there, or even to Edinburgh. Would you like me to take you away for a while? We might go to Bath, if you wish; I hear that is very fashionable now.'

Smiling, she put her fingers to his lips to silence him. 'Perhaps, when Hector is a little older.'

'As long as you are not unhappy,' he said, capturing her hand and pressing a kiss into the palm. 'I don't want you running away from me ever again.'

'I will never leave you again, you have my word on it. Why should I, when everything I want is here?'

'You know I would give you the world, if I

could, my darling, Madeleine,' he said, his lips seeking hers.

'You have given me the world,' she whispered between kisses. 'You *are* my world, Grant Rathmore.'

Ailsa, coming into the room a few moments later, saw her son and his wife locked together in an embrace, oblivious to everything except each other. She quickly withdrew again, closing the door quietly behind her.

In the hall she paused for a moment, then she lifted her eyes to the painting hanging on the wall.

'We had our doubts, did we not, Logan, when he brought home a French adventuress?' she said, smiling up at the life-size picture of her husband. 'But we need not have worried, my darling. They have weathered the storm and come home safe to Ardvarrick. Just as we did.'

* * * * *

Historical Note

When I was researching for *Rescued by her Highland Soldier*, the second book in the Lairds of Ardvarrick series, I was intrigued by the tales—some of them apocryphal—that Bonnie Prince Charlie made several visits to England in the years following his escape to France after Culloden. These include several accounts of a visit in 1750.

At that time the popularity of the House of Hanover was at a very low ebb and support for the Stuarts appeared to be growing. Stories about Charles's adventures during his escape from Scotland were read eagerly, country ladies sang songs about him and their husbands drank his health. One can easily believe that Charles was persuaded to make another push to regain the throne.

Several sources quote from Horace Mann. He

was a British diplomat in Florence, whose duties included reporting on the activities of the exiled Stuarts. Mann described a meeting in 1783 between Charles Edward Stuart and the King of Sweden, in which Charles gave details of his visit to London in September 1750. He said he had viewed the Tower of London with a Colonel Brett and met with about fifty followers in a room in Pall Mall, including the Duke of Beaufort and the Earl of Westmorland.

Dr King, Principal of St Mary Hall in Oxford, wrote in his *Political and Literary Anecdotes of His Own Times*, that he himself was invited to visit Lady Primrose at her house in Essex Street and there he was introduced to the Prince. It is also asserted that Charles was received into the Church of England—possibly in a church close to Lady Primrose's house. This would have seemed a practical move by Charles, in an attempt to win more support in England.

Dr King's *Anecdotes* suggests he told Charles there was not sufficient support in the country for an uprising and persuaded him to return 'to the place from whence he came'. However, Charles might well have received some encouragement during his visit, because in 1751 Alexander Murray hatched an audacious plot—

possibly with his brother, Lord Elibank—to kidnap King George II and his family and replace him with a Stuart monarch. However, the Jacobite plotters were reluctant to act, and in 1752 the plan was uncovered by a spy. Murray escaped and remained in exile for the next twenty years, but one of the plotters, Dr Archibald Cameron of Lochiel, was arrested and sentenced to death. On 7th June 1753 he was hanged, drawn and quartered at Tyburn, the last Jacobite to be executed for high treason.

Charles might well have returned to England several times more, but gradually his hopes of regaining the throne faded and he became increasingly bitter and depressed. He drank a great deal and alienated many of his friends and supporters. He died in Rome of a stroke in 1788 and his body was eventually buried alongside his father, mother and younger brother in the Basilica of St Peter in the Vatican, although his heart remained in a small urn beneath the floor of the Frascati Cathedral, near Rome.

Reports say that during his visit to London Charles was quite audacious and appeared at some public gatherings. There is also some evidence that the British government knew all about his visits, but turned a blind eye. Whatever the facts, these stories make a great backdrop for Grant and Maddie's romantic adventures. I hope the reader will forgive me for embroidering this novel with characters and situations from my own imagination.

COMING SOON!

We really hope you enjoyed reading this book.
If you're looking for more romance, be sure to
head to the shops when new books are
available on

Thursday 23rd June

To see which titles are coming soon, please visit

millsandboon.co.uk/nextmonth

MILLS & BOON

MILLS & BOON®

Coming next month

THE DEBUTANTE'S SECRET
Sophia James

'I like rules and manners because these are the only things that keep the world from chaos.'

He laughed at her comment and the sound was not kind.

'I cannot tell you what the secret of a successful life is, Miss Barrington-Hall, but a sure way to failure is to try and please everyone.'

'You think that is what I am doing?'

'Aren't you?'

She took in breath and answered him.

'Perhaps your way of pleasing no one has its flaws as well, Mr Moreland, for the illicit and forbidden have their drawbacks.'

'Ahhh, but they are much more fun, Esther.'

Her name was said informally and in a tone that made her heart lurch. She was prepared for neither his wildness nor his passion, and he knew it.

'I think, sir, that we have come to the edge of patience with each other, but I would like to thank you for the confidentiality you have kept concerning my past.'

'How little you know me, Miss Barrington-Hall.'

She frowned and stood her ground.

'Do you allow anyone to, or do you send people off as soon as they might guess something you may not wish them to know?'

'I've always found distance has its advantages because people can often be disappointing.'

Squaring her shoulders, Esther answered him. 'Nothing hurts more than being disappointed by the one person you thought would never hurt you.'

'Your mother?' Now he looked at her with more interest.

But she was not drawn in to making a confession. 'After disappointment there comes hope.'

'Hope to make a good life?'

'Yes, for without it one is lost, and I have been.'

These words had him stepping back.

'I am sure things will improve markedly, Miss Barrington-Hall, for you are the belle of the season with a choice of fine upstanding suitors who will do everything possible to make your life a happy one.'

She could see him retreat almost as a physical thing, a man who knew who he was and would never change. People had disappointed him, that much was for sure, so he had stopped trying to fit in to expectations and walked a path that was far from her own.

Then he was gone, lost into the throng of people on the busy street. Out of his company she felt the loss of what might have been. Once he had said to her that he wanted her to like him, but now…

Continue reading
THE DEBUTANTE'S SECRET
Sophia James

Available next month
www.millsandboon.co.uk

MILLS & BOON

THE HEART OF ROMANCE

A ROMANCE FOR EVERY READER

MODERN

Prepare to be swept off your feet by sophisticated, sexy and seductive heroes, in some of the world's most glamourous and romantic locations, where power and passion collide.

HISTORICAL

Escape with historical heroes from time gone by. Whether your passion is for wicked Regency Rakes, muscled Vikings or rugged Highlanders, awaken the romance of the past.

MEDICAL

Set your pulse racing with dedicated, delectable doctors in the high-pressure world of medicine, where emotions run high and passion, comfort and love are the best medicine.

True Love

Celebrate true love with tender stories of heartfelt romance, from the rush of falling in love to the joy a new baby can bring, and a focus on the emotional heart of a relationship.

Desire

Indulge in secrets and scandal, intense drama and plenty of sizzling hot action with powerful and passionate heroes who have it all: wealth, status, good looks…everything but the right woman.

HEROES

Experience all the excitement of a gripping thriller, with an intense romance at its heart. Resourceful, true-to-life women and strong, fearless men face danger and desire - a killer combination!

To see which titles are coming soon, please visit

millsandboon.co.uk/nextmonth

JOIN US ON SOCIAL MEDIA!

Stay up to date with our latest releases, author
news and gossip, special offers and discounts, and
all the behind-the-scenes action
from Mills & Boon...

 millsandboon

 millsandboonuk

 millsandboon

It might just be true love...